SARAH'S SECRET

*The Story of Sarah and
the Boy with a Machete*

NANCY ROGERS

ISBN 978-1-958032-34-3
Printed in the United States of America.
Registered in the Library of Congress.
2nd Edition

Page formatting and cover formatting and placement by Molly Beck, Graphic Artist

Published by Here I Am Publishing, LLC.
info@hereiampublishingllc.com
Sandi Huddleston-Edwards, Publisher
780 Monterrosa Drive
Myrtle Beach, SC 29572

Dedication

To
Janet, Allen, Sarah, and Ginger Rodgers

Contents

*To Dr. Janet Wright, my lifelong friend and research partner,
without whom this book would have never happened.*

CHAPTER I

Moments from the Massacre

Carrefour Plantation
The Colony of Saint-Domingue, Modern-day Haiti 1795

FOURTEEN-YEAR-OLD SARAH RICHARDS crawled out of the enormous feather bed and tiptoed across the cool marble floor toward a small balcony. Although it was well after midnight, Sarah was far too excited to sleep.

Earlier on in the day, Sarah and her best friend, Eliza Paget, had ended their five-day journey to Carrefour to visit her mother's island cousins, and Sarah did not want to miss a moment. She inhaled the scented air and absentmindedly scanned the horizon when something caught her eye.

Sarah leaned over the railing to get a better look, only to gasp at the sight. At the end of the allee leading to the mansion were bright red ribbons of flame racing straight toward the mansion, a dog howled in the distance, making Sarah tremble. "Mimms?" she screamed.

"What's the matter?" Mimms shouted back as she bolted from her cot at the foot of Sarah's bed.

Sarah looked at Mimms, petrified. Her words came out shaking, "There's a fire, a big one coming straight toward us! We have to warn everyone," Sarah stated in a panic-stricken voice.

"Wake Miss Eliza," the chaperone said, running toward the balcony. As instructed, Sarah did not hesitate to grab Eliza by the feet and drag her onto the floor. "Wake up! There's a fire!" Sarah exclaimed.

Eliza woke up with a jolt, her eyes blurred. All she saw was Sarah's horrified face.

"There's a fire. Hurry up," Sarah repeated in a rush.

"You tried to kill me," Eliza grumbled, fumbling with the sleeve of her dressing gown.

"I did not. Now shut up. We could die," Sarah retorted.

A commotion started to brew in the hallway. Sarah's Aunt Beatrix rushed into the room carrying her three-year-old daughter, Charlotte. "What's the matter?" she said, trying not to upset the little girl.

"There's a fire," Mimms said, motioning toward the balcony. "We've got to get out of here."

"Mon Dieu," Beatrix whispered to Mimms as they stood next to each other on the balcony.

Having grown up at Carrefour, Beatrix was aware that a wildfire was a common occurrence, given the plantation was on the windward side. However, the prevailing winds had always forced them away from the plantation in the past. Sadly, this fire was different. It was marching straight for the allee leading to the mansion.

"We've got to get to the marina," Beatrix announced, running back toward her apartment. Five minutes earlier, the estate had been as still as a tomb. Now, it reverberated with the cries of men in silk pajamas and women in expensive negligees, clutching their children in one hand and the jewelry they had worn to dinner in the other.

"Nanine!"

"Maree!" they cried hysterically summoning their servants. Hours earlier, Sarah had thought of the cousins as goddesses; now, they reminded her of bleating sheep.

While chaos engulfed the mansion in its clutches, something far ghastlier awaited them. As frightening as the fire was, something even more sinister was about to unfold in the courtyard. For it was there that the family would discover that the fire was merely a diversion, a smokescreen in the truest sense.

Eleven hundred slaves lived at Carrefour, but only a dozen had answered the fire alarm. The rest had vanished into the jungle. While the Hebert men rushed to the courtyard to fight the fire, Beatrix gave orders inside the mansion.

"Hurry!" she screamed. "Dress the children in anything you can find. We must leave the plantation, now."

"Where are we going, Mommy?" Charlotte cried.

"We're going to go on a lovely adventure," Beatrix replied. "We are going to sail down the river. Won't that be fun?"

"But the moon is in the sky. We're supposed to be asleep."

"This is a special night, darling," Beatrix said, forcing herself to be calm. "We're going to have a wonderful time, and when we get back, you can tell Papa all about how brave you were." While the women dressed their toddlers and wrapped their infants in soft cotton blankets, the older children, including Eliza and Sarah, watched the fire from the balcony.

Sarah's uncles were joined by a handful of house servants and young boys in the courtyard, where they were hurriedly preparing to fight the fire with a collection of fire buckets and hoses. Suddenly, Eliza pointed to a walkway leading to the courtyard. "Look! There are men with machetes in the courtyard!"

"Maybe they're here to fight the fire," Sarah said.

"No!" Eliza exclaimed. "They're here to attack your uncles. We have to warn them." The girls cried out and pounded their fists on the doors to the balcony, but it was too late.

The men with the machetes descended on the Hebert men like locust. The lucky ones died where they stood, including Grand-Pere, who was killed with one swing of a machete, and Beatrix's young husband, who was splayed open like a trophy fish.

It was not until that moment that the family realized that the real enemy that night was a slave uprising. The hatred of Haiti's enslaved people was generations old, but the man they hated most was Sarah's great-uncle, Louis Alexey Hebert.

CHAPTER 2

Carrefour Plantation

Forty Years Before Sarah's Visit

LOUIS HEBERT AND HIS young wife, Anne, had dreamed of escaping their lives at Carrefour to buy a house in Paris and travel the world. They were going to raise their children together and be happy.

Louis was determined not to follow his father's tyrannical footsteps, but it was not to be. Unknown to Louis, his father had already destroyed the young couple's dreams with the stroke of a pen.

Louis's father died after a fall at sixty-five, and his funeral was held at Carrefour the following day. As Louis walked to the center of the ballroom, looked down at his father's coffin, and solemnly bowed his head, a hush fell over the crown of Herbert cousins gathered there.

The blue-blooded assemblage was there to witness the changing of the guard—that defining moment when twenty-six-year-old Louis became Carrefour Plantation's new master, and Louis played his role perfectly.

Dressed in mourning attire in varying shades of gray, Louis moved across the floor as though he had stepped out of the pages of a gentleman's magazine.

"Il est tres beau," a teenaged girl swooned, followed by a whispered "Shhh!"

Louis remained unfazed. He had always had that effect on women, including the women in his own family. And then he took his seat next to his wife, Anne, nodded for the priest to begin the eulogy, and held his gaze on his father's face. Except for a pack of old warhorses standing in the back of the room, there wasn't a dry eye in the place.

It was all a charade. Louis had scarcely known his father, and most of his memories of him were those belonging to a frightened child. Louis wasn't grieving the loss of his father that day; he was mourning the loss of his dreams.

Only the day before, during the reading of his father's will, had he learned that he would be left without a franc unless, as the eldest son, he agreed to become Carrefour's new master.

The French colony of Saint-Domingue occupied one-third of the island of Hispaniola, with a Spanish-held colony known as Santa Domingo occupying the remaining two-thirds. The colonies would later become the Republic of Haiti and the Dominican Republic.

Saint-Domingue had brought enormous wealth to the French commonwealth, but Saint-Domingue was scarcely a dot on the map on the world's stage. Its isolation had enabled its colonial princes, including Louis's father, to treat their slaves with extreme brutality.

Louis didn't have the stomach for the job, and his younger brothers were still in their teens. The plan had been for Carrefour to go to an uncle and Louis and his brothers to receive annuities.

When Louis challenged the terms of the will, the lawyers remained tight-jawed, offering him nothing beyond glassy stares. All they knew was that the marching orders had been changed, and the old man was still beating the drum.

Inheriting the vast plantation would make Louis one of the wealthiest men in France, and he had a young family to support, so he had no choice. But it would come at an enormous price. It would cost him his soul, for only a soulless man could sustain an empire built on the backs of half-dead African slaves.

Following the service, Anne said, "Mari en or, you have the heart of an angel and the confidence of a young god." And then she nuzzled his neck, and he wept.

CHAPTER 3

One Year Before Sarah's Visit

Forty years had passed since that day. Anne no longer whispered words of endearment; she and Louis rarely spoke. Forty years was a lifetime. Louis Hebert was frayed around the edges, and his eyesight was dimming. However, he still held a commanding presence as he waited at the edge of the channel leading to Carrefour's secluded landing.

The midday sun was red hot. His linen blouse and the band of his white Panama were soaked through. Impeccable, however, were his boots that must have taken his bootblack hours to gin up enough spit to make them shine as they did.

Hebert's patience was nearing its end when his horse suddenly shuddered. The stagnant pluff mud at the water's edge had the viscosity of tar, and it always made the horse skittish. Hebert calmed her with a firm pat to her neck, and then he laughed.

Louis and Anne, referred to within the family as Grand-Pere and Grand-Mere, shared the mansion at Carrefour with twenty-two other family members, including nine grandchildren. And yet, this small ginger-colored mare was the only thing he really loved.

Hebert studied his reflection in the brackish water. His chiseled face, so stunning in his youth was gone now. In its place was the face of his father. A small sloop entered the channel. Oars appeared, and a line was thrown as Hebert and his horse approached the landing.

The boat's captain stepped out onto the dock and respectfully extend his hand. "Master Hebert."

"Let's get on with it," Hebert said, ignoring the captain's hand for fear of losing his balance as he dismounted. The captain ducked to miss the moving boot, wondering if the leathery smell filling his nostrils came from the saddle or the old master.

"Yes, sir," the younger man replied.

He was grateful for Hebert's disinterest in idle conversation. He had no idea what was so important about this particular cargo that the reclusive old man had shown up to accept it in person. He just knew he'd been given a bonus to make the delivery, so he agreed to do it.

But the captain was Taino, and something about Carrefour made his hair stand on end. The glittering plantation—the Pearl of Saint-Domingue—was the most opulent plantation in the French colonial empire, but there was something about it that he hated.

The chest containing the treasure was covered by a tarp and secured to the deck by ropes. Guards from the plantation, who had been sent ahead, stood on either side of it but did nothing to help the boat's three-man crew hoist the chest onto the landing.

Instead, they brandished their pistols, validating every misgiving the captain had about Hebert and his plantation. The crew scrambled back on board, eager to distance itself from Carrefour.

"Old Master's gonna get his, all right," one of the crewmen said under his breath. "He's gonna get his real soon."

The captain cut his eyes toward the man, not understanding the portent of the simple statement. And then he glanced back at the aging tyrant.

"Some money is dirtier than others, but it all spends the same," his woman would tell him back in Port-du-Paix.

CHAPTER 4

The Catherine Red

HEBERT AND HIS MARE followed the body guards assigned to carry the chest back to the mansion. The men certainly weren't overpowered by the trunk's weight, but it did require an element of teamwork, a quality not indigenous to men hired solely for their brawn.

As they continued up the path leading to the mansion, Hebert contemplated the possibility of revolt on the island. For three years, there had been pockets of insurgency on the other side of the island, but they had quailed as quickly as they had surfaced.

Hebert had considered removing his family from Carrefour for a time, but moving a household as boisterous as his was something he chose not to be involved in. Carrefour was a fortress. It was impenetrable. The family would be fine. Then his thought turned to the goings-on in Europe.

It was a subject that deeply troubled him. The revolution in France and the execution of Louis XVI and his family worried him the most. The killing of a sovereign was a sin against God and an even greater sin against the people themselves.

It could bring about another war in Europe. The Russians were also worried about the possibility of war. Hebert's solicitor had recently informed him that the Russians felt pressed to modernize their armies. It would cost a staggering amount of money, and yet, Russia—the wealthiest country in the world—was strapped for cash as usual.

To raise the money, the Russians had come up with a plan to smuggle Catherine the Great's priceless coronation crown out of St. Petersburg and to bring it to the Tower of London, where it would serve as collateral on a loan from the Irish government.

Somewhere in transit, however, the crown disappeared, and that's when Louis Hebert became part of the story. Hebert learned about the crown through a black market contact. A month later, he bought the crown for £25,000, the modern-day equivalent of nearly $4M.

Hebert knew that the honorable thing would have been to buy the crown and magnanimously return it to Russia. Some men in Hebert's shoes would have jumped at the chance to be a hero on the world stage. He, however, didn't care about such things.

All he knew was that the crown had an inexplicable hold on him that he attributed in part to his mother—a minor member of the Russian nobility. She had filled his youthful brain with fanciful tales about the glittering Russian court. That was part of it, but there was a far more compelling reason .

It centered upon his father and about making him turn over in his grave, knowing that his sickly, half-Russian son had bested him at last, and there was nothing he could do about it.

"Put it on the desk," Hebert commanded once the men carrying the trunk had arrived at the entrance to Hebert's study. "Now get out," he said, shoving money into their hands. The body guards were startled by Hebert's sudden rudeness. People treat cattle better than that, one of them said to himself.

Hebert locked the door behind them and drew the heavy silk draperies. He removed a revolver from his pocket, tossed his hat on the chair, and dropped the tarp that had been covering the trunk onto the floor beside his desk. His hands were shaking, and he was exhausted—old man exhausted.

Hebert reached for a wine glass and a bottle of Madeira sitting on a small table near his favorite chair. He chased a glassful of the pungent liquid with another and immediately steadied. And then he returned to the trunk. He inserted a small key into the trunk's golden lock and stood transfixed as he opened its lid.

Inside he discovered a patinated wooden box decorated with the crest of the House of Romanov, the double-headed eagle. It was so beautiful that Hebert could barely bring himself to touch it. The box's interior was lined with velvet, purple velvet, of course, the color of kings.

Although it was made of the finest silk, the velvet looked colorless nestled next to the dazzling crown, a masterpiece made of nine pounds of platinum, pearls, and diamonds. At its summit was the Catherine Red, the largest red diamond in the world.

A red diamond larger than five carats was considered to be a behemoth. Even Grand-Mere's red diamond was only slightly more than four carates, but this one was nearly four hundred carats. Treasured by a Chinese emperor a thousand years earlier, the diamond had taken generations to find its way to the court of Catherine the Great.

Men had been killed to possess the diamond, and women had prostituted themselves to wear it. Now, the diamond and the crown belonged to Hebert, and it was more beautiful than he had dreamed.

CHAPTER 5

Sarah and Eliza's Arrival at Carrefour

SARAH AND ELIZA HAD arrived at Carrefour aboard the Schooner Indigo, and they were watching the Indigo dock between two small Bateaux, when Sarah spotted her mother's cousin. "Aunt Beatrix!" she shouted.

"Welcome to Carrefour," Beatrix said, offering a hug. "Before I introduce you to the rest of the family, I want to take a long look at you. Has it really been four years?"

"It has," Sarah replied. "It was in Charleston, and I was ten." Then she reached out for Eliza's hand and said, "I need to introduce you to my friend, Elize Lucas Paget. This is my mother's cousin, Beatrix Hebert."

The Hebert men and boys were at a polo match in Port-du-Paix, a big grudge match, Beatrix said, but they would meet them at dinner. "Charlotte's here, though, aren't you sweetheart?" Beatrix asked, smiling down at her daughter. "Now, what do we say, Charlotte?"

"Welcome to Carrefour," the child replied, taking refuge behind her mother's skirts. Carrefour overlooked Port-du-Paix, and it was less than a half-hour's carriage ride from there to the boat landing.

After Beatrix's warm welcome, Mimms playfully shooed Sarah and Eliza toward the end of the landing and asked to speak to Beatrix in private. "I'm concerned about something that I saw on the way here," Mimms said. "There were several dozen men—slaves with machetes—lining the bank of the river. They were extremely defiant, Miss Beatrix, and I need to know what is happening here."

Although taken aback by Mimms' assertiveness, Beatrix was impressed by her concern over the girls' safety. "This has been going on for weeks," Beatrix began. "There are all kinds of rumors about their intentions, but Grand-Pere says that the slaves on this island have done this for years. 'It never amounts to anything,' he told us during supper last night.

"He said that since the slaves are little more than savages, they have to be herded around like cattle, and that makes them defiant. He said if they get too far out of control, an example will be made by executing some of them, and they'll come back in line."

"Well, I know what your grandfather thinks. Now I want to know what you think," Mimms said.

"I don't know," Beatrix replied earnestly, "but I'll admit that they frighten me. The lifespan of the typical slave here is so short that they aren't even allowed to have families. They're brought here to live in communal houses and to work until they die. As I see it, they have nothing to lose. Why do you ask?"

"Because they frighten me, too, and I promised your cousin Elisabeth to take care of Sarah and her friend."

"What are you planning to do?"

"I just asked Captain Main if we could accompany them back to Charleston in the morning," Mimms said. "He said, 'yes.'"

"What if you're making a mountain out of a mole hill?" Beatrix asked.

"I pray that I am miss, but what if I'm right? I promised Mistress Elisabeth that I would protect the girls, and although I may be wrong, I'm willing to take that chance."

As the carriage made its final turn onto the plantation's allee, Sarah held her breath. Carrefour was known for its beauty, but the words used to describe it didn't do it justice. Made out of pink brick and white stucco, the mansion was the grandest plantation house Sarah had ever seen.

The mansion had a disquieting unfamiliarity, though, and she was unnerved by the provocative stares on the faces of some of the slaves in the yard. One even stuck his tongue out at Sarah and grabbed his crotch, forcing Sarah to shield her face with her bonnet.

Had she been older, she might have put more faith in her misgivings, but she was young, and this was her first holiday, so she pushed them out of her mind as quickly as they had come. "Do you think we'll be taken for harlots if we flirt with the boys on the island?" Eliza whispered, praying that Mimms couldn't overhear her conversation.

"You don't even know what a harlot is," Sarah replied.

"I do so; it's a woman who shows her dumplings during the day."

"Her dumplings?"

"Her heavers, her boobies; don't you know anything? Boys can do really weird things with their tongues, too. Do you want me to tell you about that?"

"I certainly do not," Sarah said between her teeth. "How do you know all of this?"

"I spy on my brother and his friends," Eliza admitted.

"You eaves drop on your own brother?"

"No, I hide behind the furniture and spy. And you didn't answer my question. Don't you want to know what it's like to flirt with a boy?"

"Oh, yes," Sarah said. "It's just that since the day we were born, we've been expected to marry a man from the right family and to have a houseful of children. Half of us will die during childbirth, Eliza. Don't you want more?"

"Of course, I do," Eliza replied.

"Are you saying you don't want to get married?"

"It's not that I don't want to get married someday. I just don't want to be told that I have to."

The girls were escorted into the mansion by a noisy klatch of cousins that Sarah knew she would never get straight. Supper was in two hours, Beatrix said, giving them plenty of time to settle into their quarters at the top of the grand staircase.

Sarah had hoped to stay on the third floor, where the other children slept, but her disappointment vanished when she and Eliza stepped into their room. Despite their lives of privilege, the girls had never seen anything as breathtaking.

"It's beautiful," they said in unison.

Sprays of vanilla orchids, pink anthurium, dwarf cannas, purple passiflora, and protea had been placed through the room. The furnishings were made of burgundy-hued mahogany that Haiti was famous for.

The whitewashed walls and floors were palm wood. There was more. Mimms and the girls marveled at the lace-trimmed bed linens and matching canopy. The bed was huge and so soft that it must have contained the down of a thousand geese.

As Sarah sat on its edge, she almost disappeared. "No lumps," she said, and then she noticed something else that was new to her. The room's exterior wall wasn't solid in the usual sense. It was a series of floor-to-ceiling shutters partially concealed behind billowy muslin draperies.

"Do you ever feel guilty about being rich?" Sarah asked, looking over at Eliza.

"Everybody's rich," Eliza replied, surprised, "especially your cousins."

"Did you see Beatrix's pearls? They're as big as butter beans, and they're pink. They must have cost a fortune."

"I'm sure they did, but you changed the subject, Eliza. Everybody's not rich."

"Everybody we know is." Eliza said, bouncing on the bed.

"But don't you feel guilty? Sometimes. I look around this room and think it's not right for anyone to have so much. What did Mimms think?"

"I think it's none of my business," Mimms said.

Then with her hands mounted on her hips, she stared hard at Sarah and said, "Are we done talking about this for now?"

"Yes, ma'am," Sarah said. "We're done for now."

"I thought so."

"Mimms, I want to ask you about something else," Sarah said, joining Eliza on the bed. "I want to know what happened on the boat today, and about your conversation with Captain Main. Were you frightened by the drums?"

"No, Miss Elephant Ears, I wasn't."

"Did you talk to Captain Main about leaving the island?"

"Now what are you doing asking me about my business?" Sarah said. She was certain she'd overheard Mimms saying something like that.

"That was a private conversation, and no, I didn't say anything about leaving the island," Mimms said, preferring to spring her plans on the girls in the morning. "Now let's get you two ready for supper."

Supper was a grand affair at Carrefour, especially when there were guests, so the girls dressed to the nines. Sarah wore her favorite dress, and even Mamma would have approved of her manners that night. Her dress was pale blue, but Eliza's gown was yellow. It picked up the rusty highlights of her unruly curls, making her look like Peaseblossom.

It wouldn't have mattered what they'd worn, though. They could scarcely be seen among the women seated around them.

"Mica dust," Eliza exclaimed under her breath. "They've all been sprinkled with mica dust."

"They're wearing tiaras," Sarah whispered back. "Diamond tiaras. Mamma told me they might wear them while we were here, but I didn't believe her. Look at Grand-Mere. She's wearing a kokoshnik."

"A what?" Eliza whispered.

"It's a Russian tiara. Hers has diamonds and cabochon emeralds. And her chest, it's covered with diamonds. Aunt Beatrix's tiara is sapphires and diamonds, and Cousin Alisanne's tiara had the biggest rubies I've ever seen."

"It's like having supper inside a bank vault," Eliza whispered. "Where do jewels like this come from?"

"Russia," Sarah replied.

"They're all Russian. According to Mamma, Grand-Pere Louis is obsessed with the propagation of grandsons so he has an understanding with his sons' wives. He showers them with the finest jewelry in the world, and they stay pregnant. Mamma calls it 'an unholy alliance.'"

"Does your mother have a tiara?" Eliza asked.

"She has two; one was a wedding gift from the Heberts, and Papa gave her the other one when I was born." Sarah and Eliza were seated between Aunt Beatrix and Cousin Alisanne.

Pregnancy was certainly a fact of life in Charleston, but women in the last stages of pregnancy, as Alisanne was, seldom showed up at the supper table. They spent their last weeks in confinement that restricted them to their beds regardless of their wishes.

Sarah had grown up believing that advanced pregnancy was distasteful in some way. It was too earthy for virtuous women to flaunt or for chivalrous men to acknowledge. The Heberts didn't feel that way.

In their boisterous, good-natured way, they teased Alisanne mercilessly, and she dished out as good as she got. At one point, she stood up and marched back and forth across the room, honking like a goose. The laughter was uproarious.

Flush from their victory on the polo field, the Hebert men drank more rum, offered up more toasts, and smoked more cigars than anyone Sarah had ever seen. And the women weren't far behind. Charleston women restrained their remarks in polite company; Carrefour women didn't hold back, and the men at the table seemed to like it that way.

Eliza's great-grandmother was a big topic of conversation. One of the uncles said that he had studied her scientific findings and, as a result, turned a handsome profit growing hemp. "What's hemp?" Sarah asked Eliza when there was a lull in the conversation. Eliza shrugged her shoulders and said she had no idea.

CHAPTER 6

A Grandiose Darky

Carrefour Plantation

AFTER THEIR DAZZLING DINNER, and Sarah and Eliza were safely settled into their bed, Mimms quietly slipped out. She was counting the hours until she could get back to civilization. She intended to keep her plans from the girls as long as she could, but she couldn't put off telling Master Hebert, so she asked a servant to take her to him.

On the way she spotted Captain Main. With her brilliantly-colored attire and exotic jewelry, Mimms looked like a gypsy, according to Sarah, and she had an unwavering intuition. Back on the boat she had seen things. Something evil was just beyond the water's edge. She could feel it. Suddenly the shore was lined with shirtless men beating drums and wooden blocks with the butts of their machetes.

The pounding reached a crescendo, and then it subsided, and the men stepped back into the shadows. As they disappeared, Mimms wrapped her arms around her shoulders and shuddered.

"I want to know what's going on, Captain," Mimms said.

The captain was usually eager to speak to a lusty-looking woman like Mimms, but he was hesitant to tell her what he had just learned. Finally, he decided that she had a right to know.

"I'm a fixture on this plantation," he said, "and the servants hardly notice me, so I hear things. Tonight I learned that the entire island is about to explode. It's a slave rebellion, miss, and it is nearly here. When I leave in the morning, I'm never coming back to this plantation or to this whole bloody island."

"Do you still have room for me and the girls?" Mimms asked softly.

"We'll squeeze you in," the captain said, "but we're not going to Charleston. We're going to Cuba."

"Cuba's fine, captain. See you in the morning."

As it turned out, Mimms' conversation with Captain Main had been a waste of time. That night, some of the rebels paid a visit to the Indigo. The schooner was docked at the landing, and the rebels had overtaken the crew by swimming to the boat underwater.

A savage fight broke out, and the captain and his crew fought bravely, but they were overwhelmed. Captain Main and his men were chopped up into pieces small enough to fit into a stewpot. The decision to kill the crew had been an easy one, but the rebels argued about what to do with the Indigo. A schooner like the Indigo was worth a small fortune.

Some men wanted to sail it to Havana to sell it, but they were voted down. The boat was scuttled so the Hebert family couldn't use it to escape the plantation.

Disclosing her plans to Grand-Pere turned out to be an ugly scene. Mimms' calm demeanor usually resulted in civil discourse, but Louis Hebert bellowed like a bull when she told him her plans. "You bloody whore!" he shouted as his face turned red and his fists hit his desk. "No one does anything on this plantation without my permission, especially some grandiose darky."

"Monsieur Hebert, your grandniece and I are leaving the island tomorrow with or without your permission. If I've overreacted, I'll have to deal with my mistress once we are back in Charleston, but if I'm right, I may save your niece's life. Forgive me for any inconvenience that we may have caused you. You have been a most gracious host. Goodnight, sir."

"I haven't dismissed you yet!"

"Yes, sir, you have. Goodnight."

If Grand-Pere hadn't been three sheets to the wind and worked up about the rebellion headed his way, he would have had Mimms stopped, but he had something more important to do. He had to relocate the imperial crown to a hiding place on the other side of the plantation.

There was a knock at his door. He assumed it was Mimms returning to make her apologies. But it was a messenger with another urgent message from Sarah's great uncle at Les Cayes. "The insurrection that had been previously reported had changed over to full-scale revolt," the uncle warned.

Anarchy could reach the gates of Carrefour by the end of the week giving him four days to prepare. Hebert should have evacuated the family. He would have, but he had had no idea how dangerous the situation had become until it was too late. His brother had warned him that the channel to the sea was now in the hands of the rebels.

However, French troops were stationed throughout the island, and according to his brother, more were on the way from Antigua. Carrefour's massive gates and thick interior walls rivaled any fortress on the island, but it was going to be bloody. His servants concerned him the most.

If they joined the revolt, they could threaten his family from within. He was grateful that he had four days to get ready. He had the perfect hiding place for the imperial jewels —an overgrown cave that his father had used as a wine cellar and a place to grow mushrooms.

It was a natural cave, and it had once had a large opening, but bats had multiplied faster than the mushrooms, so his father had had the care's nature opening filled in. The cave was left with a single entrance, a narrow door disguised within the walls of one to the plantation's privies.

Only a handful of people were old enough to even remember the cave, let alone the location of its secret entrance. Grand-Pere hated to be separated from the crown, but he would rest easier knowing that even if the rebels reached the plantation, they'd never find it.

Some of his teenage grandsons were to take it there. He barely knew one grandson from another, and he didn't care. He just knew that they were strong enough to carry the trunk containing the jewelry but too young to give much thought to what they were carrying. Even though he was inebriated, Grand-Pere wasn't too drunk for one last look at the crown. But then there was a knock at the door, followed by a second. Grand-Pere jumped.

"Grand-Pere," a teenaged voice called out. It was the grandsons. The crown's spell was broken, and Grand-Pere let out a sob. He was terrified. Would his empire survive the upcoming days, or was God preparing to destroy the House of Hebert?

CHAPTER 7

Moments After the Massacre
in the Courtyard

EVEN THOUGH THE FIRE hadn't reached the mansion yet, Beatrix's apartment suddenly began to fill up with searing black smoke. It could only mean one thing: The rebels in the courtyard were inside the mansion.

Mimms was the first to comprehend the urgency. Hurriedly she pulled Sarah and Eliza away from the window and shouted "Get down!" as she grabbed Sarah by the wrist and yanked her to the floor.

"That hurt, Mimms," Sarah complained.

"You can cry about that later," Mimms replied, "but right now you're going to crawl your butt over to the door!"

"But …."

"But nothing," Mimms growled. "Now, get going."

As Mimms and the girls neared the door to Alisanne's room, they heard sounds coming from the stairs. "Mimms, the men from the courtyard," Sarah cried. "I think they're inside the house!"

"I know, I hear them, too," Mimms replied, jumping to her feet. "They're coming for us."

"But, the downstairs servants," Eliza whispered.

"They're either dead or have run away, Eliza. The fire was intentionally set; you must know that by now," Mimms replied. "We're on our own. Now, grab onto that bureau over there," she said pointing to a large chest of drawers just to the right of the door. "Let's see if we can push it in front of the door."

"Sarah, what are you doing?" Beatrix shrieked as she spotted Mimms and the girls attempting to move the bureau. "You're going to block our only way out! We have to leave before those savages find us. We've got to get to Les Cayes!"

"It's too late, Auntie," Sarah said. "They're already on the stairs."

"No!" Alisanne shrieked. "Noooooo!"

As everyone rushed to help push the bureau into place, the anarchy on the other side of the door swelled. "Where are the women?" the men chanted, pummeling the door with their fists. "We want the women!" Then the massive door began to pull away from its hinges. Mimms pushed the girls onto the floor behind the bureau, as the other women in the room tried to find their own hiding places.

Once inside, the mob found what it was looking for. Alisanne was too big to find a hiding place, so she was the first to die. Then the throng moved on to Grand-Mere and the children clustered around her. They used machetes and clubs, butcher knives, and cane hooks, lethal weapons in the hands of angry men.

The mayhem continued when a hand suddenly reached out of the darkness and grasped Mimms by her hair. She cursed and clawed at the air, and as she was being dragged backwards, she regained her balance just long enough to shove Sarah and Eliza toward Beatrix, who was crouched next to the door.

As Mimms fought for her life, Beatrix used the distraction to grab Charlotte and to lead Sarah and Eliza out of the smoke-filled room. From there they tiptoed down the darkened hallway and disappeared behind a small door leading to a narrow service stairway. "Let's hide here," Sarah whispered.

"There's too much smoke," Beatrix replied. "See how it's coming up the stairs? We've got to keep going, but I have an idea. At the bottom of the stairs, there's a tall cupboard. If we can find it in all this smoke, we can hide there, at least for a while." Then Beatrix shifted Charlotte to her other hip and made her way to the bottom of the stairs.

Then she started feeling along the wall for the door to the cupboard.

"Here it is!" she exclaimed beneath her breath, and then as effortlessly as if they had rehearsed it, Beatrix and the girls squeezed into the cupboard and closed the door.

Sarah thought her brain was going to explode from what she had just witnessed, and Beatrix fought to muffle Charlotte's cries. All Sarah could do was to hold onto Eliza as tightly as she could and to pray harder than she'd ever prayed in her life. Urine ran down her legs and she and Eliza were shaking so violently that Sarah was afraid they were going to topple over. Sarah wanted her mother.

After what seemed like an eternity, the screams from upstairs ended, only to be replaced by laughter, as the men that made up the mob began to work their way through the mansion room-by-room. They started in the main salon, where cane hooks were used to slash at Grand-Mere's cherished chandelier, forcing it to let go of its moorings and explode onto the floor.

Chairs were hurled at walls and windows, paintings were destroyed, and china cabinets were sent crashing to the floor expelling their treasurers like shrapnel. Grand-Mere's priceless stemware drew the most laughter, however, as it was thrown at the room's remaining windowpanes stem by stem. The only good thing was that the fire that had threatened the plantation earlier had failed to arrive. *Perhaps it had burned itself out,* Beatrix surmised, *or maybe it simply changed course.*

As a parting gesture, the men overturned a large china hutch in the dining room. This time the object of ridicule was Great-Great-Grand-Mere's collection of porcelain figures that had once belonged to Catherine the Great's mother-in-law, the Grand Duchess Anna Petrovna. The collection had taken the family more than thirty years to amass, only to be destroyed in the blink of an eye.

CHAPTER 8

The Boy with the Machete

BEATRIX AND THE GIRLS lost track of time during their stay in the cupboard. From the sound of things, the rebels had left the mansion during the early hours of the morning, but the women were too frightened to leave their hiding place until well into the afternoon. It was then that Beatrix insisted upon leaving.

"No, we mustn't," Sarah begged.

"I wet my gown," Eliza said. "I want to go home."

"It's all right, Eliza," Sarah said. "I wet mine, too, and we don't have to go anywhere. You and I will wait here together. We'll wait until someone comes to help us. Papa will come; he'll rescue us."

"Nobody's coming for us, Sarah," Beatrix said. "Even if they tried to find us, they'd never find us here. The house is quiet now, but the men who did this could come back, and if they do, they could set fire to the mansion. We have to leave and we have to do it now." With that, Beatrix repositioned Charlotte and timidly stepped out of the cupboard. Sarah and Eliza followed.

As they crept past the library, Sarah noticed that Grand-Pere's collection of antique maps had been ripped from the walls and torn to shreds. Grand-Pere's leather-bound first editions had met a similar fate, and the room smelled of urine and feces.

Then Sarah noticed something she'd only seen during hog killing time, a long bloody section of tissue suspended from a bamboo pike at the entrance to the dining room. "Entrails!" Sarah screamed when she saw it. "Pig's entrails!"

"Keep going, Sarah," Beatrix ordered, sickened by the knowledge that the tissue had nothing to do with entrails. It was an afterbirth, and Alisanne had been the only pregnant member of the family.

Just beyond the entrance into the dining room was a small alcove that contained a door that opened onto a narrow stairway leading down to the mansion's half-basement. "This way," Beatrix ordered. "Maybe we'll have a better chance at not being seen if we leave the house through the basement."

Grasping a narrow bannister, the women descended the stairs as quietly as insects. At the bottom, Beatrix gasped and pointed to the opening where the exterior door to the basement was supposed to be. The rebels had made mincemeat out of it. It looked as though they had kicked it in with such force that both the door and the frame surrounding it resembled kindling. "Let's go," Beatrix said, handing Charlotte to Sarah. "We're running out of time."

Taking the lead, Beatrix skillfully negotiated her way through the rubble left by the shattered door, and then she stepped into the courtyard. The fresh air smelled sweet, but the setting sun half-blinded her until something—something shiny—caught her eye. It was at that moment that a machete slashed into her neck with such force that it almost decapitated her. Sarah heard a whoosh followed by a gurgling sound, and then she saw Beatrix's lifeless body fall to the ground.

"Mama!" Charlotte wailed as she wriggled away from Sarah's grasp and threw herself on top of her mother's body. It was then that Sarah comprehended what had happened. A machete had just killed Beatrix, and the machete was attached to a boy who was standing less than ten feet away. As she studied his silhouette against the setting sun, she saw steam rising from his head and shoulders and could practically taste the blood on his clothing. This had not been his first kill of the day, and he was going to kill again if he had his way.

The boy suddenly came toward Sarah with his machete raised, and she frantically searched for a weapon. What she spotted was a three-foot section of wood that had splintered away from the basement door. It had the circumference of a fencepost and the wood was rock hard from years of exposure to the sun. Best of all, the board was still affixed to the door's lockbox and escutcheon plate. It was a formidable weapon.

As the boy crept toward Sarah, Eliza shifted her weight, preparing to escape in the opposite direction, and the movement caught the boy's attention. The boy suddenly grunted and turned his body toward Sarah. Certain that she was about to die, Sarah shouted, "Grab Charlotte and run into the fields, Eliza!"

Eliza moved toward Charlotte. The movement startled the boy, and at the last second, he turned from Sarah, and lunged instead at Eliza. Eliza screamed, and the distraction gave Sarah time to grab the doorframe.

As Sarah spun back around, she saw Eliza on the ground with the boy standing over her. He hesitated. Then he kicked her in the stomach and slammed his machete into the ground, narrowly missing her foot. Eliza did a half roll and jumped to her feet. Her eyes met Sarah's, and Sarah yelled, "Run!"

Eliza jerked her eyes toward the fields and took off. Her tattered nightgown had blood on it, but she had darted away so quickly that Sarah couldn't tell if it was Eliza's blood or the boy's. The boy now lunged at Sarah and got off the first swing, but it wasn't the measured swing of an adult killer. It was an adolescent swing that missed by a mile and almost knocked the boy off his feet.

Something inside Sarah suddenly snapped, and she became enraged. She had been raised to be a gentile young woman—a daughter of the South Carolina plantation aristocracy, but now she was seething.

Before he could regroup, Sarah took her own swing, and she proved to be far better at it than he was. She caught the boy just behind his right temple sending the brass lockbox deep into his brain. The force of the blow sent him flying, and he landed with a sickening thud at Beatrix's feet. Blood gushed from his wound, and the battle was over almost before it had begun.

At that point, the person that Sarah had been when she arrived at Carrefour would have thrown herself onto the ground and sobbed, waiting for Papa or some other male figure to rescue her. Looking back, she realized that she had been Miss Know-It-All at school, as she constantly harped about the inequities of the education available to girls and bragged about how she was going to change it someday by showing everyone what females were really capable of.

To her credit, she did identify some of the changes that needed to be made, and she was certainly willing to expose herself by expressing them, but she'd never been required to act on them until now. Talk was cheap, but squaring off against a boy intent upon killing you, was an altogether different thing. Now, she knew that courage, respect, and even opportunity had to be earned. If she wanted things to change, she would have to work for it by becoming the woman she wanted to be.

Thanks to the boy with the machete, the old Sarah was dead. "Good riddance," Sarah whispered to herself. "Good riddance." The new Sarah thought about nothing but survival, so she grabbed Charlotte and ran toward the fields after Eliza. She was strong, and she was quick, she told herself, and she didn't need anyone to rescue her. Papa had taught her that she could do anything she set her mind to, and this was going to be the ultimate test.

The boy's eye rested on his cheek, held there by threadlike ligaments. He grabbed at it and wailed. Eliza was halfway across the open field when she realized that she had forgotten all about Charlotte. She had to go back. She turned just in time to see the boy fall. Then she raced toward the courtyard.

The boy was convulsing by the time she got there, and his rantings had sent Sarah's brain into overload. "You bastard!" Sarah screamed, standing over him with her weapon. "You bloody bastard!"

"Is he going to die?" Eliza asked out of breath.

"I don't know," Sarah said.

"Then maybe we should hit him again," Eliza offered.

"You're welcome to hit him all you want to," Sarah said, handing her the doorframe.

Eliza had expected Sarah and her adrenaline-infused brain to take another good whack at the boy, and she gasped when Sarah handed her the weapon. Eliza stood motionless a long moment, and then almost against her will, she hit the boy across his legs. Eliza's lips quivered as she dropped the weapon. She'd only hit him hard enough to raise some welts, but it didn't matter. She was done.

"Beatrix is dead, isn't she," Eliza said, throwing down her weapon. Sarah didn't reply. She just stood there listening to Charlotte's cries and watching blood pool in the boy's ear. "They'll be back, Sarah. We've got to get out of here. What should we do about him?" Eliza asked, pointing to the boy.

"We leave him here," Sarah replied. And then she wrenched Charlotte away from her mother's body more harshly than she had intended and said, "Let's go."

"Where?"

"Any place but here."

Together they sprinted across the open field that surrounded Carrefour. Survival was all that mattered now, so Sarah ignored the hysterical three-year-old on her hip and kept going. She was strong and quick, and she didn't need anyone to rescue her. The boy with the machete had taught her that.

Sarah fought back today, and she wouldn't hesitate to do it again. There was no sign of the fire that had set the nightmare into motion the night before, but there was a new moon. Darkness would be their only ally.

Sarah believed that if they could get to Les Cayes, they'd be safe. A heavy carpet of cane stalk made it impossible to see the pathways leading to the plantation. She would have to rely on what she'd overheard during dinner the night before.

The plantation was due west. She remembered that much, and it was significantly lower in elevation, so she set out in the direction of the setting sun and concentrated on maintaining a downhill trajectory. Eliza stayed close behind. They came to an outcropping of striated boulders, but they skirted it fearing that they might be seen.

To avoid climbing over it, Sarah went to the left of the outcropping, and for some reason, Eliza went the other way. It was getting dark, and then it happened. The girls got separated. "Eliza," Sarah shouted in a whispered scream. "Eliza." There was no reply. What had happened to her? Sarah deposited Charlotte at the foot of the outcropping and ordered her not to move while she went looking for Auntie Eliza.

Sarah was exhausted from carrying the extra weight of a frightened three-year-old, but she had to find Eliza. Had she fallen? Was she unconscious? Had someone grabbed her, or was she dead? Sarah ran along the bottom edge of the outcropping calling Eliza's name as loudly as she dared. The darkness she'd prayed for had become enemy. She couldn't find Eliza anywhere even though she had to be so near.

Sarah rubbed her eyes with her hands and tried to catch her breath. She had no idea how to get to Les Cayes. She had Charlotte to care for, and everyone on the island wanted to kill her. The world had gone mad, but the one thing she couldn't do was give up on Eliza, so she went back for Charlotte and kept looking. It was then that she noticed a light in the distance.

She and Charlotte drew nearer, and the glow grew in intensity, hotter looking, angry. Fire! Something was on fire! She worked her way toward the flames until she spotted the silhouette of a large house. It had to be Les Cayes. "They've been here, too," she cried as she nuzzled her face in Charlotte's sweaty curls. What if they were the only ones still alive?

Sarah's eyes felt like they'd been slathered with bacon grease. She had to rest and look for Eliza in the morning. Shelter, they needed shelter—a building of some kind, a barn. Then she saw a privy built of fine red brick, with a tall pitched roofline and a beautifully carved door. There was a sign above the door: Aunt Felicia's Necessary.

Sarah knew it must have been named after Great Aunt Felicia, the fussy one in the family. Inside the privy were seven holes of varying sizes, one to accommodate every member of the family. It also had a brick floor and a long bench along one wall. It would have to do. At least they would have a roof over their heads, Sarah thought as she and Charlotte huddled together on the floor.

Sarah had never been responsible for a three-year-old before; she was little more than a child, herself. There were always a number of small children running around during family gatherings, but Sarah had never taken much interest in them. Now, she was a surrogate mother. "Mommy, I want my mommy," Charlotte whimpered. "Where's mommy?"

"Your mommy's in heaven with your papa and the angels," Sarah said.

"Is she coming back?"

"No, darling, she can't come back to us because she needs to stay with your papa, but someday you can go be with her in heaven."

"Then who will take care of me?"

"I'll take care of you, Charlotte. I'll take care of you just like your mommy did." With that, Charlotte settled into Sarah's arms, and they slept. Sarah didn't know how long she'd been asleep when she heard a sound, but it was loud enough to wake her. She heard it again. It was a scream, but not the bloodcurdling kind she'd heard at Carrefour. It was a muffled scream, a cry.

Eliza, it could be Eliza! Sarah shuddered and struggled to untangle herself from Charlotte. She crawled toward the scream. The privy was constructed of brick, but the stalls within it were made of wood similar to the stalls in a horse barn.

The sound was coming from the last stall. She crept toward it, but there was nothing there. That's when she heard another scream. Not again. She started to crawl back to Charlotte, but a voice whispered in her ear: It could be Eliza! Sarah put her ear to the side of the stall that was up against the other brick wall.

The wooden wall sounded hollow, and it wasn't a wall at all; it was a small door. Sarah ran her fingers along the edges of the door in the darkness, and then she quietly opened it. A lantern was on the other side of the door, revealing a narrow stairway leading into an underground chamber. Sarah waited until her eyes grew accustomed to the light, and then she descended the stairs on her hands and knees.

Halfway down, she stopped. Two blond-haired boys were standing over Eliza. Her hair was caked with blood, and she was whimpering, but were the boys trying to help or hurt her? Then one of them pulled up his nightshirt and pranced in Eliza's face. The whole world had gone mad. Eliza hadn't seen Sarah yet, and neither had the boys.

When they weren't taunting Eliza, they were giggling and running into each other. They were really, really drunk. Should Sarah call out, or should she try to get closer? She wasn't sure of anything; her mind was playing tricks. Suddenly, she spotted a little girl standing at the bottom of the stairs, a naked five-year-old wearing a triple strand of pearls and a glittering crown that reminded Sarah of the papier-mache crowns that English families always wore on Christmas Day.

It didn't occur to her that the crown could be anything other than a costume crown. The little girl's lips were pursed, and Sarah guessed that she was hiding something in her mouth, although she was too frightened to care. The experience was so surreal that Sarah wasn't even sure the child was real until she looked into her eyes.

Then Sarah put her finger up to her lips, and the little girl froze. Then she cautiously glanced back at Eliza and returned her gaze to Sarah. She spoke with her eyes. Help me! Come up the stairs, Sarah motioned, but do it silently. The girl complied, willing herself to caress each step.

A spider couldn't have done it more stealthily, but then spiders seldom wear Christmas crowns. The glittering crown suddenly slid off the girl's head, suspended in the air by the tangle of hair. She grabbed at it, and then she gasped as it hopped down the stairs like a pogo stick. The boys jerked their heads toward the sound and angrily met Sarah's stare.

"A girl!" they screamed.

"She's the one I want," the older of the two said in a slobbery voice. "I want to touch her tits."

As she kept a wary eye on the boys, Sarah hurriedly grabbed the little girl by the arm and catapulted her up the stains, as Eliza suddenly jumped to her feet. "Hurry!" Sarah shouted. Eliza ran up the stairs before the boys could steady themselves enough to go after her. They were still really drunk, but they weren't laughing anymore. They were clawing their way up the stairs.

Sarah pushed Eliza toward the door to the privy and was crawling after her when one of the boys grabbed her foot. She had to buy time. Five seconds, that's all she needed. The oil lamp! She seized the lamp and hurled it to the bottom of the stairs. The light exploded as Eliza, and the little girl disappeared through the doorway above her.

The smaller boy went back to fight the fire, while the older one continued to claw at Sarah's legs. She fell back a step as her fingers tore at the stair steps in front of her, and fearing that she might lose her grip, she instinctively stabbed her foot into the boy's face.

Too drunk to react quickly enough to regain his balance, the boy was hurled over the edge of the stairs. Sarah didn't stop to view her work; she darted through the doorway and slammed the door shut. *Block the door. Block the Door.* She had to block the door, but with what. Then she spotted a crude wooden latch system built into the door.

Sarah threw the latch and pushed on the door with her feet to keep it closed. She heard screams on the other side, but she couldn't open the door. She wouldn't open it. The boys might try to kill her just like the boy with the machete. Now, they were hitting the door with their fists and pleading for her to open it.

What if they were to break the latch? What would happen then? A wooden shelf the size of a fireplace mantelpiece was affixed to the privy wall just to the left of the hidden door.

"Help me, Eliza," Sarah shouted. "We've got to dislodge the shelf, Eliza; help me." But Eliza simply stood there, and Sarah didn't have time to argue. She straddled the shelf with her feet, and made it fall to the floor as smoke curled through the cracks around the edge of the door.

The shelf was heavy as Sarah dragged it into position. She had planned to put it in front of the door and keep it there with her feet, but on second thought, she decided to wedge it between the door and one of the wooden stalls. "Come on you son of a bitch!" she screamed as she kicked the shelf into place.

Sarah viewed her handiwork and filled her lungs with the damp, smoky air. Her eyes burned, and her face and hands were covered with soot, but she didn't care as long as her barricade held. She'd never see these boys again. They could die down there for all she cared.

Well, how many people could one fourteen-year-old be expected to kill in one day? Charlotte! Sarah had forgotten all about her; parenting was a new experience, so she hurriedly checked on her and smiled when she realized she was still asleep. That reminded Sarah that she had just inherited another charge, so she scooped the little island girl into her arms and whispered assuring words to her.

English didn't solicit a response, but French did. It was a small victory, but it was something. She handed the girl to Eliza, and then a debilitating thought struck her. The cave could have another entrance, and the demons could use it to come after her. And they WOULD want to get even.

Were they still in the cave, or had they found a way out. She had to know, so she crawled back to the door, put her ear to it, and listened. She heard nothing at first, and then she heard a thunderous crash. The stairway must have given way taking the boys with it.

There was a hush, and then the fire began to howl. Smoke pushed at the door and licked the bricks, circling the entrance into the passageway. The floor shook, and the walls started to crumble. The privy was falling apart. Jesus! Sarah jumped to her feet, grabbed Charlotte, and told Eliza to move. Charlotte cried out, but Sarah put her hand over her mouth. "Be quiet, Baby. You and Auntie Sarah have to find another hiding place."

"Are the bad men coming?"

"I don't know, sweetheart, but just in case, we're going to go." Just behind the privy was a large wooden dye vat filled with indigo stalks still green from the fields. It was a hiding place! Sarah quickly tossed the two little girls into the vat and started to climb in after them when she looked back at Eliza. "Come on," Sarah said, looking into Eliza's face.

It was then that she caught Eliza's blank stare. Something was wrong. Oh, God! Sarah jumped back onto the ground and said, "I need you to climb into the vat, dear. We're going to hide from the bad people."

Eliza seemed to understand, at least for the moment, so she allowed Sarah to push her up and over the edge of the vat, and Sarah tumbled in after her.

"Are we safe here?" Charlotte asked.

"Yes, we're safe here. I just need to check on something. Stay here and don't move. I'll be right back."

"All right," Charlotte whispered.

Getting to the bottom of the vat was easier than crawling to its top, but Sarah had to check on the fire. She wanted to know if the drunken boys could have survived the fire in good enough shape to come after her. She knew that there had been an explosion of some kind in the cave and that a portion of the privy had fallen in on itself, but she was astonished at what she saw.

The entire privy had been reduced to a pile of smoldering bricks. No one could have survived a collapse like that. She'd killed two boys during the past twelve hours, three, counting the boy with the machete. Who would she kill tomorrow? Perhaps she should kill an entire family or an orphanage packed with children.

Evil is as evil does. Maybe one dead body looked just like another after a while. Oh, and perhaps Sarah would be the one doing the dying next time. It would be poetic justice if you thought about it. The newspaper heading would read: Plantation Princess Turned Killer. The next day it could read: Killer Princess Dead. Sarah looked around to get her bearings before returning to her hiding place.

Les Cayes was still burning in the distance, so she knew that was west. It would be dawn any minute so that the sun would be coming up behind her. She turned, and then she gasped. The princess was indeed going to die today, and if she had to guess, it was going to happen in about two minutes.

There was a boy, another damn boy, a handsome one maybe eighteen, standing six feet from the vat. His pale blue eyes were looking right at her, and he had a machete. She was going to die, but what should she do about Eliza and Charlotte and the little girl? She didn't want to leave them alone in the vat, but she couldn't just offer them up as sacrificial lambs.

That's when the boy said, "We've got to get out of here. The rebels are on their way back. I overheard one of the field hands saying they're on their way."

"I thought you were here to kill me," Sarah said.

"No, I was looking for my cousins. Have you seen them? They're fourteen and sixteen. Blond hair. I thought they might be hiding in the cave beneath the privy. What happened to it, do you know?"

"I just got here," Sarah said, avoiding another lie. "Your cousins, were they boys or girls?"

"They were boys with blond hair."

"I haven't seen them," Sarah said. "Were they alone?"

"I don't know," the boy said. "They might have been with my sister, Ellie. She's eleven. She has blond hair, too."

"I haven't seen her, either," Sarah said as her insides screamed. OH, MY GOD! WAS SHE IN THE CAVE, TOO?

"Well, hurry up. We have to get out of here."

"I can't leave," Sarah said.

"The rebels are coming. If they see us, they'll kill us."

"Wait," Sarah said, climbing back into the vat. "I have to get something." Seconds later, she produced Eliza, Charlotte, and the little island girl. "Who are you?" she said as she handed Charlotte over to him.

"Henri Hebert," he replied. "Now run!" They raced out of the plantation yard into the nearest field, and then they sprinted about a quarter of a mile between the furrows until they came to a rocky bluff overlooking the ocean.

Delmas, another Hebert family plantation, stood in the distance, but it had been destroyed, too. They reached the edge of the cliff, and Henri called out, "We have to climb down this bluff. Hurry!"

With that, Sarah slid down the embankment taking Eliza with her, and they landed hard on the sand beach below. "There's a cave about a mile down the beach," Henri said. "Our only chance is to get there before we're seen."

CHAPTER 9

The Cave on the Beach

HENRI AND SARAH COLLAPSED when they reached the cave. Charlotte and the little island girl wept, and Eliza dropped to her knees. The cave felt like heaven. It was dark and cool, and the wet sand soothed Sarah's swollen feet. Nothing was said for a time.

Eliza was quiet, but compliant so Sarah helped her find a dry place to lie down. Eliza looked like a ghost with her soiled nightgown and glassy eyes. Her hair was caked with blood, and she seemed dazed.

"Eliza, it's me, Sarah. We're going to take you home, back to your mother." With the mention of home, Eliza's frightened eyes turned softly toward Sarah's. "We're going to go home?" Eliza whispered.

"Yes," Sarah said, knowing that she had promised a miracle. Once Eliza was settled, Sarah sat with her back to the cave. After he'd caught his breath, Henri looked over at Sarah and asked if she was from Carrefour.

"Yes," she replied. "Well, my friend and I were visiting Carrefour, but we're really from Charleston. My mother is an Hebert, Elisabeth Hebert. She and Beatrix Hebert were first cousins.

"Your father's English?" Henri said, trying to place him.

"He used to be," Sarah replied. "What's happening on the island, Henri?"

"It's a rebellion. The People are trying to take over the colony," he said. "I lived at Delmar, and I know it's been destroyed because I watched them burn the mansion. Les Cayes is gone, too. Well, I guess you know that, but I was hoping that Carrefour might have been able to hold out."

"The rebels destroyed Carrefour, too, Henri. I don't know if they set it to fire, yet, but they will."

"So where's the Carrefour family? Do you know where they're hiding?"

"They're all dead, Henri, at least I think they are," Sarah replied. "I know the men are because I saw them killed in the courtyard. I think the women and children are dead, too. Aunt Beatrix, Charlotte, and my friend and I were the only ones to escape the mansion."

"Where is Aunt Beatrix now?" Henri asked.

"She was killed by a boy with a machete."

"When?" Henri asked.

"Just as we were leaving the mansion," Sarah replied.

"Were you there?" Henri asked.

"Yes," Sarah whispered, turning her eyes away.

"Did he try to kill you, too?"

"Yes, but I hit him with a board."

"I hope you killed him."

"I think I did, but I'm not sure," Sarah said, diverting her eyes toward the rear of the cave, noticing for the first time that they weren't alone. A collection of faces, familiar ones to Henri, were staring back at her. Three of Henri's younger siblings, including his twelve-year-old sister Suzanne, were clustered together in the foreground.

In the shadows, was a young slave girl named Sookie, who was holding the baby of the Hebert family, Michael-Armand. After asking about the baby and receiving an affirmative nod from Sookie, Sarah turned to Henri and asked about the rest of his family. Where were all the grown-ups?

"They're dead; they're all dead," Suzanne interjected. Suzanne had a vacant stare similar to Eliza's. It was the kind of stare people get when they've seen too much.

Sarah hurriedly motioned to Sookie and the other children to huddle around Suzanne in an attempt to generate some warmth. Sarah didn't know how else to help the girl. They needed a fire, but that was out of the question.

40

Sarah and Sookie took turns caring for the children, except for the little island girl who wouldn't leave Sookie's side. Sookie knew a thing or two about children, but where had Sarah learned to rock a crying three-year-old or to make up stories about talking whisks and flying mushrooms. She had no idea.

Sarah had never even held a child before, and now she was Mother Goose. Maybe she had a gift, or maybe God had finally decided to take pity on the desolate remnants of the once-proud Heberts.

Sarah spent the rest of the day singing to Eliza, reliving the horror she had just experienced. Was it possible that she and Eliza had arrived at Carrefour only two days ago?

They had been on the last leg of their journey from Charleston to Haiti aboard the Indigo. Their destination was Carrefour Plantation, the home of Sarah's Huguenot relatives, known within the family as the island cousins. The girls were thrilled to be free of Madame Painchaud's Academy and traveling without their parents for the first time.

As Eliza idly dragged a stick through the water, she asked Sarah why her mother had picked Mimms to be their chaperone. "Because she trusts her," Sarah said dismissively.

"Well, I'm afraid of her," Eliza had said, and Mimms liked it that way. Creole, with features that suggested a touch of Arab blood, Mimms had a profile that could have graced an ancient coin. With her scarves and clanky gold bracelets, she dazzled. And now Mimms was dead.

Three hours into the four-hour trip, the Indigo had slowed to negotiate a narrow turn. Without warning, scores of pink ibis nesting in trees near the water's edge exploded into a flurry of wings and feathers. Sarah and Eliza screamed and covered their heads as some of the birds spilled out onto the deck. And then within moments, the jungle returned to normal, the birds flew away, and the girls entertained themselves collecting the brilliant feathers left behind.

And that's when the girls heard the drumbeats and saw the shirtless men. Mimms told them not to be afraid, but Sarah saw the look on Mimms's face. She knew that Mimms was frightened, and Mimms wasn't afraid of anything.

42

CHAPTER 10

A Stolen Boat

WHILE SARAH DID WHAT she could to comfort the children, Henri slipped out of the cave and didn't return until the following morning. As he stumbled back into the cave, he whispered to Sarah that he had bread and guarded good news, and then he motioned for her to meet him near the opening of the cave where they could speak without being overheard. "I went to Uncle Jean-Paul's plantation at Delmas to see if anyone there had survived the massacre," he said, "but they had all been slaughtered in their night clothes."

As Henri prepared to leave, however, he said he heard a sound coming from the main kitchen. When he went to investigate, he discovered Prosper, Uncle Jean-Paul's most-trusted servant. Taking an enormous chance, Henri called out to the old man and Prosper called back: "Master Henri! Master Henri!" After recounting the carnage that he had witnessed, Prosper handed Henri two loaves of stale bread and warned Henri that the family must leave the island at once. "They've already killed the rest of your family, and they will kill you, too," he cautioned.

Then he told Henri about a boat that belonged to his brother and said he would try to steal it and have it ready for Henri and the children to board after sunset. Cuba was the nearest landfall—about sixty miles. Prosper said. "It's your only chance, boy."

After speaking to Henri, Sarah was hesitant to tell the rest of the children about the possibility of escape for fear that it wouldn't come true, but she decided that Sookie had every right to know. "You're free to leave the island with the family, or you may stay," Sarah said. "The choice is yours," she told the sixteen-year-old.

"When my own baby died, my husband beat me an' sold me to the Heberts to wet-nurse the baby. My life on the island is dead," Sookie replied as she dried her tears with the sleeve of her dress. "I want to go with you."

Henri sat at the opening of the cave throughout the rest of the afternoon becoming increasingly restless as the shadows fell. Sarah kept her eye on the children and soothed and sang to Eliza.

Just then, Prosper arrived with the boat just as he had promised. "Children, wake up. There's a boat, and we're leaving the island. Come, come, we must hurry," Sarah said. Then she helped Suzanne and the younger children to their feet, and together they rushed out of the cave to see this miracle boat for themselves. It was then that she saw Eliza standing in the surf next to the boat.

"Yes, this boat is going to take us home," Sarah said, motioning to the other children. We're all going home." She put her arm around Eliza's small shoulders. Then Eliza reached for Sarah's hand and for the first time, Sarah knew that Eliza was going to be all right.

The boat was about twenty feet long, with a narrow keel running down the length of her, and there was no doubt that it had lived many lifetimes before that fateful day. It could still float, though, and it had oars and a sail, and it was filled with cans of fresh water and food that Prosper had scavenged from the kitchens at Les Cayes.

As they boarded the boat, Sarah desperately tried to properly thank Prosper, but he promptly stopped her. "If anyone sees me helping you, they will kill me. You must go now! Dieu vous assiste!"

"And may God be with you, Prosper."

Henri set sail on a west, northwesterly course. The ocean had never looked so vast, but the prevailing winds were with them, and their little boat cut through the water with ease. Sailing at night was disorienting, and Sarah worried that they would wake up in the morning to discover that their little boat had returned itself to Hispaniola. After a time, however, Sookie and Sarah spotted Polaris. To sail west, they knew that they had to keep Polaris to starboard and to pray that they would wake the next morning with the sun at their backs.

In the excitement over locating Polaris, however, Sarah had forgotten that it had been many hours since the children had last eaten. "I'm hungry," Charlotte whined.

"We're hungry, too," the younger children said in unison. So Sarah and Eliza took a quick inventory of the food that Prosper had put on board. Crammed into a flour sack, they found two crushed loaves of bread, half of a stale fruit cake, six plantains, a quart of stewed tomatoes, a bundle of dried parsley, and a pineapple far beyond its prime. Prosper had also thought to provide a paring knife, a three-gallon container of fresh water, and about a dozen kitchen rags that they gave to Sookie to use as diapers.

"If Prosper was right about reaching Cuba in no more than three days, and if we manage to stay on course and are careful with our supplies, I think we might have enough to make it," Henri said. Then Sarah and Eliza gave everyone a thin slice of bread along with a small cube of pineapple, and instructed them to suck on it very slowly before swallowing. Then everyone shared a tumbler of water, making sure that Sookie received an extra share to keep her milk flowing for the baby.

It wasn't much, but the food worked its magic, and each of the children was soon asleep, including Eliza. Sarah covered the younger ones with a tarp that Henri had found tucked inside the storage compartment in the bow of the boat, and they were finally at peace. Sarah was as exhausted as the children, but she offered to spell Henri at the helm for a few hours so he could sleep. He declined. "I'll take the first watch, Sarah," he said. "I'll wake you when I'm tired."

The first day went by in a blur as the sun beat down on them like hot coals. Sarah tended to Eliza's head that morning, hoping not to find a gaping wound that would need far more attention than she was capable of delivering. "Where does it hurt, Eliza?"

"Above my eye, toward the back of my head."

"It's right here," Sarah said, pulling Eliza's hair away from the area, "but it's not very deep. Did the boy do this to you, Eliza?"

"What boy?"

"The boy with the machete. The boy who killed Aunt Beatrix."

"Beatrix was killed?" Elisa said with tears welling.

"Yes, a boy killed her. She didn't even see him before he hit her."

"Are you certain that she is dead?"

"I'm certain," Sarah said with her voice trailing away. There hadn't been time to even think about Beatrix, or maybe she hadn't wanted to. Sarah was suddenly overcome with guilt. How would she ever explain to the family what had happened to their precious Beatrix? The only comfort Sarah could offer them was knowing that the boy hadn't taken Charlotte from them, too.

"I don't remember a boy," Eliza said after a long pause. "I only remember running through the fields and tripping. I think I hurt my head when I fell; it was a rocky place like the foundation of an outbuilding or stonewall. I can't remember."

"It must have been the privy," Sarah said.

"Maybe," Eliza replied. "I don't know."

"Well, the cut doesn't look too bad," Sarah said. "It bled a lot, but it should clean up with sea water."

"Can you believe what has happened to us, Sarah?"

"You mean the boat?"

"No, I mean Hispaniola—everything."

"Remember back in school when we planned this trip, how we tried on our island clothing for the other girls and thought how gorgeous we were going to look in our white dresses and straw bonnets? We bragged and bragged about how daring we were to be traveling to a foreign country practically by ourselves and how envious everyone was. We thought we were explorers, remember?" Sarah said. "I was going to go out with one of the overseers to see the pineapples and sugar cane growing in the fields. I wanted to kick the soil and to talk to them about manure and rainfall and insects. Now look at us."

"Well, I planned to skip that part of the trip," Eliza said. "I wanted to watch the women in the kitchens as they ground corn, and made tortillas, and carried water on their heads. Did you know there's such a thing as blue corn, Sarah? Oh, and I was going to ask to help them chop onions and chili peppers and tomatillos with their big cleavers."

"We were going to walk on the beaches and catch little fish on the jetties, and at night, we were going to dance in our beautiful dresses and meet handsome French boys," Sarah said wistfully.

"Would you have let them kiss you?" Eliza asked.

"If they were handsome enough," Sarah said.

"Sarah! Mimms would have had a fit. She wouldn't let you get close enough to a French boy to throw him a kiss, let alone kiss him on the lips. It was going to be perfect, remember?"

"I loved Mimms," Sarah said softly. "She saved our lives, you know. The last thing she did was to push us towards Beatrix."

"Had you ever seen blood before, Sarah?"

"Only course blood, never that much," Sarah said. "I'm afraid to close my eyes because that's all I can think about. Blood everywhere."

"Do you really think we'll make it back to Charleston, back to our families?"

"I do," Sarah said with conviction. "We didn't make it this far just to fail. I don't know what we're going to have to endure to get there. We may have to swim back, but we're making it home. We're going to live our lives, have suiters coming out our ears, and say damn if we want to."

That night the winds began to shift to the north. At first the change was subtle enough that Henri and Sarah did little to adjust to it. As the hours went by, however, the winds increased until they howled. Everyone was terrified. After coming all that way just to die at sea was a very real possibility, but if they fought back, they stood a chance. So Sarah and Eliza told the younger children to gather around Sookie and the baby in the center of the boat and everyone else to start bailing so that Henri could stay at the rudder.

The boat was battered throughout the night, but the following morning they woke to hear gentle waves lapping at the keel and to catch sight of the sun peeking above the horizon. "The storm—is it really gone?" Sarah whispered to Henri.

"It's really gone," Henri replied, smiling at her for the first time.

That evening, the boat was spotted by Cuban fishermen, and the rescue was underway. Although everyone was sunburned and still in their night clothes, they were alive. As the fishermen towed the boat to shore, Eliza said a prayer over their little brood, and a slight smile could be seen on Suzanne's face. They had survived.

When they reached the shallows, the men jumped into the water, grabbed the sides of the little rescued boat, and walked it to shore. Then the children were lifted out of the boat and wrapped in quilts. "The whole village must be here," Sarah whispered. At that point they were separated into groups and taken to different houses. Despite the language barrier, it all happened smoothly. Even Baby Armand seemed to understand the enormity of the moment. They were safe.

Charlotte, Eliza and Sarah were invited to stay with Ines Mejia and her daughter-in-law, Tiva, in a small wood frame house situated at the crook of a narrow lane about three hundred yards from the beach. Camouflaged from the road by towering banana trees and hedges of copper-orange hibiscus, the house looked like it had been built in stages.

In the side yard, a wooden awning protected an outdoor fireplace unlike any that Sarah had ever seen. Beside it was a long table made from plank lumber and an odd assortment of benches and chairs that suggested that Tiva and Ines did most of their cooking and entertaining out-of-doors.

Inside the house, the main room contained two narrow beds, a small table with four mismatched chairs, and a cast iron brazier that was giving off so much heat it glowed. As the girls stood as close to the fire as they dared, Tiva motioned for them to remove their clothing, and then she handed each of them a clean, dry replacement.

Charlotte was given a man's dress shirt that was so big that it made everyone laugh, including Charlotte. Eliza's outfit was a long cotton shift with drawstring sleeves, and Sarah's was a white linen dress with purple flowers embroidered along its hem and the matching sash. It smelled of lemon grass, and Sarah later learned that it had been Tiva's wedding dress, the most cherished thing she owned.

The girls lived with their adoptive families for the next three weeks until arrangements could be made to take them home. Sarah spent most of that time investigating the tropical plants that grew profusely over the island including on its pathways, tree trunks, outcropping, and rooftops. The plants she liked the best, though, were from Tiva's own garden: the Paritium Elatum Hibiscus and the fiery Habanero pepper, thought to be indigenous to Cuba.

When Grandpapa Hebert's schooner finally arrived to take the children back to Charleston, it was a teary time. They'd all fallen in love with their Cuban families, especially Suzanne, who almost refused to leave, but it was time to go home, so they climbed aboard and said their goodbyes. They arrived in Mt. Pleasant four days later, and as the crew was casting the lines to the dock master, Sarah spotted her parents.

"Mamma! Papa! I've missed you so!"

"I know, dear," Papa said, staring at Sarah in disbelief. Deeply sunburned, Sarah knew she looked much older than the gleeful child who had sat sail for Hispaniola such a short time ago. Her waist-length hair that she used to wear tied in ribbons was cinched in a knot at the nape of her neck, and it was the color and texture of corn straw. Papa said her lips were drawn and her eyes looked wider-set than he remembered.

Had it only been four weeks? It seemed more like a lifetime, Papa, said. Then he surprised Sarah by breaking into laughter. It took her a moment to figure out what the source of the laughter was, and then she remembered that she was carrying a chili plant under one arm, and a hibiscus under the other. "They were gifts from my Cuban family," she said. "Tiva and Ines gave them to me when we said goodbye."

Henri, Suzanne, Eliza, and Sarah were given a day to rest, and then Sarah's father and Grandpapa Hebert sat them down to go over the details of their ordeal.

Papa used the opportunity to also tell them what he had learned through his political connections in Hispaniola. Fifty-one members of the island Heberts were confirmed dead as a result of the massacre, he said. Then Grandpapa slowly began to read the list of those who had died. Henri and Suzanne's parents, two older sisters, and one older brother were among the dead, but Grandpapa lost his composure before he got to their names. After all, it was his family, too.

Sarah's father read the remainder of the list. When he came to Beatrix's name, Sarah closed her eyes and pictured the glint of the machete as it slammed into Beatrix's body. Henri tried not to cry, but

Suzanne sobbed. "Will we ever be able to go back to the island, Uncle James?" Henri asked after trying to console Suzanne.

"I don't think so," Sarah's father replied. "Besides, there would be nothing to return to. What happened in Hispaniola was more than a simple slave uprising. It was the start of a revolution that could last for years. In a few days Henri, we'll sit down with you again to discuss the plans that we have for your future."

"What about Mimms, Papa?" Sarah asked already knowing the answer.

"She's died," Papa said rigidly, "but we've seen to it that her daughter will always be well cared for."

"Her daughter?"

"Yes, Mimms had a seven-year-old daughter who lived with Mimms's sister. A few hours ago, the child and her aunt were given ownership of a small furnished house on Bottle Alley here in Charleston and an annual annuity of a hundred dollars."

"Is that a lot of money, Papa?"

"Yes, Sarah, that's a lot of money."

The meeting ended, but Sarah had something more to say.

"What is it, dear?" Papa asked.

"It's about Beatrix."

"Do you want everyone to stay?" Papa asked.

"Yes, Papa. I want them to stay. Eliza and I want to tell everyone what happened to Aunt Beatrix. She was killed by a boy with a machete, and then I tried to kill the boy." A hush fell upon the room that instantly sucked the air out of Papa.

Then Eliza stepped in. "She didn't do it alone," she said. "I hit him, too."

"When we walked out of the basement into the courtyard, Beatrix led the way, and she had barely taken a step when a machete slashed into her neck and she fell to the ground," Sarah explained. "Charlotte wiggled out of my arms and threw herself on top of Beatrix and that's when I saw the boy, the boy with the machete. He was about eleven, maybe twelve. I don't know, but he was a young boy. At first I thought I might be able to talk to him, but then I realized there was no sense in trying. That's when I saw Eliza out of the corner of my eye."

"Sarah whispered to me that she was going to hold him off long enough for Charlotte and me to get away," Eliza said. "Then she shouted 'Run!' I took off, but I was so scared I forgot to take Charlotte."

"What happened then?" Eliza's father said.

"While he was distracted by Eliza, I grabbed a section of the door-frame that had been torn away from the basement door. Then I looked back at the boy, and he lunged at me. His swing was wild, though, and before he had time to regroup, I hit him in the head with the doorframe. He fell on top of Beatrix, and there was blood everywhere."

"Then I came back because I had forgotten to take Charlotte with me, and the boy was on the ground cursing, and I said we should hit him again, so he couldn't follow us, and Sarah gave me the doorframe and I smacked him," Eliza said. "Sarah's right about the blood, but most of it was Aunt Beatrix's."

Papa cried, and Sarah had to fight her instincts to tell the rest of the story, but she was done. The story of the privy and the fire and the boys and the little naked girl was a million times worse, but Eliza didn't remember it, and Sarah wasn't about to tell her. She'd never tell Papa, either. He wouldn't love her anymore.

Sarah sat with her hands in her lap, too drained to speak and too disheartened to cry. She remembered very little after that. Papa said something about being proud of her, and Eliza's father thanked her for saving Eliza's life, but their voices sounded like they were coming from the bottom of a well.

Papa gave her his handkerchief, and Eliza cried in the background. "We went to see a priest," Eliza said.

"A priest?" her father asked, surprised.

"He was a priest in the village of Cajobabo. I can't remember his name, but he was really handsome, and we told him about Aunt Beatrix and the boy and everything. He told us to tell you about it once we were home."

"You both showed such courage," Papa said, trying to lighten the conversation. "But I have one more question for you. Who were the other people on the boat with you?"

"You mean Henri and Charlotte?" Sarah replied, pretending not to understand.

"Of course not, Sarah. I don't mean the younger Hebert children. I mean the island children?"

"The one my age was Sookie, Baby Armand's nurse."

"And the little girl?"

"Her name was Kai. We found her on the island," Sarah said, dodging any mention of the mushroom cave or the dye vat to avoid rekindling any memories for Eliza. It didn't work.

Eliza suddenly remembered watching Charlotte and Kai stuffing pearls into their mouths in the bottom of the indigo vat. "Charlotte was wearing a nightdress, but the little girl was naked and she was crying because she'd broken her pearls," Eliza said in a whisper.

"Her pearls?"

"Yes, Papa, her pearls." Nothing more was said. Everyone just sat like statues with their thoughts, horrified at the events but grateful for the outcome.

Finally, Sarah took her father's hand and searched his eyes for the tiniest change in the way he looked at her. Then she said, "Papa you have to be the one to tell Mamma. I can't do it. Promise me you'll tell her."

"I promise," he said. "I'll tell her once we're home." Then he hugged Eliza and shook her father's hand.

"We'll get through this together," he said.

After Papa walked Sarah to her room, he returned to Grandpapa's study, where he dispatched a messenger to Cuba with rewards for the young priest and the children's Cuban families. Then the messenger made his way into Haiti to convey a special reward to Prosper.

Prosper, however, wasn't alive to receive it. Two weeks after he'd helped the Hebert children escape the island, Prosper was hanged for stealing his brother's boat.

CHAPTER 11

Going Home

SARAH AND HER PARENTS spent another day at Hebert Plantation, but Sarah was eager to go home, so they set out for Charleston the following morning. It had been hard to say goodbye to Henri and Sookie, and Kia, and Eliza, of course, but the most challenging goodbye was to Charlotte.

"Auntie Sarah, you promised to take care of me forever," Charlotte cried. "You promised."

"Charlotte, I love you," Sarah said, shaking. "I'll always love you, but I'm not a grown-up yet, I'm only fourteen, and I have to go to school. I think a grown-up would take better care of you than I could. Auntie Anne was your mother's sister, and she loves you very much, and she has two little girls. You'll be part of a family with a mommy and two new sisters."

Charlotte was barely out of babyhood, but she was old enough to understand Sarah's argument. Besides, she liked Auntie Anne because she looked so much like her mother. "If I go to live with Auntie Anne, will you still love me?"

"Of course I will, Charlotte. I will always love you."

"Where does Auntie Anne live?" Sarah asked as Papa's carriage made its way along the allee leading away from Hebert Plantation.

"In Stono," Papa replied. "Why do you ask?"

"I just want Charlotte to be happy."

"Would you have preferred to have Charlotte live with us?" Mamma asked, reaching for Sarah's hand.

Tears dropped onto Sarah's dress, but she refused to speak. Mamma was an astute woman who knew when to quit, so she took her hand away and gave Sarah time to cry. During the rest of the ride back to Charleston, Mamma and Papa periodically attempted to engage Sarah in light conversation, but she was content to simply stare out the window.

Three hours later, the carriage made its final turn onto Hayes Street. "Hayes House," Sarah whispered. "We're home."

The servants had been waiting near the mansion's street entrance, and they fairly tripped over each other, scrambling to be the first to greet Missy Sarah. They had their suspicion, though, seeing as how she pulled such a fast one on Ol' Scratch. She looked funny, too, all different-like, older, and as browned up as a pelican.

The servants were happy to see her, but they were going to keep a close eye on her all the same. She could have been infected with voodoo spirits that could kill a person while she slept. Like those who lived in South Carolina, regular tree spirits were no match for voodoo spirits, no sir.

After getting Sarah into bed and blocking out the light by drawing the heavy damask draperies, Papa escorted Mamma into his study to tell her about Beatrix and the boy. Although he was tempted, he left nothing out so that she could understand why Sarah's nightmares were so frightening.

Papa always celebrated Elisabeth's ability to keep things to herself. However, he still reminded her that keeping the details of the massacre was imperative, especially when it came to the servants. Servants were notorious gossipers, and even the slightest slip or innuendo could bring down the House of Richards quicker than a wrecking ball.

For the first six weeks, Elisabeth Richards did everything to comfort Sarah, but nothing seemed to work, and she found herself at her wit's end. The solution was to forbid Sarah from speaking about Haiti again.

"If we don't speak of it, it will go away," Elisabeth prayed. Sarah was touched by her mother's inadvertent show of vulnerability. The nightmares were horrible enough without having to console her mother afterward.

At Papa's suggestion, a servant was stationed just outside the door to Sarah's room. When Sarah had an episode, the servant would wake Papa, who was temporarily sleeping in his study. Never was the servant to wake the mistress, and the plan worked splendidly.

Papa was always there for Sarah, and neither of them had to feel guilty about upsetting Mamma. The only other person Sarah wanted to see during that time was Eliza. They were closer than sisters now, and when they were together, it was as if they were complete. They didn't have to pretend or to reassure each other like they did when they were with their parents.

Sarah and Eliza could just be themselves. If they wanted to talk about Haiti, they did. If not, they talked about girl things, silly things. They were young, and the young heal quickly, at least on the outside. Their nightmares slowly became less frequent, and they began to feel a renewed interest in school.

When Sarah told her parents that she and Eliza wanted to go back to school for the spring semester, Mamma was reluctant, but Papa was jubilant. "You can't protect her forever, Elisabeth. It's time to let her go."

The girls stayed at Eliza's house the night before they were to move their things back into their old room, and as the hour grew late, the girls recalled the events in Haiti with a more profound sadness than they had expressed to each other before.

"What scares you the most about going back to school?" Eliza asked as she and Sarah laid side by side in Eliza's canopied bed.

"I'm not worried about facing the other girls," Sarah said. "If anyone asks me about what happened, I'm just going to tell them that I don't want to talk about it."

"Me, too," Eliza said. "Mama said the girls at Madame Painchaud's don't know very much about what happened in Haiti. They know that we were nearly killed and that we barely escaped with our lives, but it's not like they know everything."

"I'm troubled by something else," Sarah said, biting her lip. "What happened to me changed me, but I don't know exactly how. Will it make me braver throughout the rest of my life, or will it make me afraid to take chances? Will I be forgiven for what I did? Did I do the right thing, or am I evil? Will the boys' spirits find me and haunt me the rest of my life?" Sarah blurted the questions one after another, sighing at the end.

"The boys are all dead and buried by now," Eliza said, trying to soothe Sarah's fears even though she wasn't thoroughly convinced herself. She was even tempted to crack wise about Sarah making a pretty ghost but changed her mind and reached for Sarah's hand instead.

That night Sarah came within an inch of telling Eliza what was torturing her, but she held back. It wasn't every day that you set fire to your kin, and she couldn't risk losing Eliza's friendship, so she told Eliza another truth.

"I want to know if my weaknesses on the island, my failings, were because I'm a girl," Sarah said. "Would I have been more courageous had I been a boy? Maybe Madame Painchaud is right about us being the weaker sex. Maybe we were put on the earth just to have children and polish the silver."

"I think you're feeling sorry for yourself," Eliza snapped.

"I am not!" Sarah insisted.

"All right, perhaps you're not, but you're certainly underestimating yourself. Men don't second-guess themselves, Sarah. They do whatever it is they have to, and they figure they did their best."

"Do you think Henri's actions were weak?"

"Henri Hebert?" Eliza asked.

"Yes, Henri Hebert."

"We were almost capsized while he was at the rudder. Do you think it was because he was weak?" Eliza asked.

"No," Sarah replied. "Henri was extremely brave."

"His actions weren't perfect, though," Eliza said.

"No they weren't," Sarah said, "but that had nothing to do with his bravery."

"Exactly. Bravery is about doing what you have to do despite your fears. You don't have to necessarily do the right thing; you just have to have the courage to do something."

"I didn't save you," Sarah said. "Prosper did; he saved us all."

"I love you Sarah Bella."

"I love you, too."

CHAPTER 12

Madame Painchaud's Academy
For Girls

THE GIRLS MOVED INTO their old room the following morning. Sarah was eager to get back to her studies and thrilled to be back at school, but even with fresh ribbons in her hair, she wasn't the same girl.

A mirror in the far end of the room had an irresistible pull on her. When Sarah was alone, she studied herself with a critical eye. How had she changed? Were her eyes less blue, was her hair less full, and would anyone else notice how long her neck had gotten? Somethings it was as if a stranger was looking back at her, a girl she barely knew.

Madame Painchaud's academy occupied an estate that had once belonged to one of Charleston's wealthiest families, and even though the mansion had to be remodeled to be used as a school, it still had stately bones. One of Madame Painchaud's rather odd remodeling demands, however, ended up being Charleston lore.

It was rumored that during the renovation, Madame Painchaud told her contractor to extend the height of the wall surrounding the house by an additional eighteen inches.

"And then," she said, "you are to cement large shards of glass to the top of the wall. Do you understand?"

"Yes, ma'am I believe I do," he replied curiously. "What kind of glass are you referring to, ma'am? Do you mean window glass or bottle glass, or are you thinking of some other kind of glass?"

"Mr. Tanner, it is not my job to tell you what kind of glass you are to use. Just do it, and be quick about it."

Mr. Tanner's solution was to hire a local glassmaker to make fist-sized chunks of solid glass and then break the chunks into smaller shards before cementing them to the top of the wall.

Madame Painchaud seemed pleased enough, but passersby couldn't help but wonder what had prompted the demand. Papa didn't wonder, though. If something happened in Charleston, he had a way of knowing about it almost before it happened.

Sarah overheard him telling Mamma one day that Madame Painchaud had decided in reaction to an incident that had taken place a few years earlier and that her actions were perfectly understandable.

At Mrs. Potter's Academy, a girls' school that used to be on Queen Street, a student there had scaled the school wall to run away with the son of a local shopkeeper. The girl in question was barely fifteen, and the resulting scandal forced Mrs. Potter to close her doors.

No matter what Madame Painchaud had to do to maintain her school's reputation, she would do it. History would not be allowed to repeat itself, not at her school.

Sarah and her classmates lived on the third floor of the school in one large room that looked out over the city. Washstands lined one wall of the no-frills room, and petticoats suspended from clotheslines provided the only privacy. The girls' beds were on the Spartan side, rope beds that required periodic tightening with a large wooden crank kept in a garderobe.

Sarah's mattress was new, but it was still lumpy. On housekeeping day, the girls rotated their mattresses by flipping them one way and then the other, but Sarah was convinced that it only made the mattresses even lumpier.

"That's the whole idea, Sarah Bella."

"Eliza, I hate it when you call me Sarah Bella, and if you don't stop, you'll have every other girl at the school doing it too."

"No, I won't."

"How do you know that?"

"Because I know things, that's how," she giggled.

Everyone had to do chores, including cleaning their washstands and scrubbing their chamberpots with soda ash. The Middleton girls refused to clean theirs, however. Their father was the wealthiest man in Charleston, so they should be exempted from chamberpot duty.

When they voiced their complaint to Madame Painchaud, she was surprisingly gracious. She said that it was their choice, and if that's what they wanted to do, their chamberpots would be taken away, and the sisters could use the privy in the backyard.

Using a privy in the middle of the night was about the scariest thing you could do if you were a Middleton, and the privy in question was in South Carolina. Snakes and spiders thought of them as hotels, so the sisters promptly changed their minds.

The curriculum at Madame Painchaud emphasized subject matter deemed appropriate for females: French literature, English history, music theory, housewifery, sewing, dancing, and etiquette. Sarah and the rest of the girls also studied piano, botanical drawing, rhetoric, and singing that Sarah tried in vain to get out of by proclaiming that she was tone-deaf.

The girls received instruction in gift selection and gift wrapping, calligraphy, setting the table for various functions, folding napkins, avoiding water spots on crystal, identifying the different silver serving pieces, and the importance of knowing the difference between a chocolate spoon and a sugar spoon.

At one time or another, glassmakers made as many as twenty-three separate kinds of stem and other glassware, and Madame Painchaud expected her students to identify each of them with ease.

"What would you think of a mistress who served celery in a sherbet goblet or Madeira in a regular red wine glass? How embarrassing."

"Pish," Sarah whispered to Eliza. The girls were required to wear their hair parted in the middle and tied at the napes of their necks with large grosgrain ribbons. Madame Painchaud and the rest of her teaching staff wore caps made of handkerchief linen trimmed with lace. Madame Painchaud's cap consisted of a circular doily with panels on either side called spaniel's ears.

Sarah and her classmates studied fabric swatches to learn to identify the finer silks from the mundane. They learned to identify various ribbons and laces and to know the difference between everyday crochet and the finest.

They examined every nuance of the bonnet, the biggest and most important must-have of all. The girls were taught that bonnets were of critical importance, not only because they completed an outfit, but to be seen out of doors without a proper head covering would be societal suicide. The girls drooled over the bonnets featured in the ultra-chic French magazine, "Journal Des Dames et Des Mode," but they seldom had any say about their bonnets.

Their mothers picked them out because one simply couldn't make a misstep on something that important. Sarah and Eliza liked the latest fashions and knew as much about bonnets as anyone in school, except Prissy Laurens, but they were alone when it came to the belief that women were just as capable as men.

"Sarah, your papa's rich, and if it were put to a vote, you know that your mother would be named the most beautiful woman in Charleston. So why are you always carrying on about wanting to study botany and all that other boy stuff?" Prissy asked one day.

"My parents are rich and beautiful, too," Prissy pointed out, "but I've never spent one moment worrying about such things. Why can't you just be content to be a girl. Who cares if your brain isn't as big as a boy's."

"I care," Sarah said. "Besides, I'm just as smart as any boy."

"You are not."

"I am. Who makes the rules, Prissy?"

"Men, of course."

"That's my point. Just because they think they're smarter than we are doesn't make it so. Someday things will be different. Women will know that they are men's equals."

"You mean they'll grow penises!"

"No, I don't mean equal in that way. I just mean that we'll be able to choose our own paths."

"You had me worried," Prissy said. "I thought for a moment that you wanted a penis."

"Have you been listening to me at all?"

"I've listened; I just don't agree. I think there are girls' subjects and boys' subjects, and boys shouldn't study sewing, and girls shouldn't study agricultural things like botany. Have you ever seen one?" Prissy asked.

"A penis?" Sarah asked. "The answer is no."

"Well, I saw my cousin's once, and believe me, you don't want one even if they do make you smart. They're ugly."

When Sarah told Eliza about her conversation with Prissy, she just laughed and said she didn't care what the other girls thought.

"Well, you should, Eliza, you of all people. You're the great-granddaughter of Eliza Lucas, the most important woman in American history. George Washington was one of her pallbearers, for heaven's sake."

"He was interested in her worms."

"Your great-grandmother had worms?"

"She had thousands of them--silk worms. She was trying to develop a silk industry. General Washington invited her to visit him in Washington, but right after that, she got sick and went to Philadelphia for treatment. They couldn't cure her, though, and she died there. After the funeral, Papa sent the president five huge trunks of her research notes."

"But what about her research on indigo," Sarah said. "That was her most important research. Papa said it made a bunch of planters rich."

"I know, and I'm proud that I'm her great-granddaughter; it's just that in my family everyone always credits her father for having the brains, not Granny. Somehow they think she was just a dutiful daughter who did what she was told. I just get tired of it, that's all. Our family is always looking for the next male genius to crop up."

"Then change it," Sarah said. "You already have her name; be her namesake. Invent something, or grow something, or discover something for yourself. How many times do you think your great-grandmother was ignored because she was a girl? She was fourteen when she started experimenting with indigo. She was younger than we are."

"How do you know things will change, Sarah?"

"I just know."

Sarah liked her classes and excelled at botanical drawing, but she wanted to learn to grow things. She wanted to know everything about plants—when to plant them, what to fertilize them with, how to make espaliers out of them, and when to harvest them. One day she poured out her heart to Papa.

"I don't just want to be a gardener; I want to understand the science of plants. How do they receive nutrients from the soil? How do they absorb sunlight, and why do some plants need more water than others? Remember when I was little and I played in the fields at Rochambeau? I've mused that someday maybe my own children would play in gardens that were planted by me."

Papa was so astounded by Sarah's unexpected soliloquy that he couldn't think of a response, so he just looked at her and smiled. "Why don't you discuss this with Madame Painchaud," he finally managed to say. You can have all the gardens you want at Rochambeau, but I'm certain that Madame Painchaud would be happy to have a young lady so interested in botany."

Papa was wrong. During the fall term of Sarah's fourth year at the academy, she finally dared to approach Madame Painchaud about the possibility of planting a garden on a narrow strip of land that was just beyond the formal gardens behind the school.

Sarah was so excited about the prospects of caring for a garden that she burst into tears when Madame Painchaud categorically refused even to discuss the matter. "How unladylike of you to suggest such a thing," Madame Painchaud said stiffly. "Do you really expect to find a suitable husband with dirt beneath your fingernails? You are going to force me to speak to your father."

"But Madame, I'll work in a very dignified fashion. I promise to wear my hat and my gloves; I won't ever get dirty."

"Sarah, young ladies from your social class are not born to do such things. Botany and the other sciences are suited for the male brain, not the brain of a young lady. This is a man's world; the sooner you accept that, the better. Growing things beyond an occasional flower is the purview of men and their servants. Why in heaven's name do you think we have slaves?"

"What about Eliza Lucas?"

"Eliza Lucas was an anomaly, not the rule."

"I can learn to grow things, too. My brain is just as capable; Papa has told me so. What difference does it make that I am a female? The pumpkin won't know the difference."

With that, Madame Painchaud slammed her hands against her desk and looked as though her head was about to spin. "Enough! I will have no more of this. Now go."

"Mr. Richards," Madame Painchaud said during a conversation with Papa the following week, "I'm certain that you will agree that we simply cannot have Sarah dirtying her hands on, on, vegetables! Flowers, possibly but not pumpkins! I'm appalled at her request, and you no doubt feel the same."

"Quite the contrary," Papa bellowed. "I think it's a cracking idea. I loved the study of botany when I was a boy, and Sarah is a bright girl. If she wishes to study it, I'm going to give her every opportunity."

Madame Painchaud's cheeks flushed, and a small bead of sweat trickled down the left side of her neck and between her breasts, but she stood her ground. "Botany," she said after clearing her throat, "is an exclusively male-dominated discipline, and I will have nothing to do with promoting it at my school."

Papa said, "Fine." His solution was to pay a princely sum to an instructor from the Alston Academy for Boys to tutor Sarah one afternoon a week in the parlor of Hayes House.

CHAPTER 13

Sullivan's Island

THE SCHOOL SESSION ENDED, and Papa had to make an extended business trip to New York, so Mamma decided that she and Sarah should spend some time at her cousins' cottage on Sullivan's Island. Mamma packed as if they were going to China, of course, but this time they packed brand new wardrobes made of gauzy summer dresses and floppy brimmed hats.

Sarah was ecstatic about her new clothes. Since her introduction to the dreaded corset, she'd never felt such freedom. The dresses were light and airy and less restrictive, and she felt like she could float into the sky just like a kite. She and one of her Hebert cousins, who lived on the family's enormous properties in Mt. Pleasant, were strolling the beach one morning when they ran into Mrs. Hanson, whose husband owned a successful mercantile store on King Street.

The Hansons were also members of St. Philip's. Mrs. Hanson said she and her family had rented a house just down the beach. "We should get together," she said, so a few days later, the families had supper on the veranda of the Hebert cottage. Two of Mrs. Hanson's sons were there, including Robert, who was eighteen. He was friendly and good-looking, and after supper, he asked Sarah to go for a walk.

It was still light, so Mamma agreed. "But don't take long," she said. Robert knew the island much better than Sarah did, so he led the way.

It was fun to stroll the beach with a handsome young man who was chatty and seemingly interested in her.

A few minutes later, they came to a sand spit next to a small cave. The cave had appeared after a hurricane two years ago, he explained. "Do you want to go inside?"

"Oh, yes," Sarah said without a second thought. When they got inside, Robert pulled her to him and softly kissed her neck. It was Sarah's first experience with a boy. She'd never even been alone with one before. At first, it sent chills through her, but then he started to grab at her.

Sarah demanded that he stop, but he wouldn't. He pawed at her and tore at her skirts, and suddenly he was on top of her. After it was over, Robert acted as if nothing had happened. He even helped her up and attempted to straighten her hair.

"I'd like to see you again," Robert said.

"Don't' touch me!" Sarah screamed.

Robert then laughed at her and added how it was her fault for going off alone with him. Then he leaned into her ear and whispered, "You blame me for this, and I'll ruin you for good. A decent man wouldn't touch you after I get through with you. Now clean yourself up, and I'll take you to your aunt's house."

Sarah did as she was told. Robert was right; he could blame everything on her, and her reputation would never recover. She'd be lucky to find anyone who would want her after that. There was nothing she could do, so she and Robert went back to her aunt's cottage.

The sun was even with the horizon when they returned, golden and perfect as it sat there on the edge of the world. Sarah remembered that evening, thinking how everything in her entire world was again turned on its end, and yet, the sun stared back at her as dignified as ever.

Sarah was desperate to be by herself. She wanted to destroy her clothing and to scrub the filth from her skin, but most of all, she wanted to hide her face from Mamma. If Mamma were to see her face in the lamplight, she'd know what had happened.

The only thing that had saved her when she and Robert returned to her aunt's house, was that Mamma was distracted by her laughter. There was a small bathroom adjacent to the room that Sarah shared with Mamma and her maid. It had a commode and beautiful French washbasin and a porcelain sitz bath.

Sarah crept up the stairs and sprinted toward the bathroom. She wanted to cry, but she forced herself not to. The servants would notice and tell Mamma, and then the whole beach would light up with holy war between Mamma and the Hansons.

No, Sarah wouldn't cry, so she went to the washstand and looked at her face in the mirror. Staring back at her was the same injured girl who had returned from Haiti, the girl Sarah worked so hard to protect.

Sarah removed her clothes, trying not to touch them any more than she had to. They were foul and nasty, and she noticed how much sand had been trapped in them. She'd never wear them again. If she thought she could get away with throwing them away or hiding them on the beach, she would; but she had no recourse other than to add them to the stack of dirty laundry and pray that the laundresses were too busy swapping war stories to notice that they were stained with semen.

A knock came at the door, and Sarah jumped. "You all right, miss?" Mamma's maid asked. "Do you need me to scrub you?"

"No, I'm fine," Sarah replied, trying to sound cheery. "I'll be out soon. Thank you."

"You sure you don't need anything?"

"I need a dressing gown," Sarah said, realizing that she was stark naked. "Just leave it on the floor by the door."

"You sure, missy?"

"I'm sure." She returned to the mirror and pulled her hair away from her face. There was a bruise on her neck and a tiny scratch next to her eye that she could probably hide with her hair. She walked to the washstand and poured water from the pitcher into the bowl. Then she grabbed a bar of soap and a nubby washcloth and started to scrub her neck and face.

Sarah wished the water had been hotter, but even lukewarm water felt soothing against her skin. She scrubbed herself raw, but no matter how hard she scrubbed, she still felt dirty. Her nightgown was folded neatly just outside the door as she had asked.

Sarah slipped it over her head, grimacing as it slid over her defiled body, grateful that the nightgown hid her nakedness and her bruises from Mamma. She crawled into her bed before the maid had had time to turn it down for her.

"Missy Sarah, you know I'm supposed to open your bed at night," the maid said. "You could get me in trouble."

"Oh, Penny, you didn't do anything wrong. I was just so sleepy that I didn't give you time to open it. Besides, it's all messed up now, and it doesn't matter. Mamma will never know. Tomorrow night I promise to wait for you to open it properly. I promise."

"Thank you, Miss Sarah. You know how the mistress is with the rules. She's sticky for them."

"A stickler?"

"Yes, Miss—sticky."

The following week, Sarah and her mother set out for Rochambeau to stay until mid-May, when they would be forced to evacuate the plantation to avoid the summer fevers. Eliza met them there. The moment that Eliza saw Sarah, she knew something was up.

"I know something's wrong, Sarah. Fess up."

"I was attacked two weeks ago," Sarah gasped.

"Oh, Sarah. What happened? Who did it? Are you all right?"

"Remember the Hansons from King Street?" Sarah asked.

"The ones with the store and the sons?"

"Yes, Robert is eighteen. He's the one who did it."

"What did your Mamma say?"

"I didn't tell her. If Mamma knew, she'd never let me go anywhere. She already doesn't trust anyone. You know how she is."

"I know. She'd probably lock you in a room forever. Tell me what happened, Sarah," Eliza said, concerned.

Back in her room, Sarah described everything, trying to remember every detail because, strangely, it made her feel better. At the end of the story, Eliza suddenly jumped to her feet. "Oh, my god!" She said. "You could be pregnant! I didn't think of that."

"I'm all right. I"m not pregnant," Eliza. My course started yesterday. I was never so happy about anything in my whole life."

Guilded Threads

THE FOLLOWING SPRING, SARAH and Eliza celebrated their seventeenth birthdays together at Hayes House. The mansion was filled with flowers and overflowing with so many school friends and relatives that the girls only recognized half of them.

Turning seventeen was a monumental event for girls who'd grown up like Sarah and Eliza. One day they were considered too young to select their own bonnets, and the next, they were viewed as prime marriage material. *Shouldn't there be something between?* Sarah often thought.

Mamma's special gift was the loan of her tiaras for the day. Sarah's was diamonds and pearls; Eliza's tiara was diamonds and emeralds. It had been a tradition at Carrefour to wear tiaras on birthdays and other special days, Mamma said, and it seemed only fitting that the girls should wear them on their special day.

But before Mamma placed them on the girls' heads, she asked if the tiaras would remind them too much of Carrefour.

"Oh, no," Sarah replied, "That's the way I want to remember the cousins. What did you say they had been sprinkled with, Eliza?"

"Mica dust," Eliza said. "They looked like they'd been sprinkled with mica dust just like fairies. We never wanted to leave. Are you certain you want us to wear the tiaras, Mrs Richards? They must be unimaginably valuable."

"They are. They're worth more than this whole house. That's why I want you to have the fun of wearing them, dear."

"Do you think a real princess ever wore them?"

"I'm certain they were. They belonged to a princess of the blood, a sister to Alexander I."

"Did the pearls you're wearing now belong to her, too?"

"I don't know, dear. They might have."

"They remind me of the ones the little island girl was wearing, the ones she and Charlotte played with while they were in Rio Seco," Eliza said.

"Who was the little island girl?" Mamma asked.

"She was the little girl that I found in the mushroom cave," Sarah said. "Her name was Kia, but we usually just called her the little island girl."

"The mushroom cave?" Mamma asked, placing her hand on her heart.

"Yes, Mamma," Sarah said, getting nervous about revealing any unnecessary details to her mother. "I can't remember how I found the cave, but somehow I stumbled upon it the night that Eliza and I got separated," Sarah said, leaving out the part about the privy and the golden boys. "There was a lantern on the stairs. I saw Eliza, and then I saw the little island girl, but everything was spinning around me so crazily that I thought I might have imagined them. Then the little girl pleaded with me to help her, and I realized that she was real."

Sarah paused for a breath before continuing. "She looked like she belonged in a dream, Mamma. She was naked, and she was wearing ropes of pearls that came down to her knees. On her head sat a Christmas crown, except it wasn't a Christmas crown because when it fell off her head, it sounded like it was made out of metal instead of papier-mache. You don't suppose it could have been a real royal crown, do you?"

"I don't remember ever seeing a crown when I lived at Carrefour," Mamma replied, distracted by the placement of Eliza's tiara. "But I don't doubt for a moment that it could have been real. The women at Carrefour wore the finest Russian jewelry in the world. If it wasn't a Russian crown, it might have been part of a Mardi Gras costume," she said. "Lavish masquerade balls were held at Carrefour. Grand-Mere even kept trunks of Mardi Gras costumes for her guests. Perhaps that's what you saw."

"Where do you suppose the little girl got the crown?" Eliza said.

"She told Charlotte that she found it in a pirate's chest," Sarah replied. "A pirate's chest? Where? In the cave?"

"I didn't know. Eliza, I just thought that Kai and Charlotte were playing make-believe. It didn't occur to me that any part of their story could have been real."

Sarah and Eliza's formal introduction into society would take place during the coming-out ball in two weeks. Many of the fathers of the girls who were attending the ball were unimpressed, including Eliza's, who likened the whole affair to dangling meat from a hook. For Eliza's sake, though, he promised Eliza's mother to keep his opinions to himself and not to complain too loudly when it came time to pay the bills.

All of Sarah and Eliza's friends were going, of course, and when they were together, it was always the subject of conversation. Sarah was a serious student, and she was quick to get testy when she thought about how the plantation culture marginalized its women. But she had to admit that she was more excited about the coming-out ball than anyone.

Sarah and Eliza loved their gowns. "I'm going to look like a princess," Eliza announced, as she and Sarah were ushered into the salon of Madame Chloe's dress shop to see Eliza's dress. "I have worn a tiara, you know."

"All right, Princess Eliza," Sarah said. "But I don't think Eliza is a regal enough name. You'll have to change it to Elizabeth if you want to be a princess."

"Don't be so serious, Sarah. This is one of the most important events in my whole life. If I want to pretend to be a princess, I'll damn well do it!"

"Eliza! Don't talk like that. Someone will tell your mother."

"I don't care. Let's just have fun." Eliza's gown was carried into the room by two of Madame Chloe's assistants. They were holding it as if it did belong to a princess, and who could blame them. The dress fabric, champagne-colored Italian silk faille, had taken months to find its way to Charleston.

"Exquisite," Sarah's mother said upon seeing a sample of it, noting that it had cost Eliza's father a small fortune. The gown's color was perfect with Eliza's hair and with her tiny waist and delicate shoulders. Sarah knew she would catch the eye of every young man at the ball.

"Oh, Mamma," Sarah squealed when her own dress arrived at Hayes House. It consisted of more than thirty yards of cream-colored silk embroidered with hundreds of tiny French knots.

Sarah loved it, but she wasn't looking forward to the two hours it would take to get ready.

Sarah had already tried it on several times, of course, fittings, Madame Chloe called them, and Sarah had hated them because she had to stand still forever. Pinpricks, although profusely apologized for, were part of the process.

The pinpricks couldn't be avoided, so it was a waste of time to make a fuss. After all, how many ecru silk fabrics embroidered with white dots could there be? An infinite number, according to Mamma, and it was critical to select the finest among them.

The gown was made up of different pieces, including six layers of undergarments. Mamma's maid spent half the morning arranging every-thing in the proper order on Mamma's huge bed. *My, my,* the girl had said to herself. *All that lace for just one petticoat. That ain't right. If I had me one like that, I'd wear it on the outside so's everybody could admire it. My man and I would do the fancy in it, and I'd sleep in it too, so's it didn't get legs.*

The gown's first layer was a thin cotton shift, followed by a pair of cotton stockings that were the same ecru as her gown with tiny white dots embroidered onto them. Next up was an off-white, over-corset, designed to cinch in her waist, lift, and flatter her bosom.

"Mamma, I can't breathe," Sarah cried as the maid pulled at the laces on the back of the corset. "I'm going to faint dead away on the dance floor if you don't loosen it. Please!" Sarah waited for a response. She was spoiled after all, but she was ignored, and that was when she knew that this whole thing was exactly like the day she was forced to start wearing a corset. She was participating in a ritual.

Had Mamma been dressing her in armor, it wouldn't have been any more obvious. Sarah's role in the ritual was to be compliant, so that's what she did. Once Mamma was satisfied with the laces on the corset, Sarah was told to step into a pocket hoop. "Don't just stand there, Sarah," Mamma said. "Step into it one foot at a time."

Then, Mamma tied the hoop around Sarah's waist like an apron. The hoop was designed to make Sarah's waist look smaller by increasing the width of her hips. It was an optical illusion. The hoop was made out of wire wrapped with grosgrain ribbon. It was surprisingly lightweight, but it swayed from side to side when Sarah walked, and she was certain she was going to lose her balance.

An under-petticoat came next, followed by an over-petticoat. Then it was finally time to put on her gown that was a misnomer because it wasn't a traditional one-piece dress. It was made up of three separate pieces.

The first was a skirt that was intentionally slit from the center of the waist down to the floor to show off Sarah's over-petticoat. The bodice came next, and it was held in place by a series of hooks and eyes. Once that was securely in place, Mamma pinned a stomacher, a stiff panel of matching fabric shaped like a triangle, to the front of the bodice.

Then Sarah was wedged into a dressing chair, and Mamma began to brush the hair from around her face back to the crown of her head. Sarah's foot was going to sleep. "May I wear my hair up tonight?" she asked, shaking her foot.

"Of course not," Mamma replied, "and hold still. "You know as well as I do that only married women and spinsters are allowed to wear their hair off their necks. I wonder about you sometimes, Sarah. You have no sense of propriety." Then she gathered the hair at the back of Sarah's head and secured it with blue ribbons. The rest of her hair was worn loose, as was befitting a girl of seventeen.

Back on her feet, Sarah was instructed to stand still while the maid powdered her nose, placed a strand of Mamma's pearls around her neck, and helped her into a pair of beautiful silk evening slippers. Then she was given a pair of white kid gloves and a white reticule, and she was finally allowed to view the finished product.

Sarah barely recognized herself. She'd always been a gangly girl, and yet, the person looking back at her was a beautiful young woman dressed to catch a proper husband. She had to admit, though, she also felt a little bit like a cream-colored spider with little white dots. Other thoughts came into her mind that day, thoughts she kept strictly to herself.

The boy with the machete, and the Hebert cousins, and the Hanson boy were also in the mirror, and they were there to destroy her if she let them. *Not tonight,* she told them as she forced their images back into the dark place she'd learned to store such things. She'd done it a thousand times and was prepared to do it another thousand times if that's what it took.

It was getting easier all the time. A coming-out ball was a critical step for Sarah and her classmates. It was their entry into society, a crop rotation, Papa called it. The girls couldn't become debutants just because they wanted to, though. They had to be selected by a board of Charleston socialites. Papa said it was a crock of shit. Donate enough to their charities, and your little darling was a shoo-in.

Mamma disagreed. "I've worked behind the scenes to make this happen since the day you were born," she said, "And so has every other woman in this town. I've seen to it that you attended the right school, the right birthday parties, and every other social event, perfectly dressed and perfectly mannered. Nothing worthwhile is easy, Sarah."

"I feel like I'm on the auction block, Mamma," Sarah said. Mamma said that was a vulgar way to put it, but Sarah had a point, not that it would change anything.

"You'll find yourself doing the same things for your daughters," she concluded. Sarah hoped not.

The coming-out ceremony was extremely formal. The girls were even required to attend a rehearsal the day before, so there wouldn't be any mess-ups. After a five-minute ride to the society hall, Sarah stepped out of the carriage, shaking. She'd never danced with a man other than her father, and she wasn't entirely sure that she could do it without trying to lead.

As for men and sex, she had been introduced to both most brutally.

Before the rape, she'd only known what Prissy Laurens had whispered to her under the bedcovers, but her parents had always been loving toward each other, so she knew that all men weren't like the Hanson boy. She just hadn't met a good one yet.

Sarah was almost brought to tears by the sight of her classmates. Even Prissy, who had a gap between her teeth big enough to pass an English pea through, looked radiant so long as she kept her lips together. Her dress was white, Titian white, her mother insisted, and the bodice had an overlay of antique lace from her grandmother's bridal gown.

Prissy's hair was in ringlets down her back and upswept above her ears. Elisabeth Nichols was one of the smartest girls in school and one of the most standoffish. She seemed content to keep to herself when she wasn't with the more outgoing Prissy, but everyone liked her. She'd won the penmanship award three years running due to her mastery of loops and scrolls.

Sarah's handwriting looked like hen scratching by comparison. Elisabeth's dress was silvery-white, with tulip sleeves and undersleeves made of mantilla lace. It was a sophisticated gown for a coming-out dress, but it suited Elisabeth perfectly.

The Middleton sisters, who had waited an extra year to make their coming out together, were dressed in identical gowns that seemed like the oddest thing to Sarah. One sister was never seen without the other. Their gowns were made of cream-colored silk satin, and they had far more lace than anyone else's. Their sleeves had three tiers of scalloped lace. The same lace covered the bodices of their gowns and the edges of their skirts and trains. The gowns glistened in the candlelight, but the girls had snarls on their faces the whole night and looked like they'd been eating cowpats.

Eliza was the star of the show. The color of her dress made her sparkle like champagne. "You look beautiful," Sarah giggled. "I think you're the prettiest girl here."

"I think I look positively gorgeous," she replied with a twirl, "But I don't look as beautiful as you, Sarah. Let's face it; no one does."

"Do you like my dress?"

"It's perfect, but with you, it's all about your face. Tonight, you're even prettier than your mother. You're going to be fighting the men off. Are those your mother's pearls?"

"Yes, what do you think?"

"They're the color of lemon soufflé," Eliza said. "Pearls don't come in that color."

"These ones do. Mamma just told me about them. They're from the South Seas, but they have a Russian clasp. See the double-headed eagle crest stamped into it," she said, lifting her hair to expose the clasp. "That's the Romanov crest, so there's no telling who's worn them."

"Do you think Russian women ever go without their jewelry?"

"I don't know. Mamma said the royal family wears gowns with hundreds of diamonds and pearls sewn onto them, and then they wear all that heavy jewelry on top. They're known for their posture, Mamma said. From the time they're little girls, they're trained to stand very straight, so they can stand up under the weight of their jewelry."

"I'd rather do that than wear a corset," Eliza scrunched her nose and said.

"Oh, they wear corsets, too. Are you scared about tonight?" Sarah asked, reaching for Eliza's gloved hand.

"I'm terrified. I'm afraid of tripping on my dress.'"

"I'm afraid of stepping on someone's toes."

"I'm afraid of getting sick from too much punch, and I'm terrified of talking to a boy."

"We've been through worse," Sarah said, allowing herself to think about Haiti for a moment.

"We've been through lots worse," Eliza replied with a trace of sadness. "Now, let's go out there and snag ourselves some men."

A hand bell rang out, and that was their cue. The girls quickly formed a receiving line, as they had during their rehearsal, and then an elderly man, wearing a white wig and a red and blue uniform with gold ropes and epaulets, stepped to the center of the room. Then he nodded, signaling the blare of trumpets that startled everyone, with the possible exception of Mamma.

A hush fell on the room, followed by the rustle of dresses and the shuffle of feet. The man stepped forward and called out the first name: Blythe Alston.

Blythe was the epitome of composure as she walked to a designated spot on the floor and took the arm of her father. Together they circled the room as her mother and grandmother wept in the background. Blythe and her father, Captain Alston, returned to the X, and then her father turned to Blythe and bowed.

Blythe responded with a curtsy worthy of King George. It was something the girls had practiced thousands of times, but it was still intimidating. They all knew how to perform everyday curtsies because they had grown up doing them, but a royal curtsy was called for that night, and they were expected to sink to the floor.

The secret was to bend their knees to the outside as they went down and hope for the best. There were twenty-one debutants, and Sarah was number eighteen. Waiting was hard, but when her name was finally called, she followed the lead of the other girls and walked to the spot on the floor. There she took Papa's arm, and it was their turn to circle the audience.

Sarah had seen seventeen other curtsies, each performed splendidly, but the other girls didn't have James Richards to curtsy to.

"I love you," Papa whispered.

"I love you, too, Papa. I love you so much."

And then he took Sarah's hand and placed it in the hand of one of the Huger boys Sarah had grown up with. His name was Maximilian, and he was a year younger than Sarah with freckles on his adorable nose and a frog in his pocket if she knew him at all, but he looked so in awe of her that night that he made her feel like a princess.

Then, Maximilian made her laugh by squeezing her hand and flashing her his silly smile. "Max, this is serious, and you're going to get me in trouble. What will Mamma think if I start giggling?"

"You can blame it all on me, Miss Richards," he said, mocking her in a falsetto voice. "Oh, and on the subject of your mother, she was the one who asked me to be your escort. She made a lovely choice, don't you think? You'd better be nice to me, Sarah, because I'm your partner for your first dance, and I have two left feet. By the way, you're taller than me. Are you supposed to lead?"

"Very funny," Sarah replied. "You have to lead whether you want to or not."

The first dance was a traditional polonaise that Max performed perfectly. "You've been practicing."

"Your father had a little chat with me a few weeks ago. 'Son,' he said, 'Sarah's happiness means everything to me, and I'll take it as a personal affront if her first dance of the evening doesn't go well.'"

"I'll tell him you were wonderful."

"Thanks." Sarah's first introduction was to a seventeen-year-old boy with a horrific case of acne and hair tonic case that smelled like turpentine. The boy stood motionless during the exchange of names, but he did have the presence of mind to return her curtsy with an awkward bow. Then he just stood there. He didn't reach for her hand or anything. He just stood there staring at the floor.

Sarah waited, desperate to figure out how to get away from him. Maybe she could faint or pretend to be having a seizure? It was looking hopeless when all of a sudden, the boy looked at his mother, looked back at Sarah, and broke into tears.

"Oh, thank you, thank you," Sarah whispered under her breath as the boy was whisked from the dance floor by a quick-thinking servant. A sauteuse was beginning, and Sarah turned to get off the dance floor when she ran headlong into the most handsome man she'd ever seen.

"That's Percival Vaux," one of Sarah's classmates mouthed over her partner's shoulder. It only took one look for Sarah to understand why every other girl at school talked about setting her cap for him. Tall, with a breezy air of confidence and hair the same color as her own, Percival was wearing evening attire made out of raw silk, the color of inky-blue indigo.

Percival's shirt was trimmed with lace. The edges of his cutaway and waistcoat were decorated with rows of gold braid. What made his costume extraordinary, though, was that roses and grapevines embroidered with gold threads completely covered the front of the jacket and waistcoat.

Sarah didn't need carnal knowledge to know that he was gorgeous. She'd heard all about him. He was twenty-two, and she was certain that she would pee her drawers if someone that old were to approach her. Then he smiled and reached for her hand.

Sarah hesitated for a moment, remembering her ill-fated walk on the beach, but she was safe there, so she smiled and accepted his hand. Percival was noticeably taller than she was, and she loved being able to stand her full height as they made their way around the floor. They were the most handsome couple at the ball; Sarah was certain of that from the looks on everyone's faces.

Her friends watched them with their mouths ajar, the spinsters hid their comments behind fluttering fans, and some of the men watched them with broad smiles on their faces. Sarah couldn't find Mamma in the crowd, but she doubted that she was pleased. They hadn't had an age limit discussion, but Sarah expected one on the carriage ride home.

The dance ended, and Sarah's heart was pounding. She expected Percival to thank her for the dance and politely move on to someone else, but instead, he asked her for the next dance.

It was a waltz…a brand-new and controversial dance that was slower than their first dance. It gave them a chance to talk. Sarah told him about school and her parents, and then Percival spoke of his home at True Blue Plantation, noting that True Blue had taken its name from indigo.

"The truer the blue, the better the dye," he explained. "Of course, now we grow rice."

"What a shame the revolution destroyed the indigo market," Sarah responded.

"What do you mean?"

"I just meant that indigo, especially Indigofera tinctoria, is the perfect complementary crop for rice."

"Why is that?"

"Because it grows so well in the uplands," Sarah said with her voice trailing off. Percival looked at her with such directness that she knew she had put her foot in her mouth.

"How did you know that, Miss Richards?"

"Perhaps I just overheard it somewhere." Always make the man think he's smarter than you are. "I shouldn't have spoken about something I know so little about."

"You're not getting off that easily, Miss Richards. Besides, why would you apologize for knowing something like that? I've never known a young lady who knew the difference between indigo and a weed, let alone one who could identify a plant by its Latin name. I think it's wonderful."

He thought it was wonderful? Could she just be herself? Madame Painchaud would have glared daggers at her for even thinking such a thing, but then Madame Painchaud wasn't there. Before the ball had gotten underway, Mamma reminded her that it would be viewed as forward if she were to accept more than two dances with the same young man.

"We don't want tongues to waggle, do we, Sarah?"

"No, Mamma, we don't want waggling tongues," Sarah replied out of force of habit.

Her words didn't keep Sarah from doing what she wanted to on the dance floor, though. She danced with Percival all evening long, not every dance, of course. Her card had been filled out in advance, but they certainly caused some tongues to waggle.

Between dances, Sarah occasionally slipped away to the toilets. Brought in just for the ball, the toilets were porcelain basins positioned so that a servant could stand on either side of the toilet-goer to hold her dress out of the way while she peed. During Sarah's first stopover, Mamma followed her.

"Sarah," she said, ordering the servants about as if they were her own, "You've spent a great deal of time with the same young man tonight."

"Would you like me to wipe you, miss?" one of the servants interjected politely.

"No, thank you," Sarah replied.

"Yes, she does," Mamma said. "You can't do it yourself, ninny."

After an awkward moment, Mamma and Sarah continued as Mamma pulled Sarah to her feet. "I like him, Mamma, and he complimented me for knowing the Latin name for indigo."

"You and Mr. Vaux talked about indigo?"

"He told me I'm the only young woman he's ever met who knows the difference between an indigo plant and a weed. And he's taller than me, Mamma. There's probably only one boy in Charleston who would like a girl who is comfortable talking about indigo, and I found him, Mamma. I'm having a wonderful time. Please don't ruin it for me."

"I don't want to ruin anything, dear. I want you to have wonderful memories of your coming out; I just don't want you to make any mistakes." Mamma paused before pointing out, "You know we have to be especially careful."

"Why, Mamma?"

"Because…."

"Say it, Mamma. Is it because of Haiti?"

"Yes, dear, it's because of Haiti, but I'm also concerned that your young man is older than you are."

"He's only five years older, Mamma."

"That's a lot when you're seventeen. Promise me you'll think about that the rest of the evening."

"I promise not to elope tonight, Mamma."

"Sarah! Don't even suggest such a thing."

"I was just joking, Mamma."

"Well, no more jokes. This is serious business."

"I promise."

The ball ended, and Sarah and Percival parted on the dance floor, promising to meet again during one of the whirlwinds of parties, dinners, and dances that were crammed into the next six months. Percival left with friends, and every girl surrounded Sarah on the dance floor.

Eliza was the most effusive, but everyone talked at once. "I told you you'd meet a beau tonight," she said, "But even I didn't know you'd land Percival Vaux. He's très au courant."

"He's too old for you," Prissy sniped. "Oh, and he has a past."

"That's right, he kept company with one of the Alston girls last year, or was she an Allston? I can't remember. I just know that she was from Georgetown County," Lizzy Pringle said, putting on her spectacles.

"And Prissy's right about him having experience, Sarah. He courted my cousin from Columbia once. Then he moved on to my second cousin in Society Hill and another girl from there who's real snooty because her grandfather is an English baron."

"Does that make her a baroness?" someone in the back row asked.

"No, you blunderkin," Lizzy snapped.

"How do you know so much?" Eliza asked.

"I have three older sisters, two of whom are about three days away from terminal spinsterhood. My mother keeps charts on every available boy's failed and current intrigues. Papa says she pays the servants for information."

"What did you do to Mr. Vaux tonight, Sarah? He didn't look at another girl," Prissy said.

"I didn't do anything," Sarah insisted. "Well, I did bring up indigo. He seemed to like that, but I didn't do anything else."

"You talked about indigo with the most handsome man on the dance floor?" Eliza said, shaking her head.

"Mamma said the same thing."

"Well, I'm not exactly surprised. Girls are supposed to talk about the weather and mutual acquaintances. Don't you know anything?"

"That's not true," Sarah insisted. "I figured out tonight that we're no different from young men when it comes to making conversation. You should talk about things you know and things that you like." Sarah stopped briefly to look at the girls surrounding her. "It makes you more interesting if you allow yourself to be who you are. He told me I was fascinating." Sarah tried to make a point.

"So, let's get this straight. Percival Vaux found you fascinating because you talked about indigo?" Lizzy interjected.

"Not just any kind of indigo," Sarah said. "Indigofera tinctoria."

"That's it," Eliza said. "You must have put a spell on him. This is not normal. Did he say anything about seeing you again?"

"I think so. We were saying goodbye, and I was trying to impress him with my curtsy, so I can't remember exactly, but I think he said he'd very much like to see me again. 'Let's promise to see each other again,' was the way he put it, I think." Sarah's parents were hovering, and it was unnerving.

She loved them for it, though, and she was beginning to feel guilty. She'd treated the evening as a game when she knew that a reputation could be sullied forever in a matter of moments. "I have to go. My parents are waiting," she said. "Goodnight."

The ride home was sobering. Sarah admitted that she'd been flippant about her behavior and apologized profusely. "Mr. Vaux is much older than you are, Sarah, and he has quite a reputation, or so I've heard," Mamma said. "He does come from a very fine family, however."

"He is handsome, too, isn't he?"

"Yes, he very handsome, Sarah."

"Does that mean you liked him?"

"I'll reserve judgment on that for the time being. I'm not opposed to you seeing him again, but I want you to be less flirty next time. This is serious, Sarah."

"I was flirty?"

"You were flirty," Papa confirmed. "But I heard tonight that Mr. Vaux has a good head on his shoulders. Did he tell you about his plantation?"

"He told me he lived on his family's plantation," Sarah said. "His parents died a few years ago, and he runs the plantation by himself. I have to admit I like that. I couldn't have done that when I was his age." Sarah looked at Papa curiously, "Does that mean you like him, Papa?"

"It means it's a good beginning."

The Middleton's ball was coming up, which was meant to be the most lavish party of the entire debutant season. It was to be held in the ballroom of Middleton's immense townhouse. As always, everything would be over the top, including the invitations that were delivered by couriers dressed in Middleton livery.

The invitations looked like snowflakes made sparkly by silver and blue glitter. When Sarah received hers, she rushed to her room to open it, leaving a trail of glitter up the stairs. The Middleton's balls always had a theme.

This year was Winter Wonderland, an unexpected one considering that winter seldom visited Charleston. Still, everyone agreed that it was the best one ever because of the icy blue and silver decorations and the ostentatious display of crystals.

Chandeliers dripping with crystals adorned the serving tables, and along one wall, in between a series of French doors, were chandeliers the size of small trees. Ropes of crystals hung from the ceilings, and crystals resembling hen's eggs held place cards and doubled as mementos. The Middleton sisters were there, of course, and again, they were dressed in identical gowns.

However, this time, their dresses were blue that was kinder to their pasty skin than the ecru silk satin they had worn for their coming out. But with their narrow lips and long noses, they still looked like they'd been sucking lemons.

Let Percival be there, Sarah prayed, and make him remember me, and don't let him have some beautiful girl from Philadelphia on his arm, with long golden hair and curly eyelashes and a Paris frock that will make me look like a bumpkin. Her prayers were weak in the faith department. However, she was pretty sure that God didn't grant wishes that came from people as evil as she was.

Besides, the beautiful girl from Philadelphia could have offered the same prayers, Sarah concluded. Sarah hoped for a fifty-fifty chance, the same odds the other girl would have, except that Sarah was relatively certain she knew more about indigo than the Philadelphia girl did. Papa would have called it Sarah's stone ginger.

Sarah and the other debutants were escorted to the third-floor reception room, where they were told to wait until they were formally introduced.

Gilded ladies' chairs ringed the room's perimeter, and the walls were covered with marble panels inlaid with semiprecious gemstones. No wonder the Middleton girls thought they shouldn't have to clean their chamber pots. They lived in a palace. Eliza was already there, looking as adorable as always, in a raspberry-colored silk gown.

"Gosh, Eliza, you look so pretty. I thought you were going to wear your green gown," Sarah gushed.

"I was, but Papa liked this one. He's been so sweet about Mama and me and our wild spending this year. I thought the least I could do was to wear the dress he likes. You look beautiful, by the way," she said, inspecting Sarah's gown of yellow silk.

"Can you believe we're standing here wearing these fancy gowns? A month ago, we were wearing middy blouses and aprons," Sarah said.

"Oh, and those ugly shoes Madame Painchaud made us wear," Eliza said. "I hated those things, and I hate her, too sometimes."

"You shouldn't talk about her like that," Sarah said. "Goodness knows, I was at loggerheads with her more than once, but her job was to produce educated young women, and she did it."

"Marriageable young women, you mean."

"Yes, that, too, and every year she turns out a new crop. Let's not talk about this anymore," Sarah said, changing the subject. "I want to talk about who might be here tonight."

"You mean Mr. Vaux?"

"Yes, I mean Mr. Vaux. Do you think he's going to be here?" she asked, removing an errant eyelash from Eliza's forehead.

"Sure I do," Eliza replied lightheartedly. "I think he's interested in you, and he knows that you'll be here tonight. I think he wouldn't miss it."

"What if he shows up with another girl?"

"What are you talking about? He likes you. Mama even said he's smitten with you. Everyone figured that out at the coming-out ball. How bold do you want him to be? How about he scoops you up in his arms and runs away with you?"

"I'd love that."

Eliza gasped, "Sarah!"

"Have I known him long enough to be in love?" Sarah swooned.

"They say you can fall in love at first glance," Eliza replied. "But not if you're from Charleston and have parents like ours."

"I know, but when I think of him, I can barely breathe."

"You'll know by tonight, Sarah."

"I'll know what?"

"You'll know if Mr. Vaux is interested in you."

"How do you know that?"

"Because it makes sense. If he asks you to dance, he's interested. If he doesn't ask you, he's not. Now come on; it's almost nine o'clock, time for the ball."

A trumpet sounded, and it was time for the girls to take their fathers' arms. They were reminded to hold their heads high and to look about the room focusing on the tops of everyone's heads. "Don't single out anyone in particular," they were warned.

The distraction could cause them to get tangled up in their skirts. Two years ago, an Allston debutant got so knotted up in her skirts that she and her father both fell and had to be carried away on stretchers. Sarah didn't listen, of course. She was too eager to spot Percival in the crowd. *Please let him be here,* her heart was telling her.

Please. Please.

And then she saw him.

He was standing well back, but he was looking right at her. When she and Papa got to the bottom of the stairs, Sarah turned back toward Percival, and he was still looking at her.

Her heart leaped. Was this the sign Eliza was talking about? Could everything be said without saying a word?

The first dance, a polonaise, was Papa's, and Sarah laughed as they performed it, thinking about Papa teaching her the dance in his study at Hayes House. Papa was stunningly handsome. According to Eliza, he had joie de vivre, an exuberance for life, and that he did. He loved Mamma, loved his work, loved his horses, and loved Sarah, but that night, he loved Sarah best.

The dance ended, and Sarah took Papa's arm to leave the dance floor. A few steps from the edge of the floor, however, Papa felt a polite tap on the shoulder. It was Percival looking like Prince Charming and the Archangel Michael all rolled into one. Sweat popped out along Sarah's hairline and above her upper lip, and her face got so hot that she was certain that she looked like a giant strawberry.

Percival bowed deeply to Papa and introduced himself as sweat puddled in the palms of Sarah's gloves. A rivulet of sweat trickled down the center of her back, and the backs of her knees felt sweaty as Percival turned toward her to ask for the next dance.

Sarah was having a complete meltdown, and she'd just used up every ounce of sweat in her entire body on other things, so when it came time to speak, her mouth was so dry that her lips were stuck to her teeth. She couldn't say a word, so she nodded affirmatively, and Percival placed his hand on her back and led her back to the dance floor.

Sarah's ears were ringing. This beautiful man wanted to dance with her, and she was going to dissolve into the floor. In a final effort to regain her composure, she looked around the room and realized that every eye was on the two of them.

The servants, the musicians, the spinsters, her parents, the old warhorses, and the girls from school, even the Middleton sisters, were staring at them. Well, that is just great. "You're shaking like a leaf," Percival whispered.

"It's because I'm happy."

"Because of me, I hope."

"Yes, because of you."

Percival and Sarah danced every dance together that night, and except for a couple of bathroom breaks for Sarah and a quick cigar on the piazza for Percival, they spent the entire evening together. They talked about their mutual friends, of course, but mostly they talked about fertilizers and floodgates, hybridizing rice, and ways to increase the staple of fair to middling cotton.

Sarah had been boning up on cotton and rice since the coming-out ball, and she held her own. Percival said he'd like to meet Sarah's mother about midway through, and Sarah instinctively knew that asking to meet a girl's mother was a very important step.

"Are you certain?" she asked.

"Of course, I am. Do you not want me to meet her?"

"Oh, no, it's just that Mamma can be a snob."

"I'll take my chances," he said, squeezing her hand. "Let's go."

As they walked toward her parents, a hush took over the room. Elisabeth Hebert Richards was no pushover. The question that lingered in between them was, "Will Mr. Vaux survive an encounter with her, or will this prove to be Sarah's undoing?" It could go either way, the crowd whispered.

Mamma, however, was surprisingly pleasant. Sarah wasn't certain, but she had an inkling that she'd even lost her wits for a moment and was a bit flirtatious.

Sarah knew exactly how she felt. There was something about Percival that was as irresistible as grog to a sailor. Back on the dance floor, Sarah asked Percival what he thought of her mother. "She's beautiful," he said, "But not as beautiful as her daughter."

Oh, no. Sarah started sweating again, and this time she was certain she was going to ignite. Her earlobes were on fire, and her breasts were melting. Then her vision got splotchy, and she was almost sick at her stomach. "I need to sit down for a moment," she whispered.

Percival whisked her off the dance floor and sat her down on the nearest chair. "Water, she needs water," he shouted to one of the servants.

That was the last thing Sarah needed. Mamma would insist upon taking her home, and Papa would sit up with her half the night. Her head quickly cleared, though, and she assured everyone that she was perfectly fine. "I think I got lightheaded over you meeting my mother," she later confessed.

Before long, the two were back on the dance floor whirling and spinning and having a wonderful time. "Sarah," Percival whispered during the last waltz of the evening. "May I kiss you goodnight?"

"On the lips?"

"On the lips."

"Not in front of everyone," Sarah stammered. "We can go out on the piazza if you like. I can't be alone with a man," she replied.

"Are you afraid of me, Sarah?"

"Oh, no," she replied. "I'm just...."

"I wouldn't hurt you, Sarah. I'd never hurt you."

Sarah raised her chin and smiled. "All right," she said.

"I'll go with you."

Sarah and her friends had practiced kissing on the backs of their hands. Some girls even practiced on each other, but even then, she knew that kissing a real boy couldn't possibly feel the same, and she was right.

When Percival pressed his lips to hers, her lips parted, and she shivered.

"Your first kiss?" Percival asked, nuzzling her neck.

"My first real one." Now she knew what a gentle kiss could feel like, and she wasn't afraid anymore.

"May I have another?"

"You certainly may," Percival laughed, and this time he slowly wrapped his arms around her until their bodies were pressed together, and then he kissed her. This time his mouth was slightly open just as Sarah's was, and the kiss was even better than the first one.

"My parents," Sarah suddenly remembered. "I have to go; I don't want to, but I must."

"I'll dream of you tonight, Sarah."

"And I of you. Goodnight." The next morning Sarah received a spray of white calla lilies from Anson's Flower Shop. The maid wore a toothy grin as she brought them into Mamma's morning room, and Mamma motioned for Sarah to sit beside her.

"It certainly looks as though Mr. Vaux has feelings for you," she said. "Flowers aren't given lightly, especially calla lilies, Sarah. There is no doubt that he has intentions toward you, but I'm not certain what your feelings for him are."

"I want to marry him, Mamma."

Mamma was so shocked. She had to take it to her Recamier. Sarah was far too young to talk like that, she said.

"But I'm not," Sarah argued. "I've made my coming out, and now I'm shopping for a husband. I thought that's what I was supposed to do."

"Has he said anything to you to make you think he's interested in a future with you?" Mamma asked.

He hadn't said anything of the sort, Sarah admitted. She wanted to tell Mamma about the kiss, but she knew better. She could pretty much predict that Mamma would forbid her to see him again if she did.

"Write a thank you note to Mr. Vaux, Sarah, and I'll have it taken to Mr. Anson's. I want to see it before you seal it, however. This is a critical time in your relationship."

"I don't have a relationship, Mamma."

Oh, but she did. The calla lilies said it all. Didn't Sarah see the look on the maid's face when she brought them into the morning room? By the end of the day, everyone in Charleston would know she had a suitor, but mistakes could be made.

"Are you still certain this is what you want?" Mamma asked. Sarah shook her head. She wanted it more than anything. "Then we'll work to make it happen."

"Did you ever get into trouble when you were a girl?" Sarah asked.

"I'm certain I must have," Mamma replied, baffled, "But you have to remember that my childhood was different from yours. When I was small, my mother was happy and gay and very much in love with my papa, but he was away most of the time running his indigo plantation near New Orleans."

"What was the name of it?" Sarah asked. "

Petite Creole, but I never got to see it in person."

"Why not, Mamma?"

"Because," she replied. "And if you continue to interrupt me, I won't go on with the story. Do you understand?" Sarah crossed her heart and promised not to interrupt again, so Mamma continued.

"All right, then. On those times when my father would come home, Mamma would host elaborate parties.

She had so many friends back then that some of them would stay with us for weeks. Mamma never told them about Papa, though. She pretended that her life was perfect and that Papa was mad for her, and she made me promise to keep her secret. There she was with a big, protective family that loved her, but she refused to turn to them. Instead, she shamed herself, wearing low-cut dresses and lip rouge to make him stay. He wouldn't, though. Her spirit hardened over time, and her health failed. By the time I was twelve, she was bedridden. Papa started coming home less and less until he rarely came at all."

"When I was sixteen, yellow fever came to the Lowcountry, and Mamma and some of the servants came down with it. Mamma was so frail that I knew she couldn't survive, so I wrote to my father and pleaded with him to come home." Mamma stopped and looked down as she recalled the memories of her childhood.

"When he did, it was too late. He arrived on horseback three days after the servants and I had buried Mamma in the family cemetery. His clothes were tattered, and I knew he'd been crying, but it couldn't bring Mamma back."

"Were you glad to see him?" She said, "Yes," but she was also angry with him for leaving her and her mother to run the plantation. He tried to make it up to her, she said, but it didn't last. "He left the day after Christmas that year."

"Did you ever see him again?"

"Once," she said. "He came to my wedding, but he was too intoxicated to walk me down the aisle, so he was taken upstairs by one of the servants. I know some of my relatives were horrified, but I walked myself down the aisle." Sarah said she didn't know a bride could do that, and Mamma reminded Sarah that she had practically raised herself, so she didn't see any sin in it.

But how did Mamma learn the nuances necessary to become a lady? By watching her mother and the other women in the family, she said. "If I have one gift, it is my penchant for observation."

Sarah went on to ask about what happened after the wedding. "My father died soon after that," Mamma said. "I learned about his passing in a letter from a woman who described herself as my father's dearest friend. She told me that she was with him when he died and that he was very proud of me. Then she said that she and my younger brothers and sisters were eager to meet me and that I would always be welcome in their home."

Sarah was confused. Mamma was an only child; she didn't have any brothers and sisters. Ah, but she did, Mamma said. The woman who had written the letter was referring to the children that she and Mamma's father had had together, Mamma explained.

In a not-so-subtle way, the woman was telling Sarah's mother that her father had another family.

"Oh, I see," Sarah whispered. Mamma continued with her story. A few months later, she inherited her father's entire estate. Then she learned from one of the attorneys that the woman and her children were still living at Petite Creole and had nowhere else to go. Mamma had had every right to evict them, but she decided, instead, to give them the plantation and its income. Over time, they lost touch, she said, and she regretted never meeting them.

"I told you this story because I wanted you to know that opportunity has a life of its own, Sarah. It doesn't last forever."

Sarah managed to keep the kiss a secret from Mamma, but she blurted it out when she saw Eliza at church the next day. They sat together in the Paget family's box pew, and as always, they whispered throughout the sermon. Eliza was seldom lost for words, but when Sarah told her about the kiss, she was speechless. She fumbled with the hymnal for a moment, and then she demanded details.

"During the last dance, he asked if he could kiss me goodnight."

"Tell! Tell!" Eliza whispered.

"Well, we walked out onto the piazza, and he put his arms around me, and then he kissed me."

"What kind of kiss was it? Was it the juicy kind or the kind we practiced at school?"

"It was kind of in the middle," Sarah said. "But I liked it so much. I asked him for another one."

"You didn't!" Eliza exclaimed quietly.

She did, and Percival laughed. "Then Percival slowly pulled me toward him so that we were touching all over, and then he held me even tighter, and then he kissed me, and I thought I was going to die."

"Did it remind you of anything bad; you know, the Hanson boy?"

"No, it made me forget. The Hanson boy was vulgar; Percival was wonderful. Percival had his mouth open the second time, and I had mine open, too, and it made me tingly all over."

How did she know she was supposed to have her mouth open? She didn't. It came naturally, and she would have kept going, but then she remembered her parents and told Percival that she had to go.

"Oh, Sarah, do you think this will ever happen to me?"

"Of course it will. There's a wonderful man out there just waiting to meet you. You're only seventeen, for heaven's sake."

"But you met Percival at the coming-out ball."

"It was meant to be, Eliza. You just haven't met your husband yet."

"Husband! Had he proposed?"

"No," Sarah said, but if he ever did, she was going to say yes.

Six months later, Percival did propose on the way to the annual St. Cecilia Society Ball at Rutledge House.

"Sarah," he said, fumbling for her hand, "I spoke to your father this morning for permission to ask you to marry me. He laughed when I asked him and said he'd been waiting for weeks for me to bring up the subject." Percival couldn't help but smile nervously as he continued. "I told him that I swear too much, and that I drugged a horse once to win a bet and that I've been pretty well over the bay more times than I could remember. Even after all of that, he said I'd make a fine son-in-law but that the final decision was yours."

Even though it was customary for couples to announce their engagements during the St. Cecilia Society Ball, and Sarah's friends had teased her about her relationship with Percival ever since the coming-out party, Sarah was still taken by complete surprise.

"Are you asking me to marry you, Percival?"

"Of course," he said.

"Then it's a yes! It's a yes!" she cried. "But why would you want to marry me? You could marry any girl in Charleston."

"There are at least a hundred reasons," he said. "But the most important is that you're the only girl I didn't want to get away. You know I've courted other girls and that I came close to getting engaged last year, but she wasn't you, Sarah. None of the girls I've known have been like you. I suppose any of them would have made good wives, but what would we have to talk about? Do you want me to tell you a secret?"

"Oh, yes, please," Sarah replied. He'd fallen in love with her during their second dance, he said, when she started talking about indigo.

"I fell in love with you even before that," Sarah admitted. "It was the moment I saw you. Remember that beautiful blue waistcoat you were wearing that night, the one with gold embroidery all over it?"

He remembered the embroidery, but he didn't remember the color because he was as color blind as one could get. That meant he didn't know what color her gown was, either. Would she marry him anyway? She'd think about it. She said, laughing. "I have to tell you something before we tell anyone," Sarah said, whispering so that the driver wouldn't hear her. "You might want to change your mind."

"I'd never change my mind, Sarah. Tell me."

"I was attacked when I was fifteen. I wasn't seriously injured, but it made me afraid. You're the first man besides my father that I've trusted."

"Then I'll love you all the more," Percival said, putting his arm around her. "I'm so sorry, Sarah. Do I know him?"

"No," Sarah said. "At least I don't think so. His name was Robert Hanson. He is the oldest of the three Hanson boys of King Street."

"I know the family," Percival said stiffly.

"It happened on Sullivan's Island, and I think he thought it was supposed to be like that. He even said he had a nice time and asked to see me again. That was the worst part. He died last summer. He was racing his servant on the beach when his horse fell and rolled on top of him."

"I remember that," Percival said. "I heard that the servant carried Robert's body back to the Hanson's creek house, and Robert's father beat the servant within an inch of life. Hanson lost enormous respect among the men of Charleston for doing that."

"Instead, maybe the servant should have left Robert's body on the beach and stolen the horse," Sarah mused.

"That's a good plan, Sarah. That's exactly what he should have done."

The wedding date was set for Christmas Day, 1800. However, before any vows were made, Percival and Sarah were expected to sign two separate marriage agreements that embarrassed Sarah when she learned that she was the only one to benefit. The first document was an Indenture Tripartite, the legal name for a contract that involves three different people or parties. In this case, it included Percival and Sarah and Sarah's executor. The said Percival Edward Vaux would:

At all times hereafter permit & suffer the said Sarah Richards, to give Grant, sell & dispose of at her Will & Pleasure, all or any part of her sizable estate Household & other Goods, Chattles, Ready Money Debts Legacies, Jewells & and other Estate as well Real as Personal, which the said Sarah Richards, now has or hereafter may have or expect to have and may do so without the Molestation, Hindrance or Disturbance of said, Percival Edward Vaux....

"I'm not signing that," Sarah said after the document was explained to her. "Percival would never take advantage of me, and this document implies that he will."

"Miss Richards, you are the heir to two large estates. This has nothing to do with Mr. Vaux. The purpose of the document is merely to protect you."

"I'm not offended by the document, Sarah. This is business," Percival interjected. "You need to sign it to protect your heirs."

She didn't have any heirs; she pointed out.

"Our children will become your heirs," Percival said. Sarah's earlobes began to glow again at the very thought of having children with Percival. She was certain that the lawyers seated around the table laughed about her to their wives that night, but she did agree to sign the document. She didn't want to, but she did it, and Percival signed it afterward.

The next document also was designed for Sarah's protection:

South Carolina Know all Men by these presents that I, Percival Edward Vaux of Waccamaw All Saints Parish in the State aforesaid, am held firmly bound unto (the executors) of Sarah Richards of Charleston, in the full and just sum of $24,000 to be paid to the executor.... Sealed and dates at Charleston this nineteenth day of December in the year of our Lord one thousand, eight hundred years, in the twenty-fifth year of the Sovereignty and Independence of the United States of America.

It went on to say that if Sarah were to be preceded by Percival, the $24,000 would be paid to Sarah. The amount would have enabled Sarah to own estates of her own and still be left with a hefty sum.

"This sounds like a prepaid insurance policy," she said. It was, Sarah's attorney said. "I'm as rich as Percival is, so it seems ridiculous for Percival to have to put all that money into a trust for me when I don't need it."

"You're richer than I am," Percival said, stepping in, "But it's traditional for men of my station to sign an agreement like this," he said. "Just view it as a savings account."

"All right, I'll do it, but why am I not required to put money into a trust for you?" Sarah asked as she picked up the quill. Women need to be taken care of, was the response from one of the attorneys.

"Well, this woman doesn't," Sarah said, putting the quill back on the desk. "I've decided not to sign this document unless a similar one is drawn up requiring me to put up the same amount for Mr. Vaux."

"This is highly unusual," Sarah's attorney whispered.

"I don't care, and I don't need to be taken care of. Is it all right with you if I don't sign the document, Percival? I'll sign it if you want me to, but not because the attorneys want me to."

"Don't sign it," Percival said, laughing. "Gentlemen, I think we're done here. Good afternoon."

As Percival and Sarah left the meeting room, he squeezed her hand and said that he was proud of her for standing her ground. Perhaps she was wrong. She was beginning to doubt her conviction.

"Don't," he said. "You are who you are, and that's why I love you. It was important for our future children for you to sign the first document, but the second one didn't matter one way or the other." Did she embarrass him? "On the contrary, I was proud of you. I like that you are a modern girl and that you stand up for yourself. Promise me that you'll teach our children to be just like you."

"I promise," Sarah vowed.

CHAPTER 15

The Josephine Dress

"Mamma, why did I let you talk me into getting married on Christmas Day?" Sarah whined as she stepped out of her petticoats in front of a large mirror that had been set up in Bishop Wither's study. "Nobody's going to come; I just know it."

"For heaven's sake, we've gone over and over this," Mamma said as she draped Sarah's petticoats over a chair. "You're getting married on Christmas Day because the women in our family have always gotten married on Christmas Day, and in Charleston, nothing is more sacred than maintaining family traditions. In two hours every seat in this church will be filled.

"Everyone has made special plans to return to the city earlier than usual this year because this wedding will be one of the biggest social events of the whole year. Sometimes you are so unappreciative of your social position that one would think you'd been raised by wolves. Now hurry up; we have a lot to do to get you ready."

They had bickered over the details of the wedding ever since the announcement was made. Except for the color of Sarah's gown, that they both agreed should be Tuscan ivory, they had argued about everything. The biggest disagreement by far had been over the style of the dress. Mamma insisted upon a traditional gown similar to the one Sarah wore during her coming out, and Sarah wanted to wear the new Josephine dress, a high-waisted empire-style gown that was all the rage.

They compromised.

Mademoiselle Jolie, a protege of Madame Chloe, was allowed to bring a collection of sample gowns to the Hayes House mansion so that Sarah could try them on. Beyond that, Mamma made no promises. The arguing erupted even before Sarah was cinched into the first gown, when she accidentally ripped out a side seam attempting to raise her arm.

"The sleeves are extremely fitted on these gowns," Mademoiselle Jolie warned as Sarah stepped into the second gown. "They're quite lovely, though, don't you think?"

As Sarah stood before the mirror, being careful not to move, Mamma scrutinized her image with a practiced eye, and then she let out one of her patented gasps.

"This gown is practically see-through," Sarah exclaimed. It was an idiosyncrasy of the gown, Mademoiselle Jolie explained. To flow properly, the gowns had to be made of fabric that was both gauzy and sheer. For example, the dress Sarah was modeling was made of muslin, French muslin, of course.

"I look positively naked," Sarah said. They were all like that the dressmaker replied. That's why they had to be worn over flesh-colored bodysuits.

"Bodysuits? I don't even know what that is, but it sounds like you could get awfully sweaty in something like that."

"You might glisten a little," Mademoiselle Jolie replied.

When pressed, she admitted that one of Madame Chloe's larger customers did puddle up a bit, although she was quick to point out that the problem had been successfully masked with perfume. However, the feature of the dress that did the most to push Mamma over the edge was the neckline.

"Look, Mamma," Sarah said after studying herself in the mirror. "I have cleavage."

"The décolleté is très provocative," the dressmaker said as she watched Sarah preen and waltz around the room. "When the gowns are worn to garden parties, the sunlight shines right through them. Well, shall we say, the men seem to love them."

If Mademoiselle Jolie had her wits about her, she would have known to have taken her cues from Mamma rather than from a star-struck eighteen-year-old girl like Sarah. By the time she realized her mistake, however, it was too late.

Beneath Mamma's serene exterior, she was seething. "I will not have my daughter walking down the aisle looking like a trollop," Mamma said in a voice one register above a whisper.

"Sarah, take off that gown this moment, and you," she said, pointing to the horrified dressmaker, "leave this house this instant!" Mademoiselle Jolie ran out of the house while Sarah tearfully pleaded her case.

"It's not the dark ages. It's almost 1801, and this is the latest fashion. The ladies magazines are all showing this dress, and this is what I want." An astute woman, if there ever was one, Mamma knew that Sarah was willing to go to war to get her way, so she agreed to a compromise.

Mademoiselle Jolie, however, was not a part of the deal. She was banned from the house forever. The next day Madame Chloe and three of her senior assistants marched into the townhouse, like geese toward the chopping block. It was quiet enough to hear a pin drop, and as the nerves set in, plenty were dropped.

The tension in the air was thick enough to burn Sarah's eyes. Everything was on the line for Madame Chloe. Her entire reputation hinged upon smoothing the ruffled feathers of Elisabeth Richards, and they were plenty ruffled.

Under Mamma's watchful eye, Madame Chloe went into high gear, substituting medium-weight silk for the traditional muslin and adding a chemisette to make the neckline more respectable. Long white opera gloves with pearl buttons were ordered to cover Sarah's arms (an absolute requirement for a young bride), and a train was added to the back of the gown to make it more formal.

Madame Chloe suggested a mantilla of Belgian lace worn over Madame Richards's pearl and diamond tiara for a headpiece. With an affirmative nod, Mamma agreed, and the die was cast. As Sarah looked at herself in Bishop Withers' mirror, she had to admit that it had all been worth it. She'd never seen such a beautiful gown, and she looked every inch a bride.

There was something she wanted to do before the wedding got underway, however. She wanted to take one last look at the sanctuary. She stepped out of the bishop's office, tiptoed past the raised pulpit, and looked toward the narthex at the front of the church. To her surprise, she spotted Bishop Withers halfway down the aisle, and he was walking straight toward her. "Sarah," he said as she ran to join him.

"This is going to be one of the most beautiful weddings St. Philips has ever seen. The sanctuary looks lovely, and so do you, my dear. You and your mother have certainly outdone yourselves." The magnificent church that towered above the Charleston skyline was decorated with garlands of magnolia, cedar, holly, and pine boughs held together by enormous crimson bows.

Matching wreaths adorned each of the family box pews, and near the altar at the front of the church, stood two large candelabras, each holding dozens of tapers.

"I had very little to do with this," Sarah said. "You know Mamma. I was allowed to select the ribbon, but she picked out everything else. I do think it's beautiful, though."

The bishop did too, he said, and by the way, he was very fond of Sarah's young man. Sarah smiled, but then she took a deep breath and stared down at the worn marble floor. She had something else on her mind but was hesitant to speak of it aloud. Finally, she said, "May I ask you an important question, Bishop Withers?"

"Of course you may," he replied, sensing that Sarah was about to disclose something intimate. Interlocking her fingers beneath her chin, Sarah struggled to find the right words. "Is it a sin to hide something from your husband?" she asked.

"That depends upon what you want to hide," he said.

"It's about when I was in Haiti," she said, knowing that Bishop Withers knew about her time on the island except, of course, the part about her offing her cousins in the mushroom cave. "I don't think there is any need for you to bring that up unless you wish to," he said. "Do you want to tell him?"

"No, I never want to talk about it again," Sarah said, feeling as though a huge burden had been lifted from her shoulders. "Thank you so much."

And then she turned to walk away when she suddenly stopped and pivoted back toward the bishop.

"May I ask you one more thing?"

"Certainly."

"Is it a sin to be as happy as I am?"

"No, Sarah," the bishop replied, offering up one of his trademark belly laughs. "It's never a sin to be happy, especially on your wedding day. Now, off with you, or you'll be late."

Back in the bishop's study, Mamma made a face at Sarah for having left the room. Then she kissed her on the cheek. The two young servants giggled. "Sarah, Papa and I love you more than you will ever know. You are our only child and we couldn't be more proud of you than we are at this moment. What joy you've brought into our lives."

"I love you too, Mamma," Sarah replied. "I'm sorry we've been at such odds." It had been fun, though, Mamma said, smiling.

"Yes, Mamma. It's been great fun."

"But I'm not done."

There was one last thing, Mamma said, handing Sarah a velvet box. "These are for you," she said as Sarah timidly opened the box.

"They're your wedding pearls, Mamma."

"They're your pearls now."

Sarah and her father prepared to walk down the aisle less than an hour later, and the church was overflowing just as Mamma had predicted. The city's great families, including Eliza's, were all there, and stuffed into their expensive family pews like cigars in a humidor. Halfway down the aisle, Sarah turned to Papa and handed him a small note. "Put it in your pocket, Papa, and read it after you sit down. It's from me."

When it was time for Sarah to let go of Papa's arm, her legs were numb, and her insides were rubbery. Then Percival reached for her hand and flashed her one of his crooked little smiles.

"I love you," he whispered, and despite Bishop Withers' assurances about sin and happiness, Sarah was certain she was going to die on the spot. The service was beautiful, and everything came off without a hitch, except for Papa and his crocodile tears.

Blame it on Sarah's note: "Papa, I have always loved our walks together, but this one was my favorite."

CHAPTER 16

True Blue Plantation

THE MOMENT SARAH SAID I do, she became the mistress of one of the finest rice planation in the Lowcountry. Percival had inherited True Blue from his parents, William Vaux and Elisabeth Pawley, who had died three years earlier.

Percival was twenty at the time, and his only sibling was eighteen-year-old Mary, a young bride living on John's Island.

"The boy's too young to run the plantation," his fellow planters whispered behind his back. "In a couple of years, True Blue will be on the auction block and one of us will end up paying top dollar for it."

Percival had surprised them all.

To reach the plantation from Charleston, Percival and Sarah boarded a small schooner for the three-hour sail up the South Carolina coast. "Are we almost there?" Sarah asked as the town of Georgetown came into view.

"Not yet," Percival replied. "Once we get to Georgetown, we'll have to take a ferry across Winyah Bay, and then it will be another two hours by carriage. We usually make the last leg of the trip by boat, but this is the first time for you to see True Blue, and I want you to see it at its best."

They'd just returned from a six-week honeymoon trip to Boston and Philadelphia, and Sarah was exhausted. Still, the moment the carriage passed between the plantation's elaborate gates, she could barely contain her excitement.

The avenue leading to the big house was a quarter of a mile long, and it was flanked by live oaks more than a hundred years old. The mansion's exterior was white clapboard with long black shutters, and the entire house sat on top of a foundation of vaulted chambers. Six chimneys punctuated the mansion's roofline, and the same brick as in the chimneys had been used to build the dependency kitchen.

"It's even more beautiful than Rochambeau, Percival." Sarah exclaimed. "Are we really going to live here?" Sarah asked as the driver helped her down from the carriage.

"It looks like an English picture card, doesn't it?" Percival just laughed because it wouldn't be long before Sarah would learn that there was nothing pastoral about a rice plantation. True Blue was always in perpetual motion.

The first week was dedicated to unpacking, and Sarah was astonished at how much there was. She'd already unpacked six steamer trunks filled with her trousseau and half a dozen crates containing portraits of her parents and some of her books and dolls and other childhood things that she couldn't part with.

She'd seriously underestimated how many wedding gifts there were, though. "There must be two dozen crates full of wedding gifts," she said to Percival one afternoon. "It'll take weeks to unpack them."

It was going to take longer than that, he said. More than a dozen more at the landing hadn't been moved to the big house yet.

"Oh, Percival, you're so sweet," Sarah said, putting her arms around his waist. "You've been away from the plantation so long that I know you have too much catching up to do to worry about me.

"I just want you to be happy here, Sarah. Tell me that you are."

She was deliriously happy, she said pulling Percival down onto the bed.

Did that mean what he hoped it did?

"Lock the door and I'll show you."

Miss Hannah

According to tradition, Percival's responsibilities were strictly limited to the production of rice. South Carolina planters followed the rules no matter what, and that meant everything else fell squarely on Sarah's shoulders.

Sarah had come from a long line of planters just as Percival had. His mother and grandmother before her had been plantation mistresses. Unlike them, however, Sarah had spent most of her childhood at boarding school.

She knew the last styles in bonnets and parasols, she could conjugate French verbs, and thanks to Papa, she had been tutored in botany since the age of twelve, but she scarcely knew the difference between a tub of lard and a tub of lye soap.

Thank God for a solid, caramel-colored woman named Hannah. "Lord help us all," Sarah heard Hannah say under her breath after their first meeting. Years later, Hannah admitted that although her new mistress was a pretty little thing, when it came down to running the plantation, she was as green as skunk cabbage.

"I don't have time to be teaching that child or anybody else's child," Hannah complained to her husband, Blue Russell, that evening. "I don't have a choice, though, so's I might as well get on with it."

Hannah became a mammy to the white folks when her mother,

Rebecca Mae, was forced to retire from the job due to rheumatisms. Rebecca Mae had been mammy for thirty-five years, but she got too crippled to keep going, so Master Percival had given her permission to retire following the death of his parents.

At twenty-eight, Hannah knew she was stepping into mighty big shoes with a husband and two baby girls. Rebecca Mae was the thing of legends, but as it turned out, so was Hannah. Hannah worked long hours caring for her white family, but she was no fool. She walked a fine line.

One of Master Percival's cousins, for example, had recently teased her about being the black sheep of the family, as if she would find the remark endearing in some way.

She wanted to call him the ignorant fool that he was, but instead, she smiled all around, slapped her thighs, and blurted out, "My, you is a caution with that one." Hannah didn't have white skin, and she wasn't blood kin to anybody in the big house. She wasn't a servant, either; she was a slave just like everyone else on the plantation.

Master Percival and his parents had always treated her with respect; that part was true. Maybe they had even loved her in their way, but Hannah knew that slavery was against God's law and that the words love and slavery couldn't be used in the same sentence. Her white family only loved that part of Hannah that she was willing to reveal, not her true self. That part she was keeping to herself.

CHAPTER 18

Too Many Chili Peppers

EVERY NEW PLANTATION MISTRESS, including Sarah, quickly learned that women prepared the food, cared for the children, cleaned the houses, sewed the clothes, and did the laundry. They made the soap and candles, stuffed the sausages, and put up the jam. They also weeded the gardens, canned the vegetables, and baked the bread.

Sarah had a household staff to do the actual labor, of course, but it was her job to organize everything right down to the smallest detail. The looks on the maids' faces told the whole story. They'd rolled their eyes at her; she'd seen them. She sounded like a schoolgirl.

Sarah's day began in the plantation kitchen, going over the menu with Hannah and doling out the necessary spices. Then it was on to the big house, and the provisions pantry that Percival said should have had a revolving door.

Staples were stored there: barrels of rice, beans, and corn; casks of molasses; sacks of brown sugar, flour, salt, cornmeal, soda ash, and baking soda. Glass amphoras, some three-feet-tall, contained olive oil, vinegar, and syrup made from sorghum. Brasiers were stored there, too, as were candle and butter molds, rug beaters, butter churns, and winnow baskets.

Copper and silver were cleaned with quicksilver at a large table in the center of the room; hard-to-get things like pineapples and coconuts were stored nearby. Sarah's slant-topped desk stood beneath a large window. It was there that she kept her ledger books and extra keys. She also stored spices there.

Practically anything could be grown in South Carolina, except for some of the most important spices. They came by ship from around the world, and by the time they found their way into Sarah's kitchen, they were practically as valuable per ounce as gold. So they were kept in her desk under lock and key, and she kept the key on a chatelaine pinned to her dress.

Curry spices were stored there, like nutmeg, cinnamon, clove, allspice, peppercorns, paprika, and saffron. Garlic, cilantro, tarragon, rosemary, mint, chutney, sage, thyme, oregano, and onion grew profusely in Sarah's herb gardens. Sarah dreaded assigning duties to the household staff. She'd grown up with servants, of course, but dealing with an entire household staff was intimidating.

"They just stand there and stare at me," she complained to Hannah at the end of the first week. "I can't do this."

"Then you learn yourself to do it," Hannah said. "You're the only one who gives orders around here, lessen, of course, I do it. It's your job. They're not staring at you, Miss Sarah, they're waiting for you to say something. Tomorrow, you call them in, and you tell them something, even if it's wrong."

The next morning, that's exactly what Sarah did. "Janet and Juni, you start in the master's study, but don't move any of his papers," she said in her most authoritative voice. "And remember, if Master Percival comes into the room, stop what you're doing and leave. Then you can move on to cleaning the banisters and the front hallway."

Sarah talked to the laundry staff next. Did they need additional soap or borax? "We'll be needing some soda ash come next week," the head laundress replied awkwardly. She'd order some today, Sarah said, moving on to the head seamstress.

"Sister Jacob, I'll be ordering new fabrics soon, and you and I can discuss on another day what you need in the way of notions."

"Yes, ma'am," a startled Sister Jacob replied. She'd be doing that.

"If there's nothing more, you can all get to work," Sarah said, turning to walk away. "Oh, and Hannah, I have some things to discuss with you.

If you'll follow me to the landing."

"Yes, ma'am," Hannah replied in a stammer. If something was used on the plantation, it was made on the plantation. That included brooms, casks, hams, and several varieties of vinegar along with laundry soap, shampoo, insect repellent, shoe polish, hair dye, spot remover, and silver polish.

Sarah had recipes for everything, including a potion that promised to bring a victim back from the dead, although she hadn't had a chance to use it yet.

Once the more mundane chores were done, she could move on to one of the few places she was completely at ease, her gardens. Her favorite plant confounded Hannah. "I've never heard of chili peppers in South Carolina, and here we have rows and rows of them," she said one morning. "I think they're pretty and all, but they are too hot to eat. Even the birds won't have anything to do with them. So what are we going to do with them, Miss Sarah?"

"I don't know," Sarah said.

"I know I planted too many of them, but they're really special to me. They came from Cuba. Maybe we can think of something to do with them." Hannah said she was outta ideas for the moment, being surprised and all about the mistress's request, but she'd think on it.

Sarah kept a particularly close eye on her orchards; they were so immature that they were constantly under assault from birds and insects, and once the fruit was ready to pick, thievery was so rampant that she had to post guards. Sarah developed a system for everything.

Apples, for example, were first inspected for worms and bruises. The blemished ones were tossed into the apple butter pot, and the unblemished ones were individually wrapped in old newspapers and stored in the cellars beneath the big house. She stored potatoes there, too, but onions and garlic were woven into ropes and suspended from the rafters in one of the barns.

Soft-skinned fruits like plums, pears, and peaches had to be processed right away. Cucumbers, beets, watermelon rind, and okra were sliced and layered into crocks and pickled. During one of the pickling days, Hannah and Sarah were in the throes of steam and pickle jars and fruit flies when Hannah had an epiphany. "Miss Sarah, remember when we talked about what to do with the chili peppers? Well, I got an idea. Why don't we pickle them up with vinegar and salt just like we do with regular pickles?"

"Then we could strain off the peppers, and package up the juice in little toilet water bottles—the ones with those little shaker tops. What do you think?"

"I think that's a wonderful idea, Hannah. And if it's really good, maybe we could start a business and sell it on the river," Sarah exclaimed, clapping her hands.

"Oh, nah, Miss Sarah. You and Master Percival got a go-zillion dollars. You don't need to be starting a business," Hannah said scoldingly.

"Why not?" Sarah replied. "Men start businesses everyday. Why can't women do the same?"

"I don't know why, but it ain't proper," Hannah argued. "And another thing, your Mamma would fall over dead if she heard you were even thinking about something like this."

"Then we won't tell her," Sarah said. "I know that at this point it's a silly idea, but just think how much fun it would be if if it were to be successful. We could call it Mammy's Pepper Sauce."

"Mammy's Pepper Sauce?" Hannah almost fainted. And the notion of naming a business after her was more than she could stand. Her resolve left her brain as quickly as the blink of an eye, and she got the giggles.

If Miss Sarah didn't mind too awful much, she said, could they call it Hannah's Pepper Sauce, instead, being that was Hannah's name and all? Of course, it was up to the mistress, she added, thinking she might have overstepped her bounds, but Sarah was delighted.

"Hannah's Pepper Sauce it is," she exclaimed. "Now I've got to figure out how to order toilet water bottles."

"Miss Sarah, we got to make the sauce, first," Hannah cautioned. "I don't know anything about pickling peppers. We ain't even picked them up, yet."

"A minor detail," Sarah said, headed toward the Cuba garden. "A minor detail."

A few days later, Hannah stopped by Sarah's morning room. Her concerns had returned. "Miss Sarah," she said, "I've been thinking, and I've decided that this is utter audacious, you and me starting up a business together. What do you think folks'll say, me being one of the People and all?"

"I like the fact that it's audacious," Sarah replied. "It's about time women did something on their own," Sarah said. "It's way past time. What's audacious is that a wonderful, smart woman like you was born into slavery, not that we've started up our own business. Someday things are going to be different, Hannah."

Was she talking about women or slavery? Hannah asked shyly. "I'm talking about both," Sarah replied. "I'm tired of women like me growing up thinking that their sole purpose in life is to become a wife and mother. I'm just lucky my father didn't feel that way and neither does Percival, but that's what my classmates and I were taught every day. And you, well, I don't have to tell you how unfair your world is. It's going to change, though. It might take some time, but it's going to change. I know it is," she said.

"Freedom for the People would surely be a wondrous thing, Miss Sarah," Hannah replied almost inaudibly. Little did she know that for her own family, at least, it would happen within her lifetime.

Sarah and her staff put up more than fifty gallons of pepper sauce that they set to aging in empty bourbon casks stored in a small cellar beneath the house.

Sarah couldn't resist boasting to Eliza, especially about the pepper sauce.

"We put up several barrels of pepper sauce made from the chili pepper plants I brought back from Cuba—remember," she wrote, reluctant to bring up the past. "We pickled the peppers, and now we're storing the liquid off the peppers in bourbon casks. You should see it—it's a beautiful red color and hot enough to burn your tongue.

"Once it's aged, I think it will be delicious on practically everything, I think I'll like it best on speckled beans, okra and fried eggs. It was Hannah's creation, and I doubt that you've ever seen anything like it before, so I'll send you some once we've bottled it. Percival thinks we might be on to something. If it's as good as I think it's going to be, I'm going to send a batch with one of the boys from the plantation to see how well it sells at the market in Charleston. I'm going to be sure to send some samples to the naval outfitters there. Percival said with the miserable food sailors have to eat while they're at sea, they'd probably use it by the gallon. Then he laughed and said that it might be hot enough to even kill weevils," Sarah wrote.

Eliza wrote back, "I'll take a gallon."

And then she wrote to her mother and was sadly disappointed with a response that was filled with criticism.

Darling Sarah,

I am very proud of the way in which you have so boldly embraced your responsibilities as mistress, but starting a business is very out of character for a lady of means and will be frowned on in polite circles. Scrupulous though you may be, you could bring dishonor to your husband and to his good name.

I suggest that you rethink your notion of managing a business in your position. Women weren't made to fit into the marketplace, Sarah. Money, although necessary, is dirty business. Women are to be nurturers and the glue that holds families together.

As for partnering with your servant, that concerns me the most. To do so suggests equality between the races, Sarah, and it is a thing not to be done. I have always taught you to be kind to your slaves and other servants and to treat them as the precocious children that they are, but there is a chasm between the two races that was never meant to be crossed. To behave other-wise is against God's law.

Love to Percival,
Your Loving Mother

CHAPTER 19

Swamp Fever

SARAH CRIED WHEN SHE read her mother's letter and wasn't altogether certain why. It was a letter she could have predicted would come. She could have written the letter herself, but to see her mother's criticism on paper injured her spirit.

Times were changing; that was the one thing Sarah was certain of. The old ways wouldn't last forever. She understood Mamma's concerns, but she also knew that she and Hannah were strong, capable women. Someday women would be congratulated for running businesses and for using their brains for things other than making applesauce and babies. Perhaps that time just hadn't come yet, but there was nothing wrong with being on the forefront.

She'd recently read a newspaper story about sisters who started a perfume business together in Philadelphia and another who ran a housekeeping company in Boston. There were laundresses in Charleston, and boarding house owners and milliners and certainly not the least, Madame Chloe. Of course, there were also brothel owners and prostitutes and barmaids, but that didn't dampen Sarah's determination to be both a lady and a business owner. Just because it was uncommon didn't make it wrong.

One of the most challenging things about living at True Blue was that by mid-May at the latest, the entire household was forced to flee the plantation. The threat came from a deadly fever known as swamp fever. (Percival didn't know that a hundred years later, it would be identified as mosquito-born malaria.)

Percival believed that the fever came from invisible gasses that bubbled out of the pluff mud along the river. Wherever it came from, he said, it always arrived on the plantation in late spring and didn't leave again until after the first hard freeze. It was a killer, and it was random in its selection of victims, but it especially targeted children and old livers.

"We evacuated Rochambeau, too," Sarah said, "but I've never heard of swamp fever."

"Your papa plants cotton at Rochambeau. They have fevers along the Ashley River—they might even have something like swamp fever there, but it's not as deadly as it is here in rice country. By mid-May we have to be off the plantation."

"Where will we go?" Sarah asked.

"We could go anywhere," he replied.

"Some of the planters take their families to the mountains of North Carolina or Georgia. My parents used to alternate between our townhouse in London and a rented country house in New York State, but my favorite is Pawleys Island."

"Does the fever go there?" Sarah asked.

"No," Percival said reassuringly.

"I know it sounds impossible, but it's true. We have a house there on Sweet Grass Cove that I think you'll like. It's white clapboard like this house, but it has piazzas on all four sides, and it has huge windows that let in the ocean breezes.

"People call it the wedding cake house. It's much cooler there than it is here at True Blue," he said, "and you don't have to dress up. The men go without ties and the women wear white cotton dresses and straw bonnets. The little children play on the beaches and in the inlets, and the older ones ride horses and fish from dinghies. Oh, and the food—it's wonderful there.

"For dinner we can have fresh shrimp and crabs, fried flounder and deep-fried balls of cornmeal called hush puppies. I love the island so much I'd want to live there all year long if I didn't have to run the plantation."

"If we have to leave the plantation because of the swamp fever, what happens to the People? Don't tell me they have to stay."

"Most of them do," Percival replied. "Hannah and her family and the other house servants and their families will go with us; we have houses for them there. The rest of the People will remain on the plantation."

"What about the fever?" Sarah wanted to know.

"Adult slaves don't come down with it much, and even when they do, they usually survive," Percival replied. "Every year, though, it takes some of the children. Last year we lost Becky and Old George's twelve-year-old daughter along with three infants. It's sad business, Sarah, but I can't change it. This is rice country, remember."

"I know," Sarah replied. "Without rice we starve."

CHAPTER 20

Eliza's Visit

AFTER WORKING FOR MORE than a year and a half to find a husband, Eliza's prospective suitors had all been duds. The cream of the crop was the rain boy with the stinky hair tonic, and he never went anywhere without his mother.

How on earth could anyone as adorable as Eliza be expected to spend time with someone like that? Sarah's solution was to invite her to Pawleys Island for an extended stay at Sweet Grass Cover. "The house is filled with white wicker furnishings with canvas cushions, and there are muslin curtains at the windows," Sarah wrote.

"Every morning Hannah and I fill the cottage with fresh wildflowers, and the little children among us are invited inside to place their favorite seashells on the windowsills.

"Bring straw bonnets with oversized brims," Sarah advised in her correspondence, "and be prepared to go barefoot on the beach, just like we did on Sullivan's Island."

Eliza arrived aboard the Charming Betsy, a three-masted schooner under full sail, and it was a breathtaking sight as it sliced through the choppy inter-coastal waters that led directly to Percival and Sarah's landing.

It was the first Sunday in June 1801, and it was a beautiful day, unlike the muggy ones Sarah had grown accustomed to. Sarah spotted Eliza sooner than she had expected, although it was no wonder since she was hanging over the side of the boat like a puppy climbing out of a box.

Eliza's straw bonnet had emerald green ribbons that matched her green and white day dress. She reminded Sarah of the clover that grew with abandonment beneath the apple trees in her new orchard. She had missed Eliza so.

"Eliza!" Sarah cried, waving to her like a six year old.

"Sarah!"

The schooner glided along its path toward the landing with ease, despite the choppy waters. The captain was a crusty fellow who Percival had known since he was a child, and it was he, Percival said, who had transformed Percival's adolescent cursing into an art form.

Percival was a master-curser, he boasted, but he was prudent about when and where he used it like a gentleman. The stables at True Blue sat on hollowed ground. "Horses and dogs have held cursing in high esteem for generations," Percival had insisted earlier that morning.

"That was ridiculous, Sarah said.

"My dear, a tawdry display of brassy words is good for them. It perks up their ears and keeps them on their toes. As for humans who might be offended, they probably shouldn't enter my stable or anyone else's for that matter, without an invitation."

Was he telling her not to come to the stables? "Of course, not," he said. "I'm just warning you that if you come unannounced, I might be engaged in an important conversation with one of my horses."

"Fair enough," Sarah said, surprising him. Just then, Eliza was deposited onto the landing and rushed toward Sarah with open arms.

"It's been ages. I've missed you so."

"I've missed you, too, Eliza."

Eliza and Sarah laughed at the amount of luggage the deckhands were bringing off the schooner.

"How many dresses did you pack?" Sarah said.

"I don't know for sure. Mama helped me, and you know how our mothers are; they believe in packing everything you could possibly need."

"Don't tell me you brought a chamber pot." Sarah said, giggling. She did, she admitted. "How embarrassing."

"Don't be embarrassed; my mother would have done the same thing."

"Eliza Lucas Paget, you're looking bloody beautiful," Percival said as he approached the landing. "Bloody beautiful. Did you finally find yourself a beau during all of those parties and balls and teas and whatever else we were all invited to?"

"Percival, what an awful thing to say. She just got here and you're asking her if she's found a beau."

"It's not an awful thing to say," Percival said. "That's what the fuss was all about; it was to pair up. We did have some good times, though, especially during race week, didn't we? Eliza, remember when your bonnet took off, and that young ruffian returned it to you demanding a kiss?"

"You were so gallant, Percival. I thought for a moment you were going to challenge him to a duel, and then you kissed him on the lips, instead. I thought I'd die laughing."

"Do you still need a beau?"

"Why, Mr. Vaux, I certainly do. Do you have one up your sleeves?"

"In fact, I do. I have a couple in mind, but we'll talk about that later. Right now I have to talk to one of my horses. Goodbye, ladies."

"Did he say he was going to go talk to one of his horses?"

"It's a long story. I'll tell you all about it later. Now let me show you around the creek house." Eliza's things were carried to the cottage while she and Sarah strolled the creek walk. Eliza asked her when they had moved to the beach.

"Three weeks ago, and we love it here," Sarah said, holding her skirts above her knees and spinning around like a three year old. "It's beautiful, and it's filled with the oddest things you've ever heard of. We have bogs and pollies and spits and Polly wiggles. We also have two ghosts. The Gray Man is a tattered-looking man who appears on the beach to warn people of upcoming storms. Alice is the ghost of a young woman who died of a broken heart. She's buried at All Saints, just down the road from True Blue. It's too dangerous though to visit her grave in the summertime because of the fever."

"Does she travel with a white rabbit?"

"No, she's quite alone, really, and her story is very sad. Let's not talk about sad things. Let's talk about fun things."

"Then let's talk about men, Sarah."

"Oh, that's what I wanted to tell you," Sarah said. "There are some handsome men spending the summer here. I thought it would be like the boonies, but it's not. This is rice country, and everybody here is really rich."

"Only Chinese people eat rice," Eliza said, pulling her hat down over her eyes.

"That's not true. Percival says that the whole world loves rice, and that it makes a lot more money than cotton," Sarah said. "The families here stay to themselves, though, and they intermarry like rabbits. The only outsiders they bring in are English brides. I have no idea how I ended up here, but everyone's been really nice to me."

"Maybe you can pass me off as an English princess," Eliza said, picking a flower near the water's edge.

"Don't get too close to the creek, Eliza; there are alligators living there."

"Alligators were everywhere," Eliza quipped.

"Well, these ones live in a hole right beneath your feet," Sarah said.

"Let's get back to the subject of men," Eliza said. "I saw three good-looking unattached men at the St. Cecilia Society Ball, but I never could find anyone to introduce me to them. I wish I had had the courage to just walk up and say, 'Hi, I'm Eliza Paget and I'd like to dance with you, you big hunk 'o cheese,' but it doesn't work that way, does it?"

"I've missed you so much," Sarah said, throwing her arms around Eliza's tiny shoulders. "I'm so glad you've come."

"Me, too, but I didn't know the trip would be so long. I thought we were there when we reached Georgetown and was disappointed when I was told that I had to go aboard another boat.

"I finally made it, though, and I'm planning to stay a long time if you'll have me. The cottage is beautiful," Eliza said. "It looked like a wedding cake."

"That's what people call it, the wedding cake house," Sarah said. "I guess it's aptly named. I do love it, though. I wish we could live here year round. We decided to have supper on the beach to celebrate your arrival, and everything is going to come from the sea or the creek."

"What about the cornbread things you told me about?"

"Oh, hush puppies," Sarah said. "We'll have a bucketful of them. You can't come to Pawleys Island without having hush puppies."

"Sarah, I need to talk to you about something really important," Eliza said as she motioned for Sarah to follow her along the beach. Eliza's steps became brisk, and Sarah had to hurry to catch up. Once there, she sensed that Eliza's mood had darkened and that she was engulfed in sadness.

"I'm pregnant," Eliza said, "and I can't have the baby. My parents will disown me."

"Oh, Eliza. What happened? Who's the father?"

"James Paget, my cousin from Philadelphia. He and family were staying with us last Christmas, and he came into my room one night. I told him to leave, but he wouldn't. I didn't fight him like you did the Hanson boy, though. I've always had a crush on James, and he didn't hurt me or anything. I know it was wrong, but I didn't stop him, Sarah. I'm so ashamed."

"Maybe you just think you're pregnant. What makes you think you are?" Her breasts were swollen, and she'd missed her last four courses, she said.

"If you're pregnant, it's God's will," Sarah argued.

"No it's not. If you'd gotten pregnant by your cousin, would you have thought it was God's will?"

"No, I would have thought it was the work of the Devil."

"Well, that's how I feel," Eliza said. "If God loves me, he couldn't possibly want me to have my own cousin's baby out of wedlock."

Maybe she'd feel differently after the baby came, Sarah said.

"I won't, Sarah, I never will."

"What else can we do?" Sarah said.

The People had ways to end pregnancies, Eliza reminded her.

"You'd go to hell for that."

"Maybe," Eliza said, she didn't know anything anymore. She just knew that if she was pregnant, she couldn't bring such scandal to the family. Maybe it was a sin; perhaps it wasn't, but she wouldn't blame Sarah if she didn't want to help her.

"What do you mean if I help you?"

"Every plantation has a medicine woman," Eliza said. On her father's plantation in Stono, they had a woman and her daughter who practiced medicine together.

"At True Blue, the slave woman who treats the People is Ophelia," Sarah said, "but they don't call her a medicine woman; they call her a healer."

It didn't matter, Eliza said. Would Sarah agree to help Eliza see her?

"What for?" Sarah asked.

"To tell me if I'm pregnant," Eliza said.

"They could do that?"

"I think so; they put a frog on your belly or smell your urine or something like that, and then they know."

What would happen if she was pregnant? She'd cross that bridge when she got there, she said.

"Will you help me or not?"

"I won't help you kill your baby, Eliza, but I'll help you speak to Ophelia."

Bile rose in Sarah's throat at the very idea of lying to Percival. She'd never been untruthful to him, except for the lie of omission about Haiti, but Eliza was in such dreadful shape, Sarah had to do something.

Ophelia! She'd ask Ophelia to come to the creek house to teach her about herbs. There was certainly no lie in that. Sarah was a plantation mistress, and she was expected to doctor everyone on the plantation until a real doctor could be summoned. Anything she could learn from Ophelia would be enormously helpful to her. If Eliza wanted to ask Ophelia something while she was here, Sarah would simply leave the room.

Ophelia was wide-eyed when she was helped down from the wagon that made its daily run between the plantation and the creek house. She had no idea why she had been summoned to meet with the mistress, other than that she was told to bring her doctoring kit, and she was mighty curious.

"Good morning, mistress," she said when she saw Sarah exiting the kitchen.

"Good morning, Ophelia," Sarah chirped. "I'm so glad you could come. I need lessons on doctoring, and I thought we might as well get started today.

"This is my friend, Miss Paget," Sarah said, motioning to Eliza. "Eliza, this is Ophelia."

Giving doctoring lessons was right up Ophelia's ally. She was confident when it came to doctoring and midwifery, and she liked being in a position of authority.

"I'll do what I can," she said, adjusting her turban.

"Hand me my medicine bag off the wagon," she said to the driver, "and be careful, there's important stuff in there."

Hannah's cottage was offered up as a meeting place, and it was ideal. Ophelia started the lesson by spreading the contents of her bag onto the bed. Most of her tools, as she called them, were fashioned from ordinary household things.

The largest tool was akin to a pair of tongs, although Ophelia's were made of two large rice spoons soldered together. The tongs were part of her midwifery tools, she said, noting that it had helped her deliver countless babies.

Another tool resembled a crochet hook and another a large needle with an eye big enough to thread fishing line through. Sarah later learned that she was right about it being a needle but that Ophelia threaded sheep guts through it instead of fishing line.

"Nothing's better than sheep guts when it comes to stitching up wounds," she said. She also had a collection of spoons and small knives that had been cut down from larger ones. "I like to keep my knives real sharp," she said, demonstrating how easily one of them removed the hair from the back of her arm.

The tools, however, were only a small part of her collection. Drawstring bags sewn from flour sacks took up the rest of the room in her bag.

"Herbs are magic," she said, peaking her eyebrows at Eliza. "Herbs can fix almost any kind of sickness there is."

"Let's begin with herbs," Sarah suggested. "Why don't you tell us what each of the herbs is for, Ophelia? Do you mind if we take notes," she said, producing a pencil and paper from her apron.

She didn't mind at all, she said empirically. If she got to going too fast, just tell her to slow down, and she'd be happy to. The first bag contained spearmint leaves that were easy to identify because of their minty fragrance. "Spearmint leaves and spearmint oil is good for aches and pains, it's a good heart tonic, it's a nice perfume, and it can be used as a bug repellant," Ophelia explained.

Another good cure-all was chamomile. Grind it up and make a tea out of it, she said, and it would not only make little ones sleep, but it was a good tonic for the rheumatisms.

"Now, this little jar has mustard oil in it. It helps bust up boils, and it kills the crud that can grow between your toes. This other herb here is feverfew. I use it to treat fevers and headaches.

"I recon you recognize ginger root; it's good for the blood. Oh, and this little plant is aloe vera. If you break off a leaf like this, you can use it to salve up a burn."

"Do you grow all of these herbs?" Sarah said, amazed.

"I do, miss. I grow them all over the plantation. Some of them need lots more dampish soil than others. On visitation days, I usually visit my sister who lives at Silver Hill."

She's a better gardener than me, and if I can't grow a thing, she can, Sarah thought to herself.

"Now the next bunch of herbs I'm going to show you are from my birthing bag. You have to be careful with these herbs because if you ain't, you can cause a miscarriage."

At the very thought of a miscarriage, Sarah gave Eliza her pencil and paper and made her excuses, saying that she had just thought of something that needed her attention.

"I'll be back in a few minutes," she promised.

Sarah's departure did little to slow Ophelia's lesson, Eliza said later. As Sarah exited the cabin, Ophelia lined up five herbs side by side: motherwort, St. John's wort, pennyroyal, mugwort, and blue cohosh.

"Now all of these herbs are female herbs. Pennyroyal helps in child birthing, blue cohosh is for monthly distress, St. John's wort is good for when you have the miseries, and motherwort is good if you need a good long piss, although you have to be careful. Take too much of one of them or mix them, and it could cause a miscarriage."

Sarah stayed away for almost thirty minutes because she didn't want to walk in on a conversation that she couldn't repeat to Percival. Nothing was worth that, even Eliza, as much as Sarah loved her.

When she went back into the cabin, Eliza was helping Ophelia put everything back into her medicine bag.

"You missed some important stuff, miss, but Miss 'Liza wrote it all down for you."

"Thank you for coming, Ophelia," Sarah said.

"We'll meet again soon so you can teach me even more. I've heard you're the best medicine woman on the river."

Well, Ophelia said she didn't know if she was all that good, but she tried. As Ophelia headed back for the plantation, Sarah asked Eliza if she got the information that she had been looking for. She did, she said with an affirmative nod, but she was beginning to doubt if she could go through with it.

CHAPTER 21

What Did You Take, Eliza?

Seconds later, Eliza let out a scream and doubled over in pain.

"Let me get you to bed," Sarah said.

"It hurts too much, Sarah! Leave me on the floor."

So Sarah covered Eliza with a small cotton blanket that she found at the foot of Hannah's bed, and she knelt beside her.

"What did you take, Eliza? What did Ophelia give you?"

Eliza said she didn't take anything. She swore it. And then she calmly said that God was punishing her for even thinking about taking her baby's life, and she was certain that she was going to die.

She wasn't going to die, Sarah promised, but it did look like she was going to lose the baby. "Look at the blood between your' legs, Eliza!"

Sarah ran out into the yard, screaming for Percival and Hannah; then she told one of the younger boys to run after the provisions wagon and bring back Miss Ophelia.

Hannah was there in the blink of an eye, but Percival must have been away from the house because he didn't answer Sarah's cries, so she rushed back to Eliza.

"What happened?" Hannah said, horrified by the blood.

"I think Eliza's having a miscarriage," Sarah replied.

"Go out in the yard and watch for Ophelia's wagon," Sarah shouted. So Hannah rushed out of the cabin, and Sarah turned her attention back to Eliza.

"Eliza, what did you take?" Sarah cried. "You have to tell me what you took."

"Ophelia gave me a little packet of leaves to make into tea, but the packet's over there on the bed. I didn't take it, Sarah. I didn't have time."

She was right; there hadn't been time. Eliza was having a spontaneous miscarriage. The towels Sarah had stuffed between Eliza's legs only a few moments earlier were already soaked, and Eliza's color was ashen. She was going to bleed to death if she didn't get help.

Percival rushed into the room. "What happened?" he shouted.

"Eliza's having a miscarriage!"

"A miscarriage?"

"A miscarriage and we need Ophelia!"

"The provisions wagon is just coming into the yard, Sarah. Ophelia will be here in a minute."

"Eliza, Ophelia's here. She's going to take care of you."

"What happened?" Ophelia said as she rushed into the room and threw her hat on the table.

Miss Eliza was having a miscarriage, Sarah shouted.

"But the medicine I gave her didn't have time to work, and most of the time, it doesn't work, anyway."

"She didn't take medicine, Ophelia. This is a natural miscarriage."

"Spontaneous," Ophelia said, more to herself than to Sarah. "They can be tricky."

Ophelia squatted down on the floor beside Eliza and opened her legs. "You're going be just fine, missy," she cooed. "You're going be just fine."

Hannah arrived with fresh towels, and Ophelia studied the tissue she found on one of the filthy ones. "The baby's passed," she mouthed to Sarah and Hannah.

"Its little body is in the towel. Now we need to get Miss Eliza to push out the birthing cord. She won't stop bleeding 'til she does."

"You're going to have to push, Miss Eliza," Ophelia shouted, breaking the hush in the room. She was too tired. She couldn't do it.

"Oh yes, you can," Sarah demanded. "If you want to live, you're going to push like you're squeezing out a whale. You've been through worse.

Now start pushing!"

With that, Eliza repositioned herself on the floor and started pushing and screaming and pushing some more.

"Here it comes," Ophelia shouted. "It's here. Now we need to push on her stomach, plug her up with some fresh towels and wait."

"What are we waiting for? I thought the cord was delivered."

"It was," Miss Sarah, "but she'll still die if the bleeding doesn't stop. We won't know 'til she pinks up," Ophelia replied.

"We should know by morning. Now let's get her into bed and wrap her up good, and do some praying."

Sarah stayed with Eliza until she settled down enough to sleep, while Hannah took over Sarah's housekeeping duties. Ophelia said she'd stay with Eliza, so Sarah could take a rest.

When Sarah walked out of the cabin, Percival was sitting in the yard on a chair he'd brought out of the kitchen. "How is she?" he asked.

"Ophelia says we won't know for a while," Sarah said, arching her back. "She lost so much blood."

"Did you know she was pregnant, Sarah?"

"She told me this morning. Her cousin came into her room one night, and she couldn't make him stop. She just can't bring such scandal to her family. If she dies, he will have murdered her.

"She was a virgin, Percival. He stole that from her, and I want him to pay."

"It would be impossible to prove, Sarah. He'd deny it, and that would be that. You can only prove rape if there's a witness. That's just how it is. So what happened to cause the miscarriage?"

"I don't know, Percival. Ophelia says it could have been a plat-eye, but it was more likely that something was wrong with the baby. I don't know if that's true or not. At this point, it doesn't even matter. It just matters that Eliza gets better."

Percival was staring into Sarah's eyes with the intensity of a judge. He knew. She knew he knew.

And then he asked her if Eliza's pregnancy had anything to do with Ophelia's visit? It had been a stupid plan, and she was glad he'd seen through it. She didn't want any more secrets between them.

"I asked Ophelia to come here today because Eliza wanted to know if she was pregnant and if she was, to answer some questions she had about aborting the baby."

"Oh, Sarah, no."

"It's true, Percival. I didn't want to do it, but Eliza had no one else to turn to, so I asked to see Ophelia."

Percival wanted to know if Ophelia had given Eliza anything.

"She did, but Eliza didn't take it. Ophelia told me that the herbs that she gave Eliza have to be infused into tea, and if they work at all, they will take several days.

"This was a spontaneous miscarriage, Percival. I think it happened because Eliza was so desperate."

"You shouldn't have called for Ophelia, Sarah."

"I know, but in a way, I'm glad I did because if she hadn't been here, Eliza could have died. I wanted to help her, but that wasn't the way to do it.

"I offered to let her stay with us until the baby was born, but she was so worried about her parents finding out that I don't think she would have done it. I was afraid she might end her life. Women shouldn't have to carry the burden of something like this all by themselves. It's not right."

"That's the way it is," Percival said. "That's another lesson you must promise to teach our daughters, someday."

"I love you, Percival."

"I love you, too, Sarah, but don't ever keep anything like this from me again. This could have damaged our family's reputation. Mother used to say that a good reputation takes a lifetime to build and a moment to destroy."

"Mamma used to say the same thing," Sarah said, placing his face between her hands. Let me get back to Eliza. Say a prayer for her, dear."

Sarah stayed at Eliza's bedside the rest of the night. She hated inconveniencing Hannah and her family, but Eliza couldn't be moved. Ophelia also stayed, getting as much rest as she could in Hannah's rocking chair.

Light crept into the cabin from the early morning sun, and Ophelia stood and unfurled her long arms like a swan opening its wings. Then she came over to Eliza's bedside and knelt.

"Baby Girl," she whispered, "It's time to wake up, time to greet the day."

Eliza didn't move at first, so Ophelia gave her a little shake. Then Eliza's eyes got to fluttering, and she raised her left shoulder. Then she opened her eyes and stared into the smiling face of Ophelia.

"Good morning, Miss 'Liza," Ophelia said. "You had yourself a long nape. It's time to join the world for a little while. Smile at Miss Sarah and Old Ophelia."

Hannah arrived with soup and weak tea. "Miss Hannah's brought you some soup," Ophelia said. "'Help you settle your stomach and get well."

"Where...."

"You're in Hannah's bed at the creek house," Sarah explained. "You came to visit yesterday. Do you remember?"

"Ah, yes, Pawleys Island. The creek house, but why am I in bed?"

"You got sick yesterday. You got sick, and now we're taking care of you."

"What happened?"

"You lost your baby," Ophelia said, momentarily exposing her gentle spirit.

She wasn't pregnant anymore?

"No, Miss Eliza, the baby's gone, but you can have more babies someday. Right now, we need you to sit up a little and to sip this broth," Ophelia said in her doctor's voice.

"Can't get well until you eat a little something. Her color's beginning to come back, Miss Sarah," Ophelia said as Hannah stepped into the room, "and the bleeding's behaving more like course blood now.

"I think we're out of the woods."

"Where's the baby?" Eliza whispered, taking everyone by surprise.

"Can I see it?"

"I don't think you should think on that, honey," Hannah said, moving closer to Eliza's bed.

"What do you mean?"

"Well, when Ophelia give me the birthing towels yesterday, the baby was in one of them, and it didn't look very much like a baby."

What did Hannah do with it? Sarah asked, reaching for Eliza's hand.

"I wrapped it up real nice in a pillowcase and put it in this box," Hannah said, revealing a box the size of a shoebox. I didn't know what else to do with the little thing."

"That was very thoughtful of you," Sarah said, softly.

"Mammy's right, Miss Eliza," Ophelia said, regaining her position of authority.

"Tell you what we're going do, you're going get some sleep, and we're going to leave the little baby's box right here beside you. Take your time about wanting to see it, child. You take your time," she said, placing the box next to Eliza.

"How can I ever thank you?" Eliza whispered to Ophelia.

"I always tell my patients to name one of their babies after me," she replied. "That would do me just fine."

"And Hannah, how kind of you to think of the baby. I don't know how I'll ever thank you." She already had, Hannah whispered.

Ophelia stayed on another night just to be on the safe side. Still, Eliza was so much improved that Sarah permitted Ophelia to return to the plantation the following morning.

Eliza accepted Sarah's invitation to stay another month and was back to her old self in no time. She didn't look inside the box, but she buried the baby in the cemetery at True Blue in a tiny coffin made by the plantation carpenter.

The funeral was shorter than Eliza had planned, but it was at the height of the fever season and too dangerous to linger, so everyone's prayers were brief. Even so, it made Eliza feel better knowing that a Christian burial would assure the baby's entry into heaven.

Someday soon, she'd have a proper headstone made. As Hannah, Ophelia, Sarah, Percival, and Eliza left the cemetery, Eliza gave Sarah a faint smile, and Sarah knew that everything was going to be all right.

"I've decided to go home tomorrow," Eliza announced over supper that night. "When I get there, I'm going to tell my parents everything."

"Are you certain you want to do this?" Percival said, putting down his fork.

She was certain, she said. She didn't do anything wrong, and she wasn't going to keep it a secret any longer.

"It'll be hard, Eliza. You'll probably be sorry more than once," Sarah said, reminding herself of her own secret. It wouldn't be as hard as keeping the secret, Eliza argued.

"What about your cousin?" Percival asked.

"I'm going to beg my parents not to confront him, Percival. You were right when you said that it would be my word against his. Confronting him would only bring scandal to our family. It's not the outcome that I would have wished for, but it's just the way it has to be."

Sarah leaned over and kissed the top of Eliza's head as Percival raised his glass of Madeira. "To the two bravest women I'v ever known."

"To Eliza," Sarah said.

Eliza kept her plans and returned home. As the schooner pulled away from the landing, Sarah had a medley of thoughts. She was proud of Eliza's determination to tell her parents about her cousin and the subsequent miscarriage, but she was concerned.

"Do you think she's going to be all right, Percival?"

"Yes," he replied as he walked Sarah back to the house. "It all depends upon her parents' reaction, of course, but I can't imagine turning her away for something she didn't bring upon herself. If she were my daughter, I'd support her no matter what had happened."

"Do you still think her cousin will get off scot-free?"

"He already has."

A week later, Sarah received this letter:

Dearest Sarah,

It took all the courage I could gather, but last evening I told my parents everything. Mama cried, and Papa blustered, but they were both wonderful to me.

Papa wanted to storm out the door to challenge my cousin in person, but I talked him out of it. It didn't make it any easier for him, but he understood the logic of letting it go. Scandal stinks just as bad when served on a silver tray, Mama often says, so what's done is done.

Thank you for everything. You saved my life again, and I'll be indebted to you and Percival forever. Enclosed you will find two Half Eagles that are intended for Ophelia and Hannah. Papa said if Percival doesn't feel that it's fitting, however, he will certainly understand.

love you both and hope to see you soon.

Eliza

P.S. Percival, I have a big favor to ask of you. Soon you will receive a small crate from White's Granite Works on Meeting Street. It's the baby's crypt stone.

Would you emplace it for me? I didn't want its little grave to go unmarked, even one extra day.

Six weeks later, freezing temperatures put an abrupt end to the fever season, and the family eagerly moved back to the plantation. The following day the little crypt stone arrived, and Percival took it by wagon to the cemetery that very afternoon.

It was the smallest memorial stone he'd ever seen, small enough to carry by himself, so he went alone. As he positioned the crypt stone over the tiny grave, he relived that frightening day that the baby was born and cried as he left the cemetery. The inscription on the crypt stone read:

To
My Precious Baby
1801

Catherine the Great's 1762 Coronation Crown.
Credit: ITAR–TASS News Agency/Almay Live News.

True Blue Plantation's historic marker. Credit: Nancy Rogers.

St. Phillip's Church in Charleston. Credit: Jeannie Rogers

The interior of St. Phillip's Church.
Credit: Janet Wright.

A colonial plat of True Blue Plantation.

The People's Chapel at Mansfield Plantation.

The cemetery at True Blue Plantation before the restoration.
Credit: Janet Wright.

The original laundry house at Mansfield Plantation.

A small slave cabin on the grounds of Hobcaw Barony in Georgetown, SC. Credit: Nancy Rogers.

18th and 19th Century findings from True Blue Plantation.

Latta Plantation in Huntersville, NC.
Credit: Latta Plantation Foundation 2019.

Percival Vaux's new headstone 2004.
Credit: Nancy Rogers.

Sarah's completed grave shines in the sun.
Credit: Nancy Rogers.

Alice Flagg's grave at All Saint's Cemetery in Pawleys Island.
Photo credit: Wikimedia Foundation Inc.

Bill Sheehan spent many long days restoring Sarah Vaux's grave.
Credit: Nancy Rogers.

A floodgate referred to in the Lowcountry as a "trunk."

CHAPTER 22

Mamma and Eliza

THE FOLLOWING APRIL, ELIZA and Sarah's mother traveled to True Blue together to keep Sarah busy during her month-long laying-in before the birth of her first baby. Sarah was surprised that Mamma had invited Eliza to come along.

Mamma usually liked having Sarah all to herself, but Mamma loved Eliza almost as much as she did Sarah, and she knew that Eliza would be good company.

Mamma and Eliza arrived at the plantation by schooner in mid-afternoon, and while Mamma was escorted to the main house, Eliza excused herself to visit the cemetery.

On the way to True Blue, she'd told Sarah's mother about the baby and the miscarriage. It was a big risk. Eliza had no idea what Elisabeth Richards's reaction would be. Elisabeth Richards could have turned her back on Eliza. Instead, she embraced her, and together, they cried. "I've lost four babies of my own," Elisabeth whispered, "and my heart was broken each time. I am so sorry, dear."

"You're not angry with me?" Eliza blurted out.

"Of course not, Eliza. Why ever would you think that?"

"Because when I thought I was pregnant, I told God I didn't want it," Eliza sobbed. "It's my fault the baby's dead."

"Eliza, I blamed myself with each of my miscarriages," Elisabeth said.

"I shouldn't have eaten oysters; I shouldn't have gone out in the night air; I shouldn't have looked directly into the sun; I shouldn't have laughed. I know now that it was God's will. Perhaps my babies were imperfect in some way and weren't capable of surviving. I'll never know, but I do know that you have to make peace with yourself," she said as Pawleys Island came into view. "It wasn't your fault. You were eighteen, and you were innocent."

"If finding peace means that I have to forgive my cousin, I'm not doing it," Eliza said. "I'm never going to forgive him."

"Forgive him? I think you should be able to drag him through the streets, but you can't. Don't worry about forgiving him. The only person you need to forgive is yourself."

The walkway from the landing to the big house was beautiful. It led past trellised primroses, fields of early daffodils and crocus, and espaliered fruit trees in Sarah's budding orchard. Small children were weeding the flower beds as Mamma and her servant made their way to the big house. As the women passed, the children performed awkward little bows.

"Good afternoon, children," Mamma said.

"Sarah!" Mamma cried as she stepped into Sarah's room. "I've missed you."

"Mamma!" Sarah said. "You've come, but where's Eliza?"

"She went to the cemetery, first," Mamma replied, trying not to sound unnecessarily concerned.

"Eliza must have told you about the baby," Sarah said.

"She told me on the way here."

Would she be all right?

"I have every faith, dear. She just needs time. And so how are you, my lovely pregnant daughter? You look ready to pop!"

"That's exactly how I feel," Sarah said, holding her belly.

Suddenly Eliza rushed into the room, teary-eyed and looking a mess, but she was flashing a huge smile and was obviously on the verge of having a bad case of the giggles. "You look like you swallowed a watermelon!" she said, reaching for Sarah.

"Just don't tell me I look like I could pop because I might just do it," Sarah said, laughing. "What did you think of the little headstone now that it's in place, Eliza? I hope you were pleased."

"It's perfect, Sarah. His little grave is perfect. I feel good about him being here, and thanks' to your mother, I feel much better about myself. I didn't kill the baby. I loved him."

"You called the baby he. Eliza."

"I know. He was a boy."

How did she know? She just did.

It was impossible to say who talked more and who was happier to see whom at that moment. Mamma was chattier than Sarah had ever seen her, and she was filled with a million questions about Sarah's pregnancy.

She wanted to know about every little pain and twitch and flutter. She broke out in tears when she felt the baby move and fell in love on the spot.

"Mon Dieu," she whispered.

Eliza, on the other hand, was brimming with confidence, and much prettier than Sarah remembered. She walked around the room and oohed and aahed over the smallest details.

She was used to opulence, of course, but she immediately understood that there was something quite special about True Blue.

"It's beautiful here," she said. "The river, the plantation, and this room. Percival must be as rich as a sultan."

"Eliza!" Mamma admonished.

"She's just kidding, Mamma."

"No, I'm not. He's one of the most handsome men in South Carolina, and now I see that he is outrageously rich on top of it all, and I don't even have a beau."

"Percival's working on that, Eliza," Sarah assured her.

"I'm being a pill, aren't I?" Eliza said, kissing Sarah's cheek. "I'll behave, I promise."

Having two extra women in the house was bound to have been stressful for Percival, but he managed not to show it. Of course, had Sarah not been pregnant, they would have been in Charleston celebrating the racing season, but Sarah's confinement took precedence over everything, so they stayed at True Blue.

Sarah was beside herself, having to stay in bed for an entire month. "I'm not sick. I'm just pregnant. I want to walk outside and see my gardens. Please let me get up."

Mamma would have none of it. She'd lost four babies despite her adherence to the rules of confinement, and she wasn't going to lose her first grandchild by allowing Sarah to get out of bed for anything.

"You're not getting out of that bed even if the house catches fire," she said in her sternest voice. "I'll have you carried out, first. Percival agrees with me, so you don't have a leg to stand on. We want a healthy baby. In the meantime, why don't you and Eliza play draughts or twist?"

"We've played every game ever invented," Sarah groaned. "I'm tired of games."

Then why didn't she finish knitting that little sweater? Eliza suggested.

"Because I asked my sewing woman to finish it for me," Sarah admitted.

"I kept having trouble with the collar and the panel down the front where the buttons go. She offered to fix it for me, and I jumped at the chance to have it finished in time for the baby. The next time you see Eliza, would you tell her that I'd like to see her."

Eliza breezed into Sarah's room a few minutes later and plopped down on the side of the bed. "What's up?" Sarah said she was bored.

"Well, let's see what's in the magic sewing box today," Eliza replied. "We have a yummy knitting project, a doily to crochet, and, oh, your favorite, a half-finished needlepoint tea cozy."

"Quit," Sarah demanded. "I don't ever want to pick up a sewing needle again."

The moon was full that night, and the sky was sparkling. Eliza couldn't sleep, so she strolled along the walkway near the edge of the pond at the rear of the mansion. The pond was alive with gurgles and splashes, but Eliza ignored them.

A puff of smoke caught her eye, or was it her imagination? She drew nearer, and the smoke began to swirl. Eliza was transfixed.

Was it a waterspout? Was it a whirlwind?

She shuddered when suddenly the smoke stopped spinning to reveal a young woman floating above the surface of the pond. She was wearing a nightgown made of handkerchief linen, and her hair was long and silvery.

Should Eliza cry out? Should she faint? She didn't know. That's when something magical happened. Without knowing why Eliza held her hand up in the direction of the figure with her fingers spread, the figure floated toward her and placed her hand on Eliza's.

Yellow jasmine. Eliza was overcome with the fragrance of jasmine. Then the figure smiled and disappeared. A ghost had just touched her hand! She raced back into the house with her chest-pounding and breathing in quick, shallow gasps.

"Percival," she cried,

"I just saw a ghost! A real one, I swear. It touched me!"

Percival was in his study, and he jumped to his feet after hearing the commotion coming from the foyer.

"Me thinks the woman wild, hath set me up for tomfoolery," he said, laughing at his joke. He was taken aback, however, when he discovered Eliza sprawled out on the floor.

Her dressing gown was caked with mud, and her hair looked like a bird's nest. She had just seen a ghost, she said. She knew she tended to make up stories and exaggerate things now and then, but this time she wasn't kidding. She had just seen a ghost.

"Where was your ghost?" Percival asked, helping her to her feet.

"I saw her at the pond."

The ghost was a she?

"Yes, she was a girl about twenty. I'm not making this up," she said, picking up a note of humor in Percival's voice. "This is serious. I just saw a ghost in your backyard, and you think it's funny."

"I don't think it's funny, Eliza. It's just that we usually don't have ghosts here. I'm just surprised, that's all. Would you like me to go check on it?"

Of course, she would, she said. With that, Percival ran to the preparation kitchen in the half-basement, where he rummaged through pans and stew pots until he found what he was looking for. Then he returned brandishing an iron skillet.

"I'm going to smack the shit out of her, Eliza. Then we'll fry her up for breakfast."

It wasn't funny, Eliza wailed. She had even touched the ghost's hand, and Percival was laughing at her, and he was beginning to feel like a heel.

"I'm sorry," he said, putting his arm around her.

"I was just playing. I thought you were playing. How would you feel if Blue Russell and I go take a look?"

"I'd like that," Eliza managed to say through her tears.

"Don't take the skillet with you, though, and promise you won't hurt her. I think she might be Alice, the ghost that Sarah told me about. Promise you won't hurt her."

"I promise."

Percival and Blue Russell spent the next hour wandering around in the dark searching for Eliza's ghost. They found possum tracks, a family of raccoons, and a cottonmouth, but no ghost.

"If we happen onto Miss Eliza's ghost, what are we supposed to do with it, Master Percival?" Blue Russell whispered.

"I promised not to hurt it, but we sure as hell aren't going to invite it to dinner. I guess we'll just try to shoo it away."

"That's a good idea. It beats inviting it to dinner. I don't like ghosts, no siree. I don't like ghosts."

After a time, Percival said that they'd been looking for that ghost for more than an hour, and he hadn't see hide nor hair of it. Had Blue seen anything?

"Nothing," Old Blue said.

"Then let's go back inside."

Old Blue said he was hoping Master Percival was fixin' to say that. He truly was.

Eliza was disappointed, but it didn't change anything. The following morning she rushed to Sarah's room earlier than usual, saying that she had something important to tell her.

"I just didn't want anyone to overhear us. You know how the servants talk, and your mother, I'd be horrified if she heard what I'm about to say."

"What happened?" Sarah said.

"I saw a ghost last night. I know I make up stories, but I'm not making this one up, I promise. I saw a real ghost, and it scared the bejesus out of me."

"What did the ghost look like?" Sarah asked

"It was a girl, a young woman, and she was wearing a gauzy nightgown. I walked along the edge of the pond last night because I couldn't sleep, and that's where I saw her.

"She was floating in the air, Sarah, I promise. I didn't know what to do. Then for some strange reason, I put my hand up toward her with my fingers outstretched, and you know what happened then?

"She placed her hand on mine and smiled. Oh, and I smelled jasmine, yellow jasmine. It was everywhere."

"We don't have yellow jasmine near the pond," Sarah said.

"I didn't see the yellow jasmine. I just smelled it. Then the ghost disappeared. Was it Alice?

"It must have been her," Sarah cried, noting that she wished she had seen her, too.

"You promised to tell me her story, Sarah. "Now you have to."

"All right," Sarah said, allowing Eliza to adjust her pillows.

"It all began a few years ago. Alice was a young girl about sixteen. She was the daughter of a wealthy planter who went to live with her brother in Murrell's Inlet when her father died."

"Where was Murrell's Inlet? Eliza said.

"It's just up the river from True Blue, about five miles. Anyway, no one knows how, but Alice met and fell in love with a young logger who made his living selling turpentine."

"Was he French?"

"I have no idea, Eliza. Why would you ask me that?"

"I've heard that most loggers are French Canadian. I was just trying to picture him in my mind."

"I don't know," Sarah said. "Do you want me to tell the story or not?"

"I do," Eliza said sweetly.

"All right," Sarah said. "Now, I don't know if he was Canadian or not, but let's assume he was from South Carolina. Now you made me lose my place."

"You were talking about her having met the young logger," Eliza said.

"Oh, yes. When her brother and mother found out about him, they were furious. A logger was not the kind of match they wanted for Alice, so they tried to split them up by sending Alice to school in Charleston. She got sick while she was there, though, and she was brought home and taken care of by her family. Her condition worsened by the hour, and it was then that someone discovered that she was wearing a promise ring tied around her neck.

"When she was asked about it, Alice begged to see her betrothed, but her family refused."

"Then what happened?"

"She died and was buried in the graveyard at All Saints Church. But her family was so angry, they only put her first name on her crypt stone: ALICE. It doesn't contain her last name, or any mention of her family, or even the date of her death."

"It just says, Alice?"

"Just Alice."

"So why is this a ghost story?" Eliza said.

"Because her ghost can still be seen at the cemetery and other places, it seems."

"Are you sure you've never seen Alice's ghost?"

"I've visited her grave, but I've never seen her ghost."

"There's a way you can, though. If you go to the graveyard, you'll see a worn pathway leading from the cemetery entrance straight back to Alice's grave.

"It's only about a hundred yards or so, and her grave is easy to spot because people always leave things there when they visit her."

"What kind of things?"

"Mostly shells and smooth river rocks, but I've also seen coins and notes there. The most touching mementos, though, are promise rings left there to replace the one her brother took away from her."

"Get back to her ghost, Sarah. How can you see it?"

"Well, legend has it that Alice continues to visit the cemetery because she's looking for her ring. If you go there just before midnight, she'll be there, but you have to perform a ritual to make her appear.

"Starting at the bottom right-hand corner of her crypt stone, you have to circle her grave six times counterclockwise, and then you have to circle it six times clockwise, and if you end up even with the "A" in Alice at the stroke of midnight, she'll appear and thank you for visiting her grave."

"What happened to her ring, Sarah?"

"You said she's still looking for it, but you didn't say what happened to it."

"According to the story, Alice's brother threw it into the marsh."

"She'll never find it there," Eliza pointed out.

"No, she'd never find it there."

"I'm going to go see her tonight, Sarah. I have to know if she's the one I saw last night."

"You can't go to a cemetery by yourself. It's not safe. Unsavory people are sometimes seen there and, of course, there's always the danger of animals. Percival will have to send someone with you. I'm sure he will, though, if you ask him."

Eliza thought of her cousin and changed her mind. She'd do it another day, she said. She didn't want to go there with someone she didn't know.

Maybe another time.

CHAPTER 23

Did You Mark the Baby?

A SEARING PAIN HIT Sarah's back, and she stiffened. Was it time yet? "You're not even close," Ophelia said. First babies usually take their time. There were so many people in Sarah's room, she jokingly asked Mamma if she had emptied a train.

"We did no such thing," Mamma calmly replied. "By the time the baby arrives, you will be glad for the company. Mamma was wrong. Sarah wanted to suffer in silence.

Toward the end, however, she changed her mind. She would have welcomed a brass band if it could have lessened the pain. Sarah had been in labor fifteen hours, and Ophelia had filled in until Dr. Prior could get there.

In the meantime, Eliza had worked herself into a state. She no idea that the birthing process was as long as it was and as arduous, but she was more taken aback by the amount of sweat than anything. "She's lost so much sweat, Hannah."

"That's part of it," Hannah said. "The Lord knows what he's doing, Miss Eliza. Don't worry. If you do, Miss Sarah might get all scared and such, and it could slow down the baby. You just keep holding her hand and giving her encouraging words. She'll do fine."

The sweating continued, along with some swearing toward the end, but Eliza promised Sarah that it would be worth it once she held the baby. How did Eliza know such things?

She was right, of course, but where had she learned it? From her miscarriage? Probably, but Sarah loved her too much to ask. Hannah had expected Eliza to leave the room when the gory part got into full swing, but Eliza stayed. Hannah was impressed.

White women mystified her, sometimes. They were more squeamish than colored women, but when it came down to it, they could suck it up with the best of 'em.

Downstairs, the news was spread by a young servant who rushed into the kitchen shouting, "It's a boy! It's a boy! He popped out a' wailing and howling like a cork being sprung from a bottle."

"Well, thank you, Lord Jesus," Cook declared. "Can I hear an 'AMEN?'"

"It's about time for that child to be born. Maybe now we can get a little peace around here. Did you mark the baby as I told you?"

"Yes, ma'am, I did."

"Did anyone see you? Miss Hannah says the mark works instant-like, but my mama says it's got to stay on for a few minutes before it sets up good. We can't have nobody wiping it off too soon."

"Nobody saw me except Miss Hannah because I did it real quick," the girl replied.

"The baby, he spits up a little, and I was told to change him. While I had him in his cradle, I took the chalk you gave me out of my apron pocket and rubbed it hard against my thumb. Then I reached under the baby's gown and pressed my thumb right in the middle of his belly."

"Show me your thumb."

"It's still blue," the girl said, jabbing her thumb under Cook's nose. Cook didn't respond to her comment, other than to keep on rolling out her supper biscuits, so the girl waited.

Once the last of the biscuits were cut, the girl quietly placed the piece of chalk on the corner of the cook's worktable and nervously asked if Mistress Sarah would be upset with her.

"You're not going to get in trouble, child. 'Mistress'll know why you did it. There are spirits out there that can suck the breath right out of a newborn baby, but they can't get at him if he's been marked. Everybody's afraid of the spirits. Besides, the mark'll come right off with a little spit."

Hannah was upstairs fussing over Master Percival, him being young and all, but when Edward fell into Dr. Prior's hands, Percival was beaming.

"You've got yourself a son," the doctor proclaimed. "A fine son."

Then he handed the baby to Hannah, and Percival asked about Sarah. "Is she well?"

"She's just fine. She's exhausted and a little groggy, but she's just fine. You can speak to her for a moment, but be quick about it. She needs her rest."

Just then, Hannah walked up to Percival and gently placed Edward into his outstretched arms. Then Percival smiled down at the baby and took him over to meet Sarah before she nodded off.

"It's a blessed time, ain't it?" Hannah said.

"It sure is," Eliza replied.

"Who do you think he looks like?"

"Edward is a copy of his papa," Hannah proclaimed. "He even got his papa's smile."

"He is a fine boy, isn't he!" Percival said. "Promise me he's healthy, Hannah. I did so want a son." He was as healthy as a beanstalk, she assured him, but scolded him for bragging. Bragging was bad luck.

"Did you put a mark on him, Hannah?"

"The maid did, but I watched to make sure she did it right."

"I thought you were a Christian," Percival said, smiling.

"I am, but the spirits ain't Christians, and you never know when they might be passing by, and he's such a little thing. I just wanted to keep him safe."

"How long does it take for the mark to work?"

"Oh, only about a minute. Do you want me to wash it off, sir?"

The next time she changed him would be soon enough, he said.

Everyone always says that the birth of their first grandchild is one of the best days of their lives, but it sounds hollow compared to how thrilled Sarah's parents were that night.

Her father had only arrived from Charleston two days earlier, and when he walked into the house, he asked one of the servants if it was a boy or a girl. How happy he was that he'd gotten there in time.

"We waited for you to start, Papa," Sarah jokingly told him when he rushed into her room.

It was almost planting time at Rochambeau, so Sarah's father had to leave the following week, but Mamma stayed another month. Thank goodness, Sarah couldn't have made it without her. Sarah also had Hannah and Eliza to depend on.

It was a happy time. Percival was overjoyed, Sarah's parents were beaming, and Sarah loved Edward more than she'd ever loved anything in her whole life. Eliza, on the other hand, felt left out.

She was delighted for Sarah, and she loved the baby, but it only served to remind her of what she didn't have. Sometimes she'd go down to the marsh and chunk rocks. Other times she'd visit the cemetery, but she wasn't herself. Her bubbly disposition had disappeared like carbonated water gone flat. Eliza was lonely.

On a whim, Percival invited his friend, William LaBruce, to have supper one evening. It was an impromptu invitation that followed a monthly meeting of the local planters. William was the son of Laurel Oak Plantation, a mile or so south of True Blue.

William's father also owned an even larger plantation across the river, where he lived with his wife and William's younger siblings. William managed Laurel Oak for his father, with the understanding that the plantation would eventually be his.

Managing a plantation before inheriting it was commonplace. Although he'd been significantly younger than William at the time, Percival had done the same thing.

When Percival told Eliza that William was coming for supper, she was so nervous she offered to stay with Sarah rather than join everyone else downstairs.

"You're not getting off that easily, Eliza," Percival said. "I invited William over tonight because he is my friend, but I also invited him to meet you. Perhaps you two will get married and have twelve children."

"Percival," Sarah said, laughing. "Why are you always torturing Eliza?"

"Because she likes it. Right, Eliza?"

"He's right, Sarah, I do."

Sarah didn't see William that night because she was still in post-baby confinement, and it would have been inappropriate to have asked him to visit her in her bedroom.

She'd seen him several times before, however, and thought that he was handsome, not as handsome as Percival, of course, but certainly better looking than the crying boy at the coming-out ball.

Eliza thought so, too, and before long, she and William were an item. The problem for them was that the fever season would be in full swing by mid-May, and everyone had to leave the plantation, including William.

Fortunately, he also summered on Pawleys Island, but even if Eliza stayed on at Sweet Grass Cove, it was going to put a big crimp on their romance.

So Eliza and William decided to tie the knot. The wedding would take place May 1st—two weeks from yesterday.

Eliza's mother fainted when she heard the news. Fortunately, she managed to get to her fainting couch before she swooned. When she came to, she admitted that although the plan had a ring of impropriety, it was very romantic.

The wedding was to be at All Saints Church, only steps away from Alice's grave. "Will and I went to visit Alice last night," Eliza told Sarah the day before the wedding.

"Alice in the cemetery, Alice?" Sarah asked.

"Of course, 'Alice in the cemetery, Alice,' silly. We went there last night, and we circled her grave. We didn't see her, though; we didn't finish the last circle in time. You know what? That part of the cemetery is covered with yellow jasmine. It smelled like heaven.

"Do you think Alice knew we were there?"

"Of course, I do," Sarah said. "There are so many other more important things in the world that we don't understand; ghosts are easy to believe in. Eliza, are you really happy with Will? Are you sure he's the one for you?" Sarah asked, changing the subject.

"I love Will," Eliza replied. "He thinks I'm smart and pretty and funny, and he likes being with me. He told me last week that just being in the same room with me makes him happy. I love his family. His parents are so happy for us, and I adore his sisters. I understand why Mama isn't thrilled about us getting married so quickly, but she's still very happy about the match."

"What about sex, Eliza? With what happened to you, do you think you can have a physical relationship with Will?"

"We did it last night at the cemetery," Eliza said.

"When we got there, I told Will about the baby. I didn't want to begin our marriage with secrets. He cried, Sarah, and then we did it in his carriage. I didn't know for sure if I could go through with it, but it was wonderful."

"You still took a big risk, Eliza."

"I know it was stupid considering what happened to me before, but in another way, it was a good thing because I couldn't have done it if I hadn't trusted Will. Now I can walk down the aisle and know that my cousin didn't destroy my ability to be happy. This is going to be a good marriage, Sarah Bella, you'll see."

On the day of the wedding, the exterior of All Saints was congested with carriages and servants bantering about, telling jokes and killing time until the wedding ended and it was time to leave for home. Inside the church, however, it was serene and beautiful.

The brass had been polished, the wood had been oiled, and on each pew was a fragrant spray of spring flowers held together by white silk ribbons. Candles twinkled, and guests whispered. The velvety Lowcountry sunlight streamed through the ripply windowpanes and warmed the worn marble floors.

Sarah's father had travelled all night to be there, as had Eliza's parents and brother. However, the majority of the pew fillers were members of the Waccamaw family of planters, most of whom had deeper roots than the ancient oaks that surrounded them.

There was a sense of joy and family that day. Weddings do that to people. The future always seems unlimited on days like those. Eliza walked down the aisle on the arm of her father. Her gown was stunning—the color of peach blossoms, but the star of the show was her unruly golden hair peeking out from beneath her great-grandmother's mantilla.

As they made their way, the silk organza gown caught the sunlight, refracting it like a prism. William wore a dark grey suit that Percival's tailor in Charleston had made.

It was impeccable. From her seat next to Eliza's mother, Sarah could see that William's hands were shaking, although Eliza was the epitome of calm.

Sarah didn't know where Eliza had found such confidence, but she guessed it was in the back seat of a black landau two nights earlier.

Wherever it came from, it made Eliza look regal. When she approached the altar, she reached for William's hand and whispered, "I love you." From then on, Sarah was a bundle of tears and laughter. She cried even more than Eliza's parents did.

"How'd I do?" Eliza said during the reception at Laurel Oak. "Tell me you were surprised that I was so calm."

"I was," Sarah said.

"Well, I don't know how calm I was on the outside, but I can tell you one thing, I was soused."

"You were not!"

"All right," Eliza said, rearranging her mantilla.

"I wasn't drunk, but I considered downing a slug or two of gin this morning. I was so jittery that I kept kecking up my breakfast."

"Then what made you so calm?"

"I remembered how frightened I was after you and I got separated in Haiti. I thought you were dead. I remember thinking about how easy it would have been to have walked out into the open and let someone kill me, too. I kept going, though, and look how wonderful my life is now. Haiti made us strong," Eliza said. "You and I can do anything because we've already done the impossible."

Sarah was slow to respond, so Eliza filled in the time whistling. Did Sarah like her song?

"I've heard it, but I can't remember the name of it."

"'Blowzabella, My Bouncing Doxie.'"

"Eliza! That's a bawdy song! It's your wedding day. You shouldn't sing something like that on your wedding day," Sarah scolded.

"Why not? Eliza replied. "I'm planning to do some of those things when William and I are alone tonight."

"Eliza, you're impossible."

CHAPTER 24

We Is Full 'O Babies

SARAH DELIVERED HER SECOND child three months later. It was a girl this time, and Sarah named her Sarah Elisabeth.

Crankier than her free-spirited older brother, Sarah Elisabeth pouted when she didn't get her way, and despite the unbridled attention she received, it was never enough. Her peevish nature concerned Sarah.

Hanna described her best: "She's such a pretty child, but she seems so sad-like most of the time."

During each of her confinements, Sarah read voraciously. She devoured Percival's scientific magazines, current newspapers, and agricultural journals, and she kept up with the latest fashions. Everything piqued her interest.

For example, she was shocked to learn that the population of the United States had reached an astonishing six million, with an estimated population of seven million by 1810. She was also keenly interested in the new iron plow with interchangeable parts.

Iron plows were out of reach for most farmers because they were extremely costly, between ten and twelve dollars each. Sarah had an unlimited budget, and she had the oxen to pull them, so she ordered a dozen.

Soon after, Sarah and Hannah were inspecting a new order of bed linens when Sarah became lightheaded. Grabbing Hannah's hand to steady herself, she looked up at Hannah and said she might be pregnant again.

"You sure, Miss Sarah? Sarah Elisabeth isn't three months old yet, and we've got ourselves a two-year-old."

"I know, Hannah," Sarah said with a note of concern. "I'd like to have more time between them, but it must be God's will."

Just as she had predicted, shortly after Sarah Elisabeth's first birthday, Sarah gave birth to another daughter, Beatrix Anne. "We've got ourselves a parade of babies in this house," Hannah bragged all around that night.

"We is full of babies."

Round and pink, with smoky gray eyes and dark curly hair, Beatrix Anne was the spitting image of Sarah's mother, but unlike her fussy older sister, she was happy from morning 'til night.

Sarah often took Beatrix Anne with her to her gardens, propped up on a pillow in her pram. Hannah hated the idea of putting a child in danger like that, but Sarah thought the sun and fresh air were good for her, and even Hannah had to admit that the child was happiest out of doors.

"This child is exactly like you, Miss Sarah," Hannah said one day, moving the pram out of the direct sun. "Baby Girl, before we know it, you're going to have dirt on your face just like your mama." Nobody doubted that Beatrix Anne was like her mother, but she was a bigger risk taker than Sarah had ever been.

She loved playing hide and seek even when she was the only one playing. She would hide anywhere, but she was particularly fond of the fowl house and the carriage barn, and one day Sarah's dinner guests caught Beatrix Anne skinny dipping in the fountain at the end of the allee leading to the big house.

Soon after, she was found perched on the roof of the dependency kitchen. The roof was constructed of clay roof tiles held in place by their own weight and overlapping shape. Since they weren't firmly attached to the roof, Beatrix Anne's rescue was going to be dangerous for everyone involved.

Within moments a crowd had formed, and everybody had a different plan. However, the only plan that had a chance of working was proposed by a giant of a man named Jacob.

Jacob specialized in roofs and rafters and such, so he wasn't squeamish about heights or ladders. He planned to extend his longest ladder to the edge of the roof and to coax Beatrix Anne to move toward the ladder an inch at a time. Jacob would be at the top of the ladder, ready to grab her.

Percival hurriedly gave his approval, and since no one had a better idea, Jacob and a kitchen helper named John Henri set up the ladder. Watching Jacob rattling his ladder scared Beatrix Anne, and then she got to crying, "Mama! I want to come down."

"Jacob and John Henri are going to get you down, lamb, just do what they tell you to do," Sarah shouted back.

"Come on, little girl; come on over to old Jacob; go slow-like, now," Jacob said from his perch at the top of the ladder. "Just scoot your little butt on over to Jacob so I can get you off that roof. I know those tiles is hot, Be-trix, but I know you can do this." So with Jacob's encouragement, Beatrix Anne moved from one tile to the next as everybody on the ground prayed up a storm, asking Jesus to keep the tiles from dislodging and starting an avalanche.

It took more than ten minutes of coaxing, scooting, and crying before Beatrix Anne got within reach, and just as Jacob started to grab her, one of the tiles broke loose and shot off of the roof, catching John Henri right in the top of his head.

John Henri's job had been to steady the ladder, but when the tile bounced off his head, he let out a yelp like he'd been shot. Then he let go of the ladder, but it stayed in place, and it was a good thing because Beatrix Anne went sailing off the roof along with another roof tile, just as Jacob grabbed her by the foot. And then he pulled her to his chest and gently handed her down to Percival at the bottom of the ladder.

Everyone started hugging and kissing Beatrix Anne, and emotions ran rampant. Percival and Jacob did a little dance together while John Henri ballyhooed about the hole in the top of his head.

A young kitchen helper named Turnipseed caught the worst of it, though. Her job had been to watch Beatrix Anne, but she let her get out of sight. Turnipseed was most likely going to get a whipping from Cook and another one from her granny when she got home.

She was lying facedown on the grass near the steps leading up to the kitchen, boohooing and screaming over and over that she "didn't mean to get the baby kilt!"

She also said something about Jesus, but it got lost in her tears, and it wouldn't have helped anyway because Cook appeared at the kitchen door with her whopping strap in her hand.

Turnipseed looked up at her and let out one last cry. Then she seemed to accept her fate. "How many licks?" she asked, lifting herself off the ground.

"Five," Cook replied.

"I thought it'd be more," Turnipseed said.

"Well, the baby didn't get kilt," Cook replied.

"How many licks would I have gotten then?" the girl asked.

"I don't know, child. 'Just be glad Jacob caught her."

Cook took Turnipseed to the whopping place around back, while Sarah, Hannah, and Beatrix Anne went into the kitchen to get a look at the newfangled machine that had just arrived. It was called an icebox refrigerator, and it meant that eggs and milk and other dairy products could be kept in the kitchen rather than the ice house.

"It's amazing, ain't it?" Hannah said, running her hand over the top of the icebox.

"It surely is," Sarah replied, "truly amazing."

"Reckon there's anything left to invent?" Hannah said.

"I'm certain there must be, but this is one of the best."

Beatrix Anne was five and a half, and she was spending almost as many hours in the gardens as her mother. Sarah even ordered a miniature set of garden tools for her, and Beatrix Anne loved them.

One afternoon Percival stopped by to see how they were doing. "How are your new tools, Bea?"

"I love the shovel and the wheelbarrow and the rake, Papa, but I think the spade needs some sharpening," Beatrix Anne replied without looking up. Next time we order tools I could use one of those pointy hoes like the People use."

"Anything else?" Sarah said, laughing. She'd like to have her own garden someday. "I'll look into it," Sarah said.

"Papa, I have a question for you," Beatrix Anne said.

"A question?"

"Uh-huh. I want to know where angels live?"

"Well, they live in heaven with Jesus," Percival said, looking at Sarah. "Why do you ask, darling?"

"I just wanted to know. Do they come down from heaven to visit us sometimes?"

"They might," Percival said.

"Have you ever seen one?"

"Yes, Papa, I saw one last night."

"What did you see?" Sarah asked, certain that the angel must have been the ghost of Alice.

"What did the angel do?"

"Nothing, Mama. She just smiled at me and tucked in my covers. She was shiny."

"What did she look like, darling? Was she a young woman?" Sarah asked. "Kinda," Beatrix replied.

"She was real nice. She put her arms around me and touched my fingers, and then she fixed my covers."

"Percival," Sarah said, putting her arms around Beatrix Anne. "What does this mean?"

"I don't know," Percival said. "I've heard that angels sometimes visit earth just before there is a death, but if this was Alice, I think it had to have been a dream. It was just a little girl's dream."

The next day Beatrix Anne ran a fever and was promptly put to bed. "I don't feel good," she said throughout the day.

"I know, darling, but Hannah and I will take good care of you until you're better," Sarah assured her.

Sarah did everything she could to keep her word, but she couldn't stop thinking about Ophelia—what would Ophelia do? Last year Ophelia had fallen on the stairs at the entrance to the People's Chapel. She'd had fallen so softly that she shouldn't have been injured in the slightest. Everybody said so.

But the fall turned out to have been a tragic one because Miss Ophelia was never the same after that. These days she was content to sit in her rocker on the small porch that her sons had added to her cabin. She rocked and smiled and laughed sometimes, but she seldom spoke, and when she did, the words came out like her mouth was full of toffee.

Miss Ophelia's brain had become addled, taking with it her sixty years of medical knowledge. It was a blow to every living soul on the plantation but to none more than Sarah.

Sarah and Hannah took turns placing warm mustard plasters on Beatrix Anne's chest for four days. The light hurt her eyes; she said so they covered the windows with quilts to keep the room dark. Beatrix Anne was so small and precious that Sarah was tempted to scoop her up and run, just as she had with Charlotte in the cane fields in Haiti.

"Please don't take Beatrix Anne from me," she cried into her pillow. "I am the evil one. I'm the one who took a life. Don't take my innocent child!"

On the fifth day, Beatrix Anne woke up with a sore throat and a dangerously high fever. Sarah rushed downstairs to find Percival. "We need to send for Dr. Prior," she cried. "Tell him to hurry."

Two hours later, the messenger returned with bad news and an exhausted horse. "Dr. Prior's misses done give me this note," he said reluctantly. Then he handed the note to Percival and backed out of the room. The note read:

Percival,

Dr. Prior was called away on another emergency at Long River Plantation on the Pee Dee this morning. I'll send someone to tell him about your daughter, and I'm sure he'll be there as soon as he can. Until then, you'll have to manage without him.

My prayers are with you,

Annie Prior

Percival stayed in Beatrix Anne's room throughout the night as Hannah and Sarah applied fresh poultices of wormwood and sweet milk to Beatrix Anne's chest and swabbed her throat with paregoric. Her condition steadily worsened, though, and Sarah noticed a large abscess forming inside Beatrix's throat.

Two hours later, the abscess broke, and Beatrix threw up globs of slimy goo. It was the third day of November 1808. Beatrix had lived five years, seven months, and twenty-seven days and everyone in the household was certain that today would be her last.

Dr. Prior arrived a few hours later and examined Beatrix Anne and made the most astonishing pronouncement. The child would live. Beatrix Anne would live! "God worked a miracle," Hannah cried, and there wasn't a dry eye in the house. God had indeed performed a miracle.

Beatrix Anne steadily improved, but it was another week before she was strong enough to sit up in bed and to eat one of Cook's special cheese biscuits. As Sarah and Hannah coaxed her to eat, Sarah asked Hannah if she thought that losing a child was a punishment from God?"

"No, Miss Sarah, God doesn't do such things. When God takes a child, it's because the child is so pure in its heart that he needs the child in heaven," Hannah replied. "He makes angels out of pure little children. Before you come to the plantation, Miss Sarah, I lost my own baby girl," Hannah said, about to reveal a rare look into her private life. "Her name was Rosebud, and she was a perfect little child until she got the whooping cough."

"How old was she when she passed, Hannah?"

"Three months and four days. She'd be almost six years old today. Maybe she's up in heaven taking care of other little children. When I get to heaven, Rosebud's going to be the first person I look for. Then I'm going to look for my granny."

"Tell me about your granny," Sarah said.

"Ah, naw, Miss Sarah, you don't want to hear about her."

"But I do, Hannah; tell me about her."

"Well, she wasn't much of a specimen. She was small and hunchbacked, but she lived to be an old liver, so she must have done something right. Granny Becca knew just about everything, but the most important thing she knew was about dyeing, not the human kind of dying, but dyeing fabrics."

"She used to go off into the woods all day looking for ingredients for her potions. Then she'd come home and hang everything she collected from the ceiling of her cabin. When a person was to ask her to dye something, all she needed to do was to ask what color they wanted."

"What did she use to make red dye?" Sarah asked.

"Oh, the best reds come from berries and beets and red oak leaves.

Granny even made dye out of the skins of tomatoes and plums. She said the yellow dye was a pretty easy one because it can be made out of lots of things, including dandelion flowers, safflowers, marigolds, and sumac bark. Even sunflowers and red clover make good yellows. Let's see, for your greens," she said, thinking back to the old times, "it depends on the kind of green you want. Spanish moss and onion skins, lilies of the valley make apple green dye. Spinach leaves, snapdragons, and lilac flowers make darker green."

"What makes brown?"

"Oh, that's easy—walnut shells. It's a strong dye, so you don't have to use vinegar to set it, like a lot of other dyes."

"Vinegar?"

"Well, once you get the fabric the color you want, you rinse it good with water, and then you put it in a pot of water and white vinegar and boil it up, so it sets up good. If you don't, the dye will stain your skin and fade out in the wash. Some colors you have to set with water and salt. It just depends."

"Well, I don't have to ask you about blue dye," Sarah said.

"You surely don't," Hannah replied. "We got more wild indigo on this plantation than we can use. It makes the prettiest blue, you know, but blueberries, cornflowers, and berries from the elderberry bush make blue, too, only not as good as indigo. Are you sure you want me to keep on with the story, Miss Sarah?"

"Oh, yes, tell me more."

"Granny's most powerful dye, the one she called rusty nail red, was made by digging a hole in the clay down by the pump house, filling the hole with water, and stirring the water until it worked itself into a soupy red slush. "That was all there was to it. Anything thrown into the hole would stay dyed forever. The trick was in knowing how long to leave it there before it started to rot."

Hannah and Sarah reached the house and went their separate ways. Hannah went around back, and Sarah headed for the piazza to sit in a rocker next to Percival.

"I've never been this scared," Percival said after allowing Sarah time to fuss with her skirts. "I've decided that I don't want any more children."

"But Beatrix Anne is going to be fine. Besides, we have no say about how many children God has planned for us," Sarah whispered.

"It's just that we came so close to losing her that I'm afraid we won't be so lucky next time," he said.

"What are you talking about?" Sarah said, alarmed.

"I'm an arrogant and prideful man, Sarah, and I'm afraid that someday God will punish me for it," Percival said tearfully.

CHAPTER 25

Sarah's Secret

FOR THE NEXT TWO days, Percival's admission and tears ate at Sarah's heart until she couldn't bare it any longer. She had to tell him the truth about Haiti. Then he'd understand that her sins, not his, caused the evil in their lives.

She found him in his study and was relieved that he was alone. "Percival, I must speak to you," she said in a whisper.

"Now, dear?"

"Yes, right now."

So he got up and locked the door and returned to his chair behind the desk, while Sarah sat on the settee beneath the window and fumbled with her skirts.

"I was always certain that God was going to take Beatrix Anne from us," she began. "But not because of your sins; because of mine—because of the sins I committed in Haiti," she said.

Sarah's monotone voice was as foreign to her own ears as to Percival's. And then she became inconsolable. Percival rushed to her side. Hannah was in the rear hallway when Sarah began to sob, and even through the door, she heard enough of Sarah's conversation to come running.

"Miss Sarah, what happened?" she screamed through the door. "What happened? Did you seize up?"

"No," Sarah said. "I just need to speak to Percival, alone."

Hannah respectfully walked away from the door, but she didn't like being left out of anything, especially something important enough to bring on tears. Percival checked the lock on the door and took a seat on a worn overstuffed chair that had been his father's favorite.

Sarah had to tell him something that she'd kept a secret for years. She didn't have to tell him while she was so upset, Percival said. She could wait. Besides, if she was planning to tell him about the massacre back in Haiti, she could save her breath. Sarah's father had told him all about it the day he asked for her hand.

"He couldn't have told you everything because he didn't know the whole story, Percival. No one knows, not even Eliza. With her hands resting in her lap and her eyes fixed on the floor, Sarah began her narrative:

"The rebels came pouring through the gates of Carrefour," she said. "They butchered the Hebert men in the courtyard, and then they started up the stairs.

"'Make them stop, Mimms! Make them stop!' I cried.

"'Get down on the floor,' she shouted.

"She hurt my wrist, and then there were fists pounding on the door and furniture being overturned and babies crying—and the smoke—thick black smoke with hands reaching out of it, grabbing and slashing at everything they touched.

"We hid in a cupboard.

"Aunt Beatrix covered Charlotte's mouth to muffle her cries. 'Don't cry baby, don't cry baby'....

"Then the screaming stopped. There was laughter and yelling and the sounds of things being broken and the smell of urine. I had wet myself.

"We have to go," Beatrix said. It was too dangerous to stay. The rebels would return, and this time they'd burn the house down. "We have to go now."

"'No!' I cried.

"Aunt Beatrix told me to stop, and then we went down a back stairway into the basement. It was moldy, and we hid in the shadows. There wasn't a sound. Then we saw a door in the yard. It was broken, and Beatrix said there was no more time. She handed Charlotte to me, and then she was dead!

"She was dead, Percival! Her gown turned to red aspic."

"Why don't we stop now?" Percival said in a pleading voice.

"That's when I saw the boy, the boy with the machete," Sarah said, ignoring his concern. "His eyes looked like fish eyes, and steam was rising off his head. Fish eyes. He moved toward me, and I knew he was going to kill me."

"Then what happened?"

"Eliza suddenly caught his eye, and he kicked her and swung at her with his machete. He missed, though, and while he was distracted, I grabbed the doorframe. I'm not sure, but I think that's when I told Eliza to get Charlotte and to run into the fields.

"She was too frightened to even think of Charlotte, though. She just sprang to her feet and ran. That's when the boy lunged for me. His swing was wild, though, and before he could come at me again, I hit him on the side of his head with the doorframe. Then he flew backward on top of Beatrix.

"There was blood everywhere, Percival."

"What happened then?"

"He started cursing at me. I don't know. I can't remember anymore."

"Why don't we stop there, dear?" Percival said.

"I have to tell you how evil I am."

"You're scaring me, Sarah."

"I have to tell you, Percival. I can't keep it a secret anymore. My parents knew about Aunt Beatrix and the boy, but they didn't know that I killed my own cousins, Percival, and I did it on purpose. In one day, I killed two people, probably three. They're all dead, dead because of me."

Percival was stunned.

"It happened after Eliza and I got separated, and Charlotte and I found the privy near Les Cayes. We needed a place to sleep, and it had a roof, so we hid there. During the night, I heard a sound coming from the wall of the privy.

"There was a door, and someone was crying on the other side. I opened the door and found a stairway leading to a cave where the Heberts grew mushrooms. There was a lantern sitting midway down the stairway. I wanted to turn away, but I kept thinking— WHAT IF THE CRIES ARE COMING FROM ELIZA! I had to know, so I crawled down the stairs. That's when I saw the demon boys."

"The demon boys?"

"Boys with golden hair. They were drunk. Eliza was there, too. The boys were taunting Eliza, and she was crying. And there was a little girl with big eyes. She was at the bottom of the stairs, and I motioned for her to come to me.

"She did, but then the boys heard her and spun around. They clawed at us. I threw the oil lamp onto the floor of the cave to give Eliza and the little girl time to get up the stairs, and it sent flames everywhere. We crawled through the door and threw the latch.

"The boys pounded on the door and cursed and screamed, but I didn't let them out. Then the privy caught fire, and we hid in an indigo vat. I didn't know they were my cousins, but it wouldn't have made any difference. There was just so much death. Then I ran into Henri Hebert who told me he was searching for his cousins. That's when I realized that I had killed my own blood."

"You didn't set out to hurt them, Sarah. You were just trying to protect everyone. You were just a girl," Percival said, trying to console her.

"But what made me do it?"

"Because you were so frightened."

"Why did they have to die? Why did Mimms and Aunt Beatrix and practically everyone else around me die, and yet, I survived? I remember asking Mamma that question a hundred times, but she didn't know what to say, so she forbade me to speak about it ever again. If we didn't talk about it, it would go away, she said. I tried to forget, but I just couldn't."

"I know," Percival said. "Do you feel any better now?"

"Yes," Sarah said, noticing for the first time that Hannah was standing outside with her nose pressed to the window of Percival's study. "I feel better now that you know. You haven't answered my question, though. Why did they have to die?"

"I don't think they had to die, Sarah. They just did, and God spared you for a reason. He must have wanted you and Eliza and the rest of the Hebert children to go on. Perhaps the best way to honor your family is to do just that, to go on with your life. I don't know what else we can do."

Then Sarah looked at Percival and said something that took him by complete surprise. "Do you think the People will ever be given their freedom?"

"Do you mean all slaves everywhere or just the ones here at True Blue?"

"All slaves, everywhere," she said.

"Yes, I think they'll be freed someday," he said after a long pause. "I don't think it will be in our lifetimes, though. Plantations can't exist without slave labor, and without the plantations, our economy would be destroyed.

"We can't just grow anything we want to. We have to grow a crop that there are established markets for. We grow rice, of course, but planters in other parts of the world grow everything from rubber to coffee.

"Plantation crops are all labor-intensive, and they're not profitable when they're grown on a small scale. We'd starve without the slaves. If they were freed today, where would they go?"

"Back to their homes in Africa," Sarah suggested.

"People have been proposing that for years, but it won't happen. There's not enough money in the world to send all of them back to Africa, and besides, most of them were born here. How can they survive on their own unless they own land? Do you want to give them True Blue?"

"Absolutely not! True Blue belongs to our children," Sarah said. "I would never do that. I wouldn't do that no matter what."

"Then it's settled?"

"It's settled for now."

The next morning Sarah received a note from Eliza, who was laying in for her third child that she hoped would be a boy.

My Dears,

I begged Dr. Prior to let me come to you, but he said that my time is imminent ,and it would be too risky for me to travel, but you know that I am there in spirit.

We are thrilled to hear the good news about Beatrix Anne. We were so terrified. Your loving Eliza, Will, Sarah Elisabeth, and Ophelia.

Three days later, Eliza gave birth to her third daughter, Beatrix Anne LaBruce.

Sarah spent the rest of the fall thinking about her confession. Soon after, she wrote to Eliza. She cried as she told Eliza what had happened, causing her to make childish mistakes with her quill.

Errant blobs of ink dotted the page, but Sarah didn't care. A floodgate had opened. If she didn't keep writing, the gate could close, and the despair would return. Eliza was so shocked by Sarah's story that she showed up unexpectedly at True Blue one warm December morning.

"Miss Sarah, you got yourself some company," Hannah said after finding Sarah in her morning room.

"Who is it?"

"Miss Eliza."

"Where is she?"

"She's at the landing. She's telling her servant what to carry up to the big house, but the girl's a little bitty thing who couldn't carry a valise the size of a shoebox, so I sent one of the boys down to help her."

"Thank you, Hannah," Sarah said as she sprinted down the hallway toward the back stairs.

"I'm going to meet her."

When Eliza looked up to see Sarah racing toward the landing, she sat down on one of her suitcases and laughed.

"Sarah, for heaven's sake, what are you doing running with your skirts in the air? You're going to be the talk around everybody's supper table tonight."

"I don't care. I'm just so glad to see you," Sarah said, trying to catch her breath. "Why are you here? Is it because of my letter?"

"Of course, ninny. I read it about a thousand times, but I still have questions, so I decided to see you in person so we could talk."

"Well, I don't care why you're here. I'm just glad to see you."

As the women walked back toward the big house, Sarah said she'd agonized over telling Eliza the rest of the story.

"That's ridiculous," Eliza said. "It's my story, too. I'm hoping that when you fill in the blanks, maybe I can remember it better.

"After we got separated, I couldn't find a hiding place, so I just kept running," Eliza said. "Then I fell. The last thing I remember was crawling under a pile of indigo stalks. I slept, I think. My vision was all blurry, and my head hurt.

"Then I remember seeing two boys dressed in nightshirts. In the moonlight, I could tell that their faces were tearstained and sooty, and they were sneaking through the brush the same as me. They said they had a hiding place and that I could go with them, so I followed them, hoping you might be there. I don't know how I got into the cave, but when I didn't see you there, I told them I had to leave.

"I couldn't, they said, I'd be seen.

"I was going anyway, I told them, and then the older boy cuffed me and tore my gown. Looking back, I think they were planning to wait out the revolution in the cave and thought they could have fun with me. The older one had had trysts down there; he bragged about them. Oh, and there were cases of rum.

"I slept, and then they woke me by pissing on my legs. They were crazy."

"They were drunk." Sarah said.

"They were mean." Eliza added.

"I looked for you for a long time," Sarah said, "but it got so dark that I decided to wait until morning. Charlotte was only three, remember. She was too small to keep up with me on foot, so I had to carry her. She was heavy, and I was exhausted. I had to rest. Then I saw the privy, so we hid there. I slept for a while, but I woke up when I heard something.

"It was a muffled scream, and it terrified me because I thought it was you, so I followed the sound. I don't want to relive all the details, Eliza, but the truth is, after you and Kai and I got up the stairs and through the privy door, I blocked the door. The boys were screaming for me to open it, but I was afraid they might come after us.

"Then the building caught on fire, and the stairs fell in, and they were trapped. I didn't know they were my cousins at the time, but it wouldn't have made any difference, at least I don't think so," Sarah said.

"All I could think about was what they might do to us, and I couldn't take the chance. I wrote a paper about Giovanni Boccaccio once, and he was an eye witness to the Black Plague. He said that some people became extremely pious during that time, while others were so frightened that they lost their civility," Sarah said. "Some of them even abandoned their own families. I remember thinking about that when I was barricading the door to the cave."

"I don't remember any of that," Eliza said.

"It's best that you don't," Sarah said. "I wish I didn't."

"So this is the secret you've kept all these years?" Eliza asked. "I've always known that you were holding back something. I'm just sorry you had to go through it alone. When we got lost, I thought I'd never see you again."

"Me, too," Sarah said. "It was a miracle that we found each other. I just can't figure out why we survived; that's the part that bothers me the most."

"If we'd been killed and Aunt Beatrix had been the one who survived, would you have blamed her?"

"Of course not," Sarah said.

"That's exactly how Beatrix feels. She's happy that you survived and, above all, that you saved Charlotte. You know the boy with the machete was going to kill her, too?"

Percival had told her the very same thing.

"Well, he's right. Now, where's that handsome husband of yours?"

"He's probably in the stables."

"Let's go surprise him," Eliza said. So the two set out for the stables.

"Well, hello, Master Percival," Eliza said, giving Percival a come hither look.

"What the hell are you doing here?" Percival asked as he picked her up and swung her around. "You're a sight for sore eyes."

"Well, you're a sight, anyway."

"How's tricks, Percival?"

"Do you know what that term really means, Eliza?"

"If it's dirty, don't tell me because I'm going to say it, anyway."

They Found Him Behind His Desk

THE FOLLOWING YEAR, SARAH realized that she was pregnant again. It wasn't what she would have preferred, not because she didn't want another baby, but because Percival was behaving so strangely. She didn't know very much about medical things other than the usual cuts and scrapes that were daily occurrences on the plantation.

Percival seemed very troubled, and he appeared to be having extreme bouts of depression. Even with the promise of a new baby, he was often inconsolable. His step had slowed, and there were lines on his forehead and around his mouth. He complained of debilitating headaches and abdominal pains. Something was eating at his gut, he' tell Dr. Prior in private.

His favorite black rum was the only thing that seemed to cut the pain. Sometimes he'd even lock himself in his study and drink all day. Sarah would sit by the door for hours to check on him. He didn't answer her knock one evening, so she had one of the servants pick the lock. Percival was on the floor behind his desk, unresponsive. Sarah later learned that he'd had a stroke, and at five that evening, he died.

"He's gone, my dear," Dr. Prior said as he solemnly covered Percival's face with his bedsheet. Sarah made no acknowledgment. She simply continued to stroke Percival's hand.

"He's only thirty-six," she whispered, looking into Dr. Prior's pale eyes. "He can't leave us."

"He hasn't been well for some time, child. It was his time."

"I know he's been sick. I've heard his cries. I've dried his tears, but I didn't know he was going to die. Why didn't you tell me he might die?" Sarah said angrily.

"Because I didn't know until the very end, and when I told him that we should gather the family, he made me promise not to tell a soul," Dr. Prior said, looking over at Hannah. "Can you…?"

"Yes, sir. Miss Sarah," Hannah said softly. "Master Percival's gone. He's gone to heaven to be with Jesus and my little Rosebud. Let me take care of him for a little while. You need to go to the children."

"The children, I'd forgotten about the children." Sarah rose from her seat on the edge of Percival's bed and quietly made her way out of the room. That evening Percival was laid out in the east parlor.

True Blue's master was dead, and the plantation should have been a flurry of somber activity. The funeral coach would have been removed from the carriage house, polished, and spit on to make it shine.

A matched pair of Friesians would have been curried and brushed and burnished with rags, and black ribbons would have been woven into their manes. They would have worn black socks on their feet, and their patent leather tack would have been rubbed to a sheen.

Then the carriage's wheels would have been wrapped with linen to muffle the sounds they would have made as they bit into the gravel lane leading down the allee to the landing. From there, Percival's coffin would have been placed aboard a bier in the center of a small keeled skiff and covered with a starched purple shroud.

The rest of the boat would have been draped with black and purple swags made of cotton muslin kept in waiting in a special chest beneath Percival and Sarah's bed.

Little girls would have swept the path between the big house and the boat landing and gathered massive bouquets of primrose, gardenias, and hydrangeas from Miss Sarah's gardens to decorate the master's coffin.

Percival's funeral would have been planned out and carefully orchestrated. The People would have even had their funeral clothes laid out and scolded their children to be seen and not heard when Master Percival goes to be with Jesus.

Nothing was as it should have been, however. Percival had had the misfortune to die at the beginning of the fever season. All Saints Church was closed for the summer, and except for Percival and Sarah's immediate family, the other planter families along the river had fled their plantations.

A large formal funeral was impossible, so Sarah decided to hold a memorial service inside the mansion. The funeral coach would stay beneath its cover in the carriage house. The purple shroud and bunting would remain under Sarah's bed, and Sarah's beloved flowers would remain in their beds.

Sarah and her family shared their grief with a final prayer extolled during an unrelenting rain, and Percival's coffin was placed into a grave half full of rainwater. Then the priest raised his arms and beseeched the Great Almighty to bless the soul of his son, Percival Vaux. After the prayer, the priest hurriedly motioned to the family to say their final goodbyes. Rain, after all, exacted a toll on pastoral robes.

It was over.

As much as the family had loved Percival, they feared the fever even more, so they hastily made their way along the path and retreated to the waiting carriages. Sarah, the children, and servants, including Hannah, hurriedly prepared to leave the plantation when Hannah quietly retrieved a handful of letters from beneath her skirts and handed them to Sarah.

"They're Master Percival's letters to the children," Hannah said. "He gave them to me for safekeeping."

"Thank you," Sarah whispered as she put the letters into her pocket. "I didn't know."

"You weren't supposed to," Hannah replied. "There's one for you and one for the children." With that, Hannah turned back toward the house.

Sarah pressed the notes to her nose, praying to catch a fleeting scent of Percival, and then she slowly walked toward the house where she opened her letter. It read:

My Dearest Sarah,

Thank you for our lives together. How kind and loving you have been to me. There hasn't been a moment since that moment we met on the dance floor so long ago that I haven't loved you.

You will always be my Darling Sarah. Take care of the children; they love you so.

PS: I haven't forgotten my promise about Hannah.

Percival.

CHAPTER 27

Percival's Will

THE FOLLOWING WEEK, SARAH and the children gathered in Percival's study at Sweet Grass Cove, where his attorneys took turns reading the various provisions of his will. As expected Percival had been remarkably equitable with the distribution of his estate.

True Blue was bequeathed to Edward upon his twenty-first birthday, along with his grandparent's London townhouse and Percival's silver-handled pistols.

A smaller plantation known as Lower Plantation, along with the creek house, was bequeathed to the new baby, Oakhampton Plantation, the most productive of all of Papa's plantations, was also bequeathed to Edward.

However, the bulk of the estate was to go to Sarah, including his long guns, family heirlooms and jewelry, family portraits, his globe and collection of antique maps, his pocket watch, his surveying instruments, and his cherished spyglass.

With Sarah's permission, bequeathed the money Percival signed over to Sarah as part of Sarah and Percival's prenuptial agreement to Sarah Elizabeth and Beatrix Anne. The girls would also equally share a property on the Pee Dee River known as Marsh Plantation.

The attorneys then explained that Percival had made no provisions for any of his slaves, with one exception. Then they stopped reading and requested that someone find Hannah and ask her to step into the room.

Hannah arrived a few minutes later dressed in a traditional mourning dress and black kerchief. She looked puzzled by the urgency of the summons. She had diapered most of the people in the room and had rubbed salve on their skinned knees, but at that moment, she was surrounded by strangers.

"Come in, Hannah," one of the attorneys said. "You may take a seat if you wish."

"No, sir, I won't be doing that if you don't mind," Hannah replied as the door to the study was closed behind her, and she retreated into the shadows at the back of the room.

"Now we'll continue with the reading of Master Vaux's will," the attorney said, "and this part concerns you, Hannah."

I will and desire that my Negro woman named Hannah and her issue should from the time of my death have and enjoy full freedom in consideration of the faithful service performed by her to myself and children and for the undisclosed sum of money that her now deceased husband paid me for her freedom.

She shall be allowed to continue to live at True Blue Plantation, if that is her wish, and to receive an annual sum of $100 for the remainder of her natural life.

A hush filled the room. It was against South Carolina law to emancipate a slave. Percival knew it, his lawyers knew it, and everybody knew it, including Hannah.

As her weight shifted toward the wall behind her, Hannah heard nothing beyond the word freedom. Freedom for Hannah and her issue. Unless she had been rocking a fussy baby or shelling peas in the kitchen, Hannah had never allowed a member of her white family to see her seated. Slaves and their masters didn't sit together, ever.

When Edward placed a chair next to her and told her to sit down, she did it without hesitation. Today was no ordinary day. As Hannah tried to clear her head, someone in the background asked the attorneys how Percival expected them to fulfill his wish to free Hannah if it was against the law.

"Percival was a clever man," the older of the two replied. "Six months ago, he advised us that he wished to sign an affidavit stating that Hannah's husband, Blue Russell, had secretly purchased his family's freedom. Two weeks later, Mr. Russell drowned in an accident, so no one knew about the transaction except Percival."

"Will it stand up in court?" Sarah asked.

"I think so," the attorney replied, hiding his own thoughts on the subject. He opposed the idea of freeing slaves, thinking of them as little more than savages, but he had a job to do.

"They're the words of a gentleman," he said. "I don't think the courts will reverse them even though they do sound suspicious. We've seen it before. As far as we are concerned, Hannah and her daughters are free women as of this moment," he said as if he was making the final argument to a jury.

"Percival was a clever man, indeed."

I Don't Want To Be Called Mammy No More

"I'LL TAKE YOU HOME," Edward said after helping Hannah to her feet.

"No, Master Edward, I can be taking myself home," Hannah said, calling Edward by his new title. "But I thank you all the same. I'll be taking the rest of the day off if that's all right. I have a lot to think about. Oh, and before I go, I want to thank Master Percival. That was a kindly thing he done."

Hannah left the room as quickly as she had entered it, but she was a changed woman; she was free. She had waited her entire life to hear those words, and now the thing was done. She just wished that Blue Russell had been alive to enjoy it. She hoped he was up in heaven right now, laughing at the snafu Master Percival pulled on the lawyers.

They said that Old Blue paid eight hundred dollars for the freedoms, but he didn't have eight hundred dollars; he barely had two nickels to rub together most o' his life, but now his girls were free.

Now and forever free like the paper said. Hannah could go and do whatever she wanted to do for the first time, but she was nearly forty years old. She was beginning to get her mother's rheumatisms, and besides, where would she go? True Blue was her home.

Maybe freedom was for the young. Hannah's daughters were still young enough to leave the plantation if they wanted to, and the annuity that Hannah was to receive might even help her buy the pepper sauce business. What was to be done?

For two days, Hannah ignored the knocks at her door and the faces pressed against the windows of her cabin. On the morning of the third day, she stepped out onto the porch and set out for the big house. She went directly to Master Vaux's old study and knocked on the door.

"Master Edward, I'd like to speak to you if I could," Hannah called out.

She heard Edward's fifteen-year-old voice: "Come in, Hannah; the door's unlocked."

After accepting a seat facing Percival's old desk, Hannah said she was there to discuss her future plans. "And what are they?" Edward asked.

"Well, sir, I've decided that I want to stay on at True Blue if you'll have me. I want to keep on living in my own house. And I want to keep on working in the big house. But I want to be paid for my work now, Master Edward, two dollars cash money every month."

"I think that can be arranged," Edward replied, trying to sound like his father. "Is there anything else?"

"Yes, sir, there is another thing," Hannah said, but I need to talk about it with Miss Sarah."

"Was it about buying her half of the pepper sauce business?"

"Yes, sir, now that I'm legal and all. I've saved up one hundred and fifty-one dollars and fifty-five cents, and I think that's a fair price for it if you're agreeable."

"I don't want your money, and neither will Mother," Edward said, surprised. As a matter of fact, you may have the entire business. It's always been yours anyway."

"Thank you, sir; that's mighty kind of you. Oh, and there are two more things that almost slipped my mind. The first one is that I don't want to be called Mammy anymore. From now on, I want to be called Hannah."

"And the second thing?"

"Did Miss Sarah know about this—the pepper sauce business, I mean?"

"I'm pretty certain it was her idea."

"I thought so," Hannah said as she stood to leave the office. "I truly did."

CHAPTER 29

Percival's Crypt Stone

PERCIVAL'S CRYPT STONE FINALLY arrived. It was made of Vermont marble by the White Monument Company in Charleston. Sarah had selected the stone from a collection of samples sent to her. She had not taken the company's advice on an appropriate inscription, however. She'd written it herself.

The crypt stone arrived in a wooden crate aboard a straw-covered barge, and it took six men to lift it from the barge, and onto a wagon to take it to the plantation cemetery.

Percival's grave had already been prepared to accept the crypt stone, and once the men cleared the fence to get it inside the cemetery, the installation took less than a minute. It was done. The men who had carried the crypt stone tipped their hats to Sarah and then they disappeared.

The workers understood that families were happy to see them come but even more eager to send them on their way. After Hannah and Sarah's children inspected Percival's new crypt stone, Sarah kissed each of them and asked them to go back to the house.

"Are you sure, honey?" Hannah asked.

"I'm fine, Hannah. I just want to be with Percival for a little while. Don't worry."

So Hannah and the children quietly left the cemetery. Sarah was tired, and her back was killing her. She should probably be in bed; Dr.

Prior certainly thought so. The new baby wasn't due for another three weeks, but babies had a habit of coming on their own schedule, so she didn't really know. It didn't matter, though. She had to be with Percival.

She talked about the new baby, and how much she missed him, how she would always miss him, and then she awkwardly reached down to run her fingers over the beautifully engraved sentiment:

To My Darling Percival
All My Dreams Are Buried Here

Percival's death hung over the plantation like a shroud, and Sarah was scarcely able to put one foot in front of the other. When she went into labour two weeks later, everything went more smoothly than her previous pregnancies, but she missed Percival so much, she didn't even ask about the sex of the baby.

William Alston Vaux was a rolly polly baby fascinated by everything, especially things that made a noise like clocks and pot lids. Since Sarah was too distraught to respond to him as she might, he became incredibly close to Hannah. He was crawling now, and he would scurry after her on his soft little knees, and Hannah adored him. She wasn't going to go 'round blaming a little child for slavery and such.

Hannah's views on slavery hadn't changed much over the years, even though she was a freedwoman now. Slavery was still against God's law, and she couldn't see how anyone could call himself a Christian and still believe in it. Some of her views were fraying around the edges, though.

It had been more than six months, and Sarah's depression continued. Sarah's mother lived at True Blue since Percival's death, and she was worried half to death. After a particularly plucky morning when Sarah couldn't stop crying, Elisabeth hurriedly jotted off a note to Eliza and handed it to a waiting messenger.

"You are to wait for an answer. Do you understand?" Elisabeth told the man. He assured her that he understood and ran from the room. The next day Eliza's skiff glided up to True Blue's landing, and out she stepped pregnant with baby Number Five. After kisses all around, Eliza climbed the stairs toward Sarah's room, reminding Hannah of a tightroper walking a wire.

There were twenty-four steps in that stairway, and each one was a struggle for Eliza. Sarah was in a particularly black mood that morning, but she couldn't help laughing when Eliza walked into the room holding her belly like a watermelon.

"What's up?" Eliza said in her cheeriest voice.

"Nothing," Sarah whispered.

"Nothing isn't good enough, Sarah."

"All right, then how about I don't want to go on anymore, Eliza. I can't."

"Well, I'm sorry, Sarah Bella, but you don't get a choice. You have to go on; you have babies to raise. You should have thought about all of this when you were seventeen."

"But Percival…" Sarah cried.

"Sarah, when Will and I lost Meggie, I wanted to die. She was three years old! I didn't want to see Will or the other children; I just wanted to die, but then you gave me the same lecture I'm giving you now.

"You have to go on. You have to find a way. You don't have to do it all in one day, but you have to do something every day, something for someone other than yourself. It works, Sarah. I'm living proof."

"It's so hard, Eliza."

"I know, Sarah. I loved Percival, too, but we can't undo what has happened. You have to get out of that bed and go to the children. It doesn't mean that you loved Percival any less or that you've stopped grieving for him. It means that you love the rest of your family, too. They need you, Sarah. Your mother needs you, and the children need you, and I need you."

Sarah stayed in bed another two days, but Eliza's words sunk in. Eliza was right. It didn't make it any easier, but Sarah knew she was right. So she crawled out of bed and ventured down the hallway where she encountered Edward. Going on sixteen, Edward was one moment a boy, the next a man. He'd always loved bugs and insects and crawly things, and his room contained jars and wire cage filled with centipedes, spiders, crickets, lizards, bullfrogs, pollywogs, and a small garden snake.

Shortly after Papa's death, however, Edward stripped his room of his boyhood treasures. He asked Hannah to redo the room as one appropriate for a young gentleman, a gentleman who would someday be True Blue's master.

Hannah saw that the room was gentrified, as she called it, with heavy mahogany furnishings and suitable Federal-style fabrics. To do it right, though, she'd had to trouble Miss Sarah a might by asking her where she kept her catalogues for such things so that she could order the necessaries for the room.

When Edward saw Sarah in the hallway, he ran to her. "Mother, are you well now? Are you going to be the mistress again?"

"Yes, Edward. I'm going to be the mistress again. I'm sorry it took me so long to get well."

"That's all right, Mother. I miss Papa, too."

Yellow Fever

It had been a lazy evening, and the creek house was quiet, except for the ticking of the hall clock, when everyone was jolted from their beds by frantic pounding on the door to the main house.

"Who is it?" Sarah shouted from the balcony above. "What do you want?" And then she heard a commotion from the yard and saw that Hannah and several of the male servants (all of whom were brandishing shotguns) were sprinting across the yard in their nightclothes.

Sarah hurriedly ran downstairs and cracked open the door to discover a nervous young man standing on the edge of the porch with Hannah and her rolling pen close on his heels.

"I'm sorry to frighten you, ma'am, but I have an urgent message for Mistress Vaux," he said, looking back at Hannah. "It's a letter," he added, extending his hand.

"Thank you," Sarah said, accepting the letter. "Do you need lodging?"

The messenger said, no, thanks. He wanted to get as far away from South Carolina as he could. "The fever's coming, ma'am."

"The fever?" Sarah asked.

"Yellow fever, ma'am. Yellow Jack's going to kill us all."

Sarah hurriedly shoved silver into the man's hand, and he disappeared. She stared at the letter. "It's in my father's hand," she said, looking down at Hannah.

May 19, 1814

Rochambeau Plantation

Dear Daughter,

Your mother and I evacuated Charleston six days ago, but she has been taken ill. At present, her symptoms are the usual flu symptoms: vomiting, fever, and pain, but it will be many days before we know if it is yellow fever.

DO NOT COME TO ROCHAMBEAU; it is far too dangerous.

The encouraging thing is that I was exposed to but never came down with it during an epidemic in Philadelphia back in '93. And with Mamma's ties to Haiti, the odds are hugely in our favor that she's also immune.

I will send daily updates on her condition, but again, do not risk coming to Rochambeau. Stay away from Charleston, too, and don't send any of your servants there for any reason.

The city is little more than a shell of itself. The streets are empty and eerily quiet. Those who could evacuate are gone, leaving behind the poor who have no place else to go.

Farmers are afraid to come into the city, so the food price is three to four times what it should be. Thievery and crime are rampant. Storefronts have been looted, and the houses of the dead have been pillaged. Cannons are shot in the streets at night to remind stragglers that they are under martial law.

Many are hopeful that the exploding gunpowder will also purify the air and destroy the fever.

Bodies are picked up once a day by teams of men and slaves, who are paid two dollars to remove a child's body and five dollars to dispose of an adult.

The city disinfects the streets and homes of the dead with carbolic acid and sulfur, and quarantine flags can be seen everywhere. Sadly, Sarah, our loved ones are being buried in shallow, communal graves on the outskirts of town.

I'll send another messenger tomorrow. To err on the side of caution, instruct your servants to stay well away from him. I'll have him leave the message in the yard, well away from the house.

Papa

"I have to go to Mamma," Sarah cried.

"You can't do that, Missy. Your Papa warned you about that."

"But, Mamma."

"If you were to go to him, you could bring the fever back to the children. You can't risk that. Besides, your mother should be immune."

"We could send Dr. Prior."

"Your Papa says, no. Now, all we can do is wait."

Papa kept his word about sending updates on Mamma's condition. Of course, it took the better part of two days to get the messages, but at least they came with regularity.

Percival's library included a large medical text that listed the symptoms of historic plagues and epidemic diseases, and it read more like a horror story than a medical report. Sarah had no idea anything as dreadful as yellow fever existed, and the possibility of it attacking someone she loved was almost more than she could bear.

Mamma's symptoms continued for three days, and then they subsided, but she still wasn't out of the woods because that was the course the fever always took. Sarah read on.

Yellow fever subsides for up to seven days, then it reappears. The odds of dying are as high as fifty percent in someone Mamma's age. Sarah dried her tears on a tea towel, and then she continued her reading. The most common symptom the second time around, it said, was yellowing of the eyes and skin because of the shutting down of the kidneys.

Excruciating headaches, abdominal cramping, extremely high temperatures were also expected, followed by thick, black blood seeping out of lesions on the skin and body openings. Sarah spent the next seven days on pins and needles, eager to receive another message and dreading it at the same time.

Mamma had survived. She either didn't have yellow fever, or she was immune to it. Papa, however, wasn't as lucky. He'd traveled the world and spent years in Barbados and Antigua, where yellow fever commonly surfaced aboard slave ships, but he'd never built up an immunity. He died in Mamma's arms.

"Oh, God," Sarah screamed when she learned about Papa's death. "Not Papa! He was immune. The letter is a mistake. Papa can't be dead."

The threat of fever made it impossible for Sarah to travel to Rochambeau for the funeral, so she didn't get to say goodbye. Her mother and her household held a service as best they could. The People's pastor at Rochambeau delivered the eulogy, and Mamma wrote that

Papa would have been pleased.

"We'll hold our own funeral when it's safe for you to travel," she promised. "How much sadness will God foist upon us?" More than we could imagine should have been Sarah's reply because there was more yellow fever to come.

The fever visited several of the other families of Waccamaw, including William LaBruce's parents, who both died on the same day. Sarah didn't go to the LaBruce's funeral either, of course. William's parents were quietly buried on the grounds of their plantation on the other side of the river. William and Eliza didn't go, either.

In a note from Eliza, Sarah later learned that Will had gone into the woods behind their home during the hour of the funeral and cursed God at the top of his lungs. Will was broken, Eliza wrote, and I had no words to console him. Do you ever wonder if the pain of losing someone is worth the joy of loving them?

I've spent a million hours thinking about that, Sarah wrote back, "but I've always come back to the same conclusion. I'll miss Percival and Papa for the rest of my life, but I wouldn't give up one moment that I got to spend with them. It's just that it seems as though there is so much death around us."

What troubled her more was her uncertainty about what happened after we die. Was heaven absolute, or was it a product of our fear? Would we be with our loved ones someday, or was death the end of things? Would our souls soar when we die, or would they rot with our flesh?"

"They will soar, Sarah Bella," Eliza replied. "They will soar."

After reading Eliza's last note, Sarah sat at her desk to write Mamma. Sarah had written hundreds of letters to her mother but never one like this. In it, she poured out her heart over losing Papa and expressed the love she had for her mother. Sarah pictured her mother as the lost child she had been when her own father had abandoned her so long ago.

Then she met Papa. Mamma said she was safe. Papa had always been there, but now he was resting in a narrow grave in Rochambeau's small cemetery. He couldn't speak to Mamma anymore, and he couldn't protect her. She had no one except Sarah.

Sarah had been so wrapped up in her own life that she'd taken her mother for granted but no more; so she decided to ask Mamma to make her home at True Blue. Mamma's response arrived the next week, and it took Sarah by surprise.

Darling Sarah,

Thank you for your loving offer. Someday soon, I will join you at True Blue if you are still willing to have me, but for now, I want to stay at Rochambeau to be with your father. Besides, I darn't leave until the threat of yellow fever has played itself out.

I know Papa's not coming back. Please don't think that I have become unbalanced. It's just that I'm not ready to leave him just yet. I know that his soul is with the Father, but I like to think that a little part of him is still here.

When spring comes, and I must leave the plantation, I will change over my household and join you on Pawleys Island. It will be wonderful to see the children every day, but for now, I am fine, and you needn't worry.

I had no idea how much I loved your father until he was gone. He was everything to me, just as you are my darling girl.

Mamma

PS: We also need to discuss your situation at True Blue. Without Percival, you are a helpless female, and you need someone you can trust to run the plantation.

Sarah smiled a tired smile when she read her mother's postscript. She wasn't a helpless female. Everyone had been most respectful since Percival's passing, but she would need an overseer until Edward was old enough to take over the reins.

Another yellow fever wave was in the air, and Sarah refused to leave the creek house the rest of the summer. No one on their enchanted marsh left their homes. They sat and waited and waited and waited. Sarah's younger children fought and bickered over the slightest things, things they wouldn't have even thought to fight over had they been allowed to venture out of doors.

Hannah suggested that they should be allowed to play on the veranda or in the bog just behind the house, but Sarah wouldn't budge. The Fever was out there. So the little ones endured their piano lessons, dissected bugs under Percival's microscope, read every appropriate book in the library, and staged their own plays.

Edward concentrated on his required reading list for school, Sarah Elisabeth sulked, and Beatrix Anne propagated beans, blackeye peas, barley, and buttercups in the lids of mason jars. Hannah wasn't herself, either.

"Ain't been so bored in all my days," she said one day. "It ain't natural to do nothing."

But she worked so hard every day, how could she be bored? Sarah argued.

"Well, I didn't mean bored from the lack of working; I'm just weary from worrying about the Fever. I want things to get back to normal. I can't wait until tomorrow when they bring the peaches in from the plantation. We'll have lots to do, then."

"You're sure we have enough white sugar and jelly jars?" Sarah asked.

"I told the provisions man not to show up without them," Hannah replied. "That man's got the biggest sweet tooth on the plantation. He'll remember, all right."

At a time like this, Hannah sure thought a lot about her late husband, Ol' Blue. His real name was Russell, but most people called him Blue because he was so dark-skinned on the outside that his gums were dark blue on the inside.

Blue was the best fisherman on the plantation, and he used to spend all of his free time on the creek crabbing and catching fish that he could sell to other folks along the river or add to the communal stew pot.

Not only had Blue Russell been the best fisherman on the plantation, but he had been the best storyteller. He could make up a story about anything. Everyone's favorite, though, was the story of a bullfrog, a cooter, and a fiddler crab called The Bullfrog's Jug Band.

The Bullfrog's Jug Band

There was this old bullfrog down by the pond. Ol' Bullfrog he wanted more than anything to play de drum. But he was too fat to hold de drum and his arms was too short to reach de drum, so he be sad.

And then he met up with a crab. Ol' Crab was sad too 'cause he wanted to play de washboard, but his shell was too big and crusty. So they be sad together. Then they met up with Ol' Cooter.

Ol' Cooter say, "What you so sad for?"

Then the bullfrog and the crab tell Ol' Cooter their problem, and he say he sad too, 'cause he wanted to play de fiddle, but his chin can't fit with it so they all be sad tageth–er.

The next day, a dragonfly fly by and say to the bullfrog, the crab, and the cooter, "What you so sad for?" Then they tell him the story, and he said he'd think on it, and then he fly away.

The next day, Ol' Dragonfly came back to the pond with a great big ol' smile on his face.

"Why you look so happy, dragonfly?" said the bullfrog.

"Cause I think on the problem, and I figured this thing out," he say.

"Bullfrog, you is too fat to play de drum, but you're not too fat to hold a jug and to reach your lips to the jug hole.

Crab, you is too crusty to play de washboard, but you could play the fiddle real fine; and Cooter, you's carryin' 'round a washtub right on your belly."

Then the ol' bullfrog, the crab, and the cooter jump up all excited-like and thank the dragonfly for his good thinking. Then they decide to join up as de Bullfrog's Jug Band and they be happy ever after.

The moral of the story, according to Blue Russell, was not to dwell on what you couldn't do, but to celebrate what you could.

"That's the Lord's plan, chil'ren."

Ol' Blue must have told that story a hundred times before he died, but he didn't mind. He liked the way his daughters and the master's children shared their love of the story.

If they could share a story, maybe they could share other things, Blue pondered.

CHAPTER 31

Cuban Cigars

YELLOW FEVER FINALLY LOST its sting following a hard freeze, and those living along the Waccamaw rejoined the world. The newspapers and the postal mail were back on schedule, and the mail carrier delivered an entire boatload of old mail to Sarah's doorstep.

She'd heard rumors that the mail would be delivered any day, and she couldn't wait. When it finally arrived, the whole family was on the landing waiting for the schooner to dock. It took two dockworkers the better part of an hour to unload everything onto the dock, and every minute was filled with anticipation.

The first crates were from a nursery owner in Putnam, New York, and they contained ten dozen bare-rooted apple trees, twelve dozen raspberry bushes, and six dozen Concord grapevines.

Of course, Sarah didn't know when they had shipped, and she had no idea where they had been stored during the mail stoppage, so she didn't know how many of them, if any, had survived.

Another crate contained bulbs of crocus, daffodils, paper-whites, amaryllis, and hundreds of assorted tulips. At the bottom of the crate, Sarah found onions and garlic sets, along with packaged seeds for tomatoes, lettuces, kale, spinach, radishes, sunflowers, basil, and rosemary. For everything else, Sarah used her own cuttings and homegrown seeds.

As the freight was unloaded, each person in the family amassed his or her own pile. Sarah Elisabeth's pile included new dresses, a dozen pairs of new shoes, and half a dozen hat boxes. She also received stacks of notes, invitations, and letters from her thirteen-year-old friends, who were as obsessed with handmade stationery as she was. Some of her letters were even scented with perfume.

Beatrix Anne's stash was a combination of her sister's pile and her mother's. Bea's pile included the obligatory dresses and bonnets, but it also contained a fine pair of English Wellington boots that Bea and her mother called wellies. Bea also ordered seed catalogs and dozens of packages of seeds.

Her favorite packages, however, contained garden tools. She had a penchant for having her own tools that she stored in her own small garden shed. She treasured them. She also loved botanical drawings. She wasn't very good at it yet, but that didn't deter her from requesting stacks of textbooks, reams of drawing papers, and boxes of paintbrushes, paint pots, and watercolors.

Edward paced the landing, waiting for his packages and mail to be brought out of the cargo hold. He was expecting a new shooting jacket, a pair of riding boots, and news of his friends, but most of all, he was expecting a new shotgun.

Made by John Blanch, Percival's favorite London gunmaker, the shotgun had a stock of burley walnut and barrels made of twist steel. Sarah was uneasy when Percival had told her that he had ordered the gun. After all, Edward was only sixteen.

The shotgun would be nearly as long as he was tall, but Percival said that it was a tradition among planters to give their sons their first shotgun on their fourteenth birthdays and that it was high time.

When the shotgun was finally retrieved from the hold, it was given to Sarah. "Happy Birthday," she said, ceremoniously handing it to Edward.

"May I open it now, Mother?" Edward asked excitedly.

"It's your choice, but I believe it is customary for a gentleman to inspect a new weapon in the privacy of his study."

"Oh, right, Mother. May I use Papa's study when we return to the house?"

"Of course, dear," Sarah said, beaming.

As Sarah watched, Edward's pile grew larger and larger. She mournfully kept her eye on the stash that would have been Percival's. His stash contained an entire wooden crate filled with nothing but English newspapers: the *Globe, London Times* and the *Morning Chronicles and Observer*. Next to the crates of newspapers, Sarah discovered two new suits from Percival's tailor on Savile Row in London and a pair of evening shoes and boots from his bootmaker in Charleston. Dwarfing those crates, however, were individual casks containing rum and whisky and a half pipe of Madeira.

How thrilled Percival would have been to see Edward receive his new shotgun and to dig through the rest of his stash. Sarah's pile was paltry next to Percival's.

She received two gowns from Madame Chloe's; bolts of Provincial cotton from Avignon; Italian silk; laces from Brussels; a large box of lavender soaps from the Abbaye Notre Dame de Seranque; a set of European goose down coverlets and pillows; and twelve rolls of hand-painted French wallpaper for the dining room.

She also received stacks of personal mail, fashion magazines, three back issues of Agricultural Magazine, and a stack of seed catalogs.

"This is just like Christmas." William gleefully exclaimed. "It's going to take the whole day to get everything up to the house."

"It's embarrassing to stand on the landing like daft children," Sarah said wistfully.

"I wouldn't worry about that, miss," the ship's captain said after overhearing Sarah's comment. "Last week, some young women in Georgetown tried on their new dresses right over their old ones. They made the biggest mess you've ever seen, but then a happy day like this one has been a long time coming.

"I'm sorry to hear about Master Vaux. He was a fine gentleman," the captain said, removing his cap. Did you lose anyone to the fever, miss?"

"Yes, my father and some friends along the river. Once I read my mail, I'm certain to learn of others," Sarah replied.

"Did you lose anyone, Captain?"

"My daughter and her husband and two of their babies," he said, pulling a handkerchief to his face. "The wife and I are planning to raise the other young 'ens. Now we got ourselves a seven year old, a four year old, and a three year old. It's like starting again, but family's family, so we'll do the best we can."

"God bless you," Sarah said as he and his crew pulled away from the landing.

"Blessings to you, miss."

The boat made its way upstream to make its next delivery at Midway Plantation when the family watched it turn away and head back toward the plantation landing.

"Overlooked something," the captain shouted.

"One is a letter, and the other is a small package from Cuba."

"My husband's cigars," Sarah said.

"Aye," the captain said.

"Do you smoke cigars, Captain?"

"Yes, ma'am, but not ones like those. Those are made for a gentleman. The King of England smokes cigars like that."

"That is precisely why I'd like you to have them," Sarah said, handing the cigars back to the captain.

"Oh, ma'am, it wouldn't be right. I'm just a common man, common as dirt."

"Take them as a gift from me," Sarah said, "for your many kindnesses over the years."

"Thank you, ma'am."

"God's speed."

As she watched the boat make its way up the river, Sarah looked at the letter and noticed that it was from Hebert Plantation in Mt. Pleasant, and it was marked URGENT:

Dearest Sarah,

I have grave news about your mother and my precious cousin, Elisabeth. You know that she has spent the past few weeks with us here at Hebert House before moving on to be with you on Waccamaw.

There has been an accident. Your mother has died, Sarah. She died in a fall last evening. She has been experiencing several dizzy spells, and the doctor believes that she suffered one while descending the stairs.

Her death came instantly, dear, and she experienced no pain.

She is in God's hands now. We will wait for your instructions before we make any final arrangements. We are assuming that Elisabeth wanted to be buried next to your father at Rochambeau.

So sorry, my dear, Cousin Marie.

Before Sarah had even finished reading the letter, Edward saw her distress and sent a runner back to the house to get Hannah. Then he placed his shotgun on the landing and watched helplessly as Sarah collapsed, clutching the letter to her chest.

"Mother, what happened?" Edward said, wrapping his arms around her. "What happened?"

"Grand Mamma… Grand Mamma has died," she said in a whisper. "Mamma is dead."

Just then, two livery boys sprinted onto the landing with Hannah close behind. "What happened?" Hannah gasped, holding her side.

"Grand Mamma has passed," Edward said, trying in vain to hold back his tears.

"Oh, Honey," Hannah said, kneeling to touch Sarah's face. "I'm so sorry; I know how much you loved her."

"She fell… she died instantly. I should have been there. I could have protected her," Sarah screamed.

"You couldn't have stopped this from happening," Hannah said. "It was her time. It was her time. At least it sounds like she didn't suffer. She probably didn't even know what happened until she woke up in your papa's arms. She's with your papa now."

"She is, isn't she? She's with Papa," Sarah said, looking into Hannah's sad eyes. "She's with Papa."

Sarah, Eliza, and Edward arrived in Mt. Pleasant that night, and Elisabeth Richards had already been laid out in the east parlor. She was dressed in a black silk crepe gown that was part of her own extensive mourning attire. At her neck was a mourning pendant depicting a sheaf of wheat covered in diamonds and surrounded by luminescent gray pearls. Mamma once told Sarah that the sheaf was a Biblical reference to a ful-filled life. How appropriate it seemed placed at Elisabeth's slender neck.

Her casket rested on the Hebert family bier, centered beneath the room's enormous chandelier. Vases of flowers from the vast gardens at

Hebert Plantation filled the parlor with color and fragrance, but Sarah was oblivious. All she saw was her mother's exquisite face.

The service for Elisabeth Richards would be held at the plantation the following afternoon, and there was nothing to do but wait, so Edward had the servants take his mother up to the bed, and he returned to the parlor to stay with his grandmother's body.

Sarah's younger children were expected to arrive the following morning. Eliza offered to get them settled in once they arrived, but when they pulled up to the mansion, she was happily surprised to see that they were accompanied by her husband, Will.

Sarah's cousins, most of whom lived within an hour's carriage ride of Hebert Plantation, also arrived that morning. When they saw how pale and drawn Sarah was, they fussed over her in their affectionate way, but she assured them that she was well. After paying their respects, they stopped to kiss Elisabeth's hand, then joined the rest of the family in the west parlor.

"How are you doing?" Eliza asked.

"I'm fine," Sarah replied. "It's heartening to see Mamma's family. You can feel how much they loved her." Sarah heard a familiar voice. It was Cousin Charlotte, now a sixteen-year-old young woman, who was recently betrothed and soon to be married.

"Charlotte," Sarah cried.

"I'm so sorry about Auntie Elisabeth," Charlotte said, "We loved her so."

"I know," Sarah said, letting out a sob.

A bell rang, and the funeral-goers were ushered into the east parlor. So grand in size, the room had long been the centerpiece of glittering balls and family weddings but not that day.

Its mirrored walls were draped with black crepe, the hall clock had been stopped to reflect the hour of Elisabeth Richards's death, the shutters were drawn, and a black drapery had been placed over the chandelier.

The trappings of the lavish room felt alien shrouded in such somber tones, and it was only a portent of things to come. Two of Sarah's elderly aunts fainted within minutes of each other during the service; Grandpapa tripped over a lady's chair and dislocated his wrist. One of the servants backed into a pier table and broke a vase.

Sarah and the children accompanied Mamma's body to Rochambeau, while Eliza and her family returned to their home at Laurel Hill. Elisabeth Richards was buried next to her husband the following day in Rochambeau's rose garden. In keeping with tradition, she was buried to his left.

Before the arrival of Elisabeth's coffin, a team of brick masons from the plantation had prepared her gravesite. A narrow grave just large enough to accept the mistress's coffin was dug, and then a short brick wall was built around the perimeter of the grave.

Elisabeth's coffin with a black lacquer finish with a large gold cross affixed to its top was placed into the grave. Sarah and the children watched as the brick masons returned to the gravesite and placed an arched layer of bricks over the rounded surface of the casket.

Then Mamma's crypt stone was placed on top of the wall of brick surrounding her grave. Made of the finest Vermont marble, the crypt stone had been hurriedly engraved by Charleston's premier maker of headstones. Sarah selected the inscription at the bottom of the crypt stone with her papa in mind:

My darling James,
I'll never leave you
Always you'll be in my heart.
Don't forget my soul is near you
And that we'll never part.

CHAPTER 32

He Was From Barbados

True Blue Plantation

1818

This handsome man who had entered the social scene on Waccamaw in 1818 said he was from Barbados.

Everyone was curious about him, especially those related to him, who, according to him, included every expensive name in South Carolina, including LaBruce.

Eliza didn't' know what to think about him, this tall, striking man with a French accent, slicked-back hair, and a name that rolls off your tongue, Armand DuBois. South Carolinians didn't take to strangers; they preferred the familiar.

They weren't the most trusting lot, either. They had long memories and even longer noses that they were exceedingly good at looking down.

And yet, something was captivating about DuBois. It was rumored that he had a pedigree to match anyone in Charleston and a fortune to boot, but who was he exactly? No one seemed to know.

When pressed, he always declared to be related to a member of a little-known branch of the family in question, the one who lived thousands of miles away in an isolated chateau or villa in Tuscany.

He told other relatives that they were cousins through a first wife, less known. He traced his Middleton lineage to an obscure second son who took to the sea rather than playing the role of the spare to the family's millions.

Again, he was related to everybody, practically everybody, but through twists and turns and second cousins twice removed, and black sheep and runaway heiresses. They were farfetched stories perhaps but creditable enough and far more interesting than the stories in anyone else's closet.

Perhaps that was his draw. His mannerisms were gentile, and his manners were exquisite. His laughter, though, seemed genuine, but his gray eyes were unsettling.

But where had he recently come from? South Africa, he said. It had something to do with a diamond mine, someone said. They couldn't be sure, but he had also been a mariner. Wasn't he fascinating!

He'd arrived in the Lowcountry with a stack of introductions and a wad of cash and a circular tattoo at the base of his left thumb, given to him by the Maori.

After he'd made his introductions in Charleston and attended the right parties and met the right people, he then moved north to the Waccamaw, where he flamboyantly introduced himself to Eliza's husband, William LaBruce.

William was an astute man who fiercely loved his family and ran an extremely productive plantation, but he wasn't much of a fraternizer. He left that to Eliza, who could charm a fencepost; besides, a man like DuBois made it easy.

What was he doing in South Carolina? Eliza wanted to know. "Stretching my legs," DuBois said. "I've been away from civilization, far too long. I longed for the gentility of the South and its beautiful women."

Well, Eliza liked that. She was pushing thirty-six and she could use a little flattery. And so could Sarah, Eliza suddenly thought. It'd been four years since Percival had died, and Sarah had barely set foot off the plantation since then. Sarah needed some fun, and perhaps this mysterious man could provide it. She'd introduce them and soon.

"And where are you staying, Mr. DuBois?"

He'd rented a house in Georgetown, he replied.

"Well, we'll have none of that. Since you and my husband are kin, I insist that you stay with us." DuBois profusely thanked Eliza but said he couldn't possibly impose like that. Then he said he wouldn't want to impose, and then he said, "Are you certain I wouldn't be imposing?"

"Of course not," Eliza said. "I insist."

DuBois took up residence at Laurel Oak two days later. It was as though he had planned it, although he couldn't have, could he? Eliza introduced Sarah to DuBois the following Sunday. Sunday dinner was always a good way to introduce folks.

Everyone looks better after a Sunday spread, especially a picnic, so that's what Eliza busied herself setting up. It was a beautiful day, and the river reflected the pink and blue sky like a mirror.

Small tables had been set up on a crocket field that Eliza had built overlooking the river, and it was a perfect place for a picnic because it was board flat, and the chairs and table didn't get wonky.

The table was set with crystal and silver tableware, a pink linen tablecloth, and enormous lace-trimmed napkins. The Madeira was sublime and a perfect accompaniment to the pheasant and rice dish that Eliza was famous for.

William and Armand talked man talk while the service was taking place, but Eliza saw to it that she kept William occupied during the meal so that DuBois and Sarah could get to know each other.

They chatted about the river and the colors of the sky, and then they moved on to Sarah's children and Armand's stories about Africa. Had she ever been to Africa, Armand asked.

"No," she replied. When she was younger, she'd enjoyed travel, but it had been a very long time.

She should try it, Armand said offhandedly. Travel had gotten easier. And then he asked her about Percival, noting that he had heard that he'd been an extraordinarily gifted planter. True Blue produced more rice per worker and more rice per acre than any other plantation in the Lowcountry, he'd heard.

"That's right," Sarah said, studying Armand for the first time. She thought it quite odd that he would know the details of Percival's management of the plantation. It wasn't as though there was a plaque on a wall somewhere stating Percival's accomplishments.

Armand must have asked; he must have studied up on it before meeting her. Was that a good thing or a bad thing? She honestly didn't know. The evening ended pleasantly with Armand accompanying Sarah back to True Blue in a small skiff rowed by four LaBruce slaves.

Armand helped Sarah onto the landing and thanked her for a most pleasant day.

She thanked him; it had been a pleasant day, indeed. The following morning Sarah received a note from Armand, thanking her again for the lovely picnic. Perhaps we can see each other again, soon. With it, she also received a note from Eliza effusively extolling Armand's many charms and gallant demeanor.

Oh, Eliza, Sarah thought. Armand DuBois may be a charming man but gallant demeanor? After all, it was 1818, the dawn of the modern age. People didn't talk like that anymore.

A week passed, and she'd heard nothing further, so she worked overtime on her gardens. It was one of those mornings. She had dirt on her face and her hair was a mess when she looked up to see Armand walking toward her with a bouquet of peonies.

"They're from Eliza's garden," he said. "Flower shops are few and far between on Waccamaw."

"They're nonexistent," Sarah said, laughing. "I wish I'd known you were coming, Mr. DuBois," she said with a hint of reproach. "I'd have been more presentable."

"Didn't one of the poets write that a woman is at her best with dirt on her face?"

"I don't think so," Sarah said, shaking her head.

"Well, they should have because, in your case, it would be true." Sarah accepted the flowers and stepped out of her garden. After she closed the latch to the fence and turned toward the mansion, Armand followed.

"I was thinking," he said, "I think it might be a good time for you to start calling me Armand. Am I being too forward?"

"Not at all," Sarah said. "I'm not a girl anymore. Please call me Sarah. And what has brought you to True Blue today?"

"Oh, I almost forgot. I came with good news I've just purchased the Old Pettigrew Plantation across the river."

"What a beautiful property," Sarah said, stopping to look out over the river. The gardens have been untended for a while, though. You're going to need some gardeners."

"Perhaps I could borrow some of yours."

"Perhaps. I must ask you, though, I didn't know you were planning to buy a plantation. You didn't mention it during our picnic."

"That's because I just decided to do it," he said, pausing to pick a leaf off of the path. His long, lean lines always impressed women; it'd been that way since he was an adolescent, and he took every opportunity to show them off. Sarah noticed. He could feel it, but she should be impressed.

He'd bought a broken-down plantation he didn't want and didn't need, just to be near her.

"So why did you do it?"

"Because I've fallen in love," Armand said, dragging out the word love. "With the river, I mean," which wasn't at all what he meant, of course. It's beautiful here, even more, beautiful than Africa."

"What do you plan to do here?" Sarah asked, stopping at the pathway that led to the main kitchen. "You must have something in mind."

"Oh, I do. I intend to invest in a kaolin mining operation near Charleston. I'm going to build huge saltworks on the marsh here on Pawleys Island, and I intend to plant rice. The gardens may be in disarray, but the rice fields are in excellent condition. My lawyers said that the overseer is a fine chap and an experienced planter. I'm planning to give him a percentage of next year's crop."

"What a good idea," Sarah said thoughtfully. "I never thought to offer a percentage. That would certainly increase the incentive."

"That's what I thought," Armand said, stepping forward just to see what Sarah's reaction would be. Most women liked it when he stepped in, but this one was different. Without a word or a blink of an eye, Sarah took a step backward. Armand loved it. This was going to be fun. "Well, Sarah, I'm off. I have things to do to get the plantation livable." Then he smiled and turned to leave when she made her first mistake.

She asked him to stay for lunch. "It will be a light fare, just vegetables from my garden, but you are welcome to stay."

Armand declined at first; after all, he wouldn't want to impose, but he let her talk him into it, just as he always did. He was so good.

"Good," Sarah said, motioning toward the river entrance into the mansion. "Make yourself at home while I wash up," she said as she walked toward the back stairway.

"I'll only be a minute."

Armand was stunned. Some of the old ladies he'd flirted with the past few weeks had told him that True Blue was one of the finest plantations on the river, but he hadn't expected such opulence. The furnishings were gilded and upholstered in the finest Italian silk. The master's study and desk could have belonged to a prince, and the dining room was dominated by a crystal chandelier the size of a 900-pound pumpkin he's seen back in Ghana.

The large English breakfront held silver trays with glass cloches, silver dome covers, silver pitchers, and enormous silver bowls. He couldn't stop himself from oohing and aahing over the smallest thing, including a Baccarat crystal decanter set and a Royal Doulton table service decorated with hand-painted birds of prey.

In the hallway were two large prints by the touted ornithologist, John Audubon. There were also several other paintings and dozens of antique maps. On the other side of the gallery were numerous plats of the plantation.

One defined the location of every building, road, fork in the street, garden, privy, slave cabin, kitchen, landing, and barn. Another was drawn from the river's perspective, looking back on the plantation, enabling it to focus upon the rice fields, dikes, and trunks.

What a magnificent house, he thought, *exquisite in attention and detail.* It was just the kind of house he could see himself pouring port to his guests in. Once he and Sarah were married, he'd have to make some changes, of course.

The family portraits would be gone the first day, and then he'd work from there. The master's study interested him the most. Of course, after all, it would be his soon enough.

It was a bit stodgy, though, a little too traditional. The draperies had to go and so did the busts of Plato and Aristotle. He'd get rid of them under the pretense of saving them for the oldest boy, Whats-his-name?

And speaking of Edward, if that young man weren't already away at college, Armand would help him pack his bags. The last thing he needed was the nineteen-year-old heir to the throne underfoot.

And what-to-do, what-to-do with the main parlor? It was filled with the finest French and English antiques, but the arrangement wasn't pleasing to the eye, at least not to an eye as exquisite as his own.

Being a man of taste did have its drawbacks, but that was a trivial issue compared to winning over the Widow Vaux? She was lovely and quite youthful. Thank God for that, but she was also wary and skittish as a deer.

The secret to success was time. Why else had he bought that stinking plantation? He didn't know how to plant a petunia, and he wouldn't plant one if he did. *That's why we have slaves,* he reminded himself.

Gentlemen weren't made to get their hands dirty. Common, it was such a common practice for the plantation owners to set out over the rice fields each morning, as if their presence made one whit of difference.

Let it be grown by the unwashed. He didn't even like rice. Rice was for horses and the world's underbelly. Grass seed, that's all it was. But it made fortunes, including the one he was planning to take over from the Widow Vaux.

He was actually quite charmed by her. She was beautiful, had good teeth, and was young enough to give him a son or two. She was also the kind of stay-at-home girl he liked, unlike some of the shopping fiends he'd hooked up with in the past.

He couldn't see his relationship with Sarah going anywhere other than to the altar, but that wasn't what he was after this time. He'd love to lord over the plantation for a while and to sleep with a willing woman, but if that didn't happen, so be it. He needed something far more important from Sarah. He was obsessed with finding the mushroom cave at Carrefour, and Sarah might be the only person alive to help him do it. Just thinking about it made him breathless.

He'd spent the past four years preparing for this moment. He had learned about her former husband and poured over tax records and Pawley family wills. Oh, how he loved reading Percival's will. Poor thing. Everyone said he died so young.

Did anyone think to ask if he'd been poisoned?

Well, of course not. How could that even be accomplished?

Well, one COULD have put traces of arsenic into an expensive bottle of Percival's favorite Black Rum and sent it to him as a gift. But who would dream up a scheme like that, and who would be sinister enough to do it?

The Mistress Vaux would be surprised to know that Jean Armand DuBois was born Jean Armand Hebert at Les Cayes, his father's plantation on the colony of Saint-Domingue.

So far, so good, but there was one little problem with Armand's maternal line. Armand's mother was a mistress, all right, but not Les Cayes' mistress; she was Master Hebert's mistress. Armand and Sarah were cousins, even though Armand had been born on the wrong branch of the family tree.

Armand's mother, Annick, had been a sweet-spirited girl from New Orleans who'd met Armand's father, Georges Hebert, at a quadroon ball in New Orleans.

She was sixteen; he was thirty-four. Once Armand's father had decided upon Annick, and she had agreed to become his mistress, he brokered between Hebert and Annick's mother through a system known as placage.

Soon after, Annick and Hebert sailed to Haiti, where they lived at Les Cayes. Freckle-faced with pale auburn hair, Annick was a beauty, but she was completely without legitimate bloodlines, and the contract that her mother had signed was all fluff and no substance when it came to the law.

Bloodlines could be manufactured for the right price, however. Armand's first widow (herself, a quadroon) had taught him all about it.

As Sarah fussed upstairs, she weighed her feelings about Armand. She had to admit that she enjoyed his company, and she liked the fact that he was mysterious. He couldn't compare to Percival, of course.

No one could ever take Percival's place in her heart, but she was tired of running the plantation by herself, and with the children away at school, she was lonely. Armand hadn't met Hannah yet, but she'd secretly watched him inventorying the house and had taken an instant dislike to him.

This was all about money; she could tell by the way he strutted around the house, touching things as if they were his own. Hannah was conflicted. Sarah enjoyed Armand's company, and she had been lonely for so long. Maybe Hannah could put up with Armand's haughty ways for Sarah's sake. She'd think about it.

Sarah wouldn't continue to see him if Hannah really objected to him. Of course, Hannah realized that she could be wrong. It's just that she didn't trust anyone on first blush. And it would be nice to hear a man's voice and to smell the scent of a fresh cigar wafting from beneath the door to the study.

Armand met Sarah at the bottom of the stairs and escorted her to a small breakfast room at the back of the house. "I like to have lunch here," Sarah said, looking about the room. "It's the sunniest room in the house. Do you like the house?"

Armand almost replied, "You bloody well bet I like it," but he kept his composure and replied that he thought it was lovely, especially the family portraits lining the mantle in the main parlor. "Perhaps I can meet your children someday?"

When Hannah heard those words, she knew on the spot that he was up to something. That man didn't care nothing about Sarah's family or anyone else's. He was lying through his pearly white teeth.

Hannah entered the room carrying a large tray filled with greens and fresh fruit from the gardens and positioned herself behind DuBois so that she could roll her eyes at Sarah.

What did that mean? Sarah wondered. Was Hannah rolling her eyes because Armand was so handsome or because she didn't like him? "Excuse me a moment, Armand. I need to check on something in the kitchen."

"Of course," he said, jumping up to help her with her chair.

"What's the matter with you, Hannah? I've never seen you act like this."

"It's because we ain't had a scoundrel to lunch before."

"I'm shocked at you, Hannah. You don't even know him."

"I know enough to know that he ain't no gentleman, and he ain't no Master Percival."

"No, Hannah, there will never be another Percival, but I enjoy Mr. DuBois's company. Please try to be nice to him. I really expected you to like him. Will you try?"

"I'll try, but I still won't like him. He's a scalawag or something. Something ain't right about this. His hair's all slicked down, and he's got them French ways."

"Hannah, Mamma had French ways."

"Well, that was your mama. This is a greasy Frenchman. I wonder how you say, *lizard* in French?"

"That's enough, Hannah. Have Cook serve us the rest of our meal. I'm afraid you might poison his soup."

"Well, I just might do that," Hannah said, headed for the preparation's kitchen. "I just might do that."

Sarah had planned to give Hannah's impression of Mr. DuBois a great deal of weight. Hannah had good instincts. She knew things, but she hadn't given Armand a chance. Without intending to, Sarah suddenly felt protective of Armand. She was on his side, in his corner, in his confidence. Big mistake.

Lunch went swimmingly, as did many others. A month later, Armand asked Sarah to accompany him across the river to see the Pettigrew Plantation. Perhaps she'd have some suggestions for the gardens, he said.

She'd love to, she said, glaring through the window of the main kitchen at Hannah. Then she shouted "Hannah," and that liked to have made Hannah prostrate herself on the floor. "I need my shawl," Sarah said.

"Well, I'll be sending somebody up to get it," followed by "your highness" that she said under her breath.

Sarah and Armand had a wonderful afternoon studying the dilapidated state of the Pettigrew gardens. Sarah assured him that they would turn around with the proper care and fertilizer. Then he started expounding on the fabulous properties of elephant dung that he'd learned about from the Maharaja of Lumpur, who was his dearest friend.

"I didn't know you'd spent time in India," Sarah said, picking up on the part about the Maharaja. Before his years in Africa, he said, noting that the Maharaja insisted that dung from Indian elephants was far superior to dung from African elephants because Indian elephants had a passion for mangos.

"Mangos, the very idea," Sarah said, laughing.

That's when DuBois saw his opportunity. He wrapped his long arms around Sarah and kissed her softly. Sarah acted as if she'd been shot but only a glancing wound. Being in a man's arms felt natural and safe, so she stood on her tiptoes, put her arms around his neck, and returned his kiss.

"You taste like mangos, my dear."

"Very funny," Sarah said, smiling.

"Well, what would you think about a long-distance romance?" DuBois said.

"Long-distance?"

"Well, we do live across the river from each other. I'd say that was long enough."

"We'll see," Sarah said.

DuBois then took Sarah back to True Blue, offered up a hearty good-bye, and got into his skiff for the return trip to Pettigrew Plantation. As she walked back to the house, Sarah spotted Eliza's boat heading her way.

"Sarah," Eliza shouted.

"I've missed you," Sarah shouted back.

Sarah said she hadn't missed her all that much once Eliza stepped onto the landing. She'd missed the gossip about Mr. DuBois.

"Well, that is the truth of it," Eliza admitted.

"You must, must tell me the latest, Sarah. After all, it was I who introduced you."

"I like him," Sarah said, cutting to the chase. "I like him very much. I think he's interesting, and I enjoy his stories. I've given this a lot of thought. I mean about where our friendship might go from here, and I think I might want to marry him."

"No!"

"Yes. I'm not getting any younger, and he's good company. The children's inheritances have been settled, and I have my own money. I don't need a man to take care of me, but I miss the company of one."

"Will you ask him to sign a marriage agreement?"

"Of course, I wouldn't marry him without it."

"When did he propose?"

"He hasn't yet, but I'm certain he's working up to it."

"Have you told the children?"

"Not yet. I wanted to see what you thought first."

"He's not Percival," Eliza said, "but I think he's charming company, and I think that's enough. We're into the third act, you know."

"Yes, it's the third act."

Edward was away at school, Sarah Elisabeth was staying with friends in Charleston, and ten-year-old Beatrix was visiting her Hebert cousins in Mt. Pleasant, so after Eliza left, Sarah wrote letters to each of them. She'd met someone, she said, not a replacement for their father, but a man she enjoyed spending time with.

Sarah didn't speak to William, of course. He was barely five and far too young to understand what was going on. Sarah was grateful that he still greeted each day as a new adventure. Since everyone was planning to be on the plantation during the Christmas holidays, perhaps that would be a good time for them to meet Armand and to tell her what they thought.

Sarah had always been a woman who thought for herself, and she had become even more independent since Percival died. Because of that, her children had never given any thought to the possibility of her remarrying.

It didn't sit well with them at first. They saw it as a betrayal of their father's memory, but after a few weeks, they all came to the same conclusion. Papa was never coming back, and their mother had a right to be happy. They urged her to follow her heart.

Sarah felt better. She'd been holding back because of her concern for their feelings. Now, if she could just get Hannah on the bandwagon, but Hannah wasn't budging. Why did she feel such animosity toward Mr. DuBois?

Hannah said she didn't know why, but Sarah wasn't buying that. She knew Hannah too well. "It just ain't right," Hannah said when pressed.

"Do you mean that it's not right for me to consider getting married again, or that Mr. DuBois isn't the right man?"

"Both," she said.

"If you want me to respect your opinion, you have to be more specific."

She couldn't do it, she said. She just didn't like Mr. DuBois. He had some fancy ways, and he always said the right things, but Hannah just thought he had a black heart is all.

Sarah said that wasn't much to go on and certainly not anything she could hang her hat on.

"I like his company," Sarah said. "He's a gentleman, and he's been very respectful. He's even told me he likes you."

Hannah humphed out of her nose and said, "Well, la-de-da," but there wasn't anything else to say. Besides, maybe she was wrong. She doubted it, though, 'cause she was pretty used to being right.

Would she at least try to be pleasant to Mr. DuBois?

She would, she said, but she'd have to wear her actress face.

"Your actress face?"

"The face I wear when I have a hard time being pleasant. I've got it on now," she said, smiling her Cheshire Cat smile.

CHAPTER 33

Mistress DuBois

THE FAMILY HAD GATHERED for a late supper on a sparkling December night. The children had only been home a few days, but they had settled back into the rhythm of the plantation like sleepy children crawling into a warm bed.

DuBois was there, sitting at the head of the table, and he said he had something say. "During the past several months, I've fallen in love with your mother," he said, reaching for Sarah's hand. Then he looked around the table and asked each of the children for their permission for them to marry.

William, of course, was five, so he didn't say much of anything, and Edward was clearly uncomfortable with the unexpected role reversal. On the other hand, Sarah Elisabeth wasn't thinking about her mother's happiness; she thought of her own.

She was only months away from her seventeenth birthday and madly in love with this mysterious man who had found his way to their table and hadn't shown her the least attention. And now, he was declaring his undying love for her mother.

Sarah Elisabeth was convinced that every boy on Waccamaw was madly in love with her, and yet, this man treated her like a child. She was mortified, but she said yes and raised her glass in anticipation of Edward's toast.

"To family," he proclaimed.

"To family," everyone followed in unison.

Then the children discretely excused themselves from the table, leaving Sarah and Armand alone. The room was filled with sprays of magnolia, rosemary, and fragrant evergreens; crystal bowls brimming over with pinecones, quince, oranges, and persimmons and the intoxicating scent of pineapple, cinnamon, and ground nutmeg.

DuBois turned to Sarah and said, "I think we should make it official. I know that you were very much in love with the children's father, but I would hope that you could learn to love me, at least a little."

Sarah was lost for words. "I care very much for you, Armand," she finally managed to say, surprised by the lack of enthusiasm in her voice. *I must care,* she told herself. *I've had months to think about this. Surely I care for him.*

DuBois continued. "Will you marry me, my dearest Sarah."

"I will," Sarah replied less hesitantly. "I will."

Hannah's mother had taught her that decent women never spit, but Hannah let out a big one that night. When she heard Miss Sarah proclaiming her love for the lizard, Hanna spat on the door leading into the dining room. It was a big wad, too, and she watched it drip down the door. She wasn't going to clean it up, either. She was going to leave that spit there forever.

The wedding date with the charming DuBois was set for New Year's Day. Armand had suggested Christmas Day, but Sarah's heart knotted up at the very thought. Besides, there had to be enough time for the lawyers to work out the marriage agreement. Sarah's fortune was no laughing matter.

A few years earlier, Madame Chloe had expanded her Kings Street shop to include a beautiful bridal shop. Sarah's first wedding dress had taken weeks to make, but this time, she and Eliza and Sarah Elisabeth traveled to Charleston to buy a readymade one.

They looked at more than a dozen gowns, each modeled by one of

Madame Chloe's young assistants. Sarah Elisabeth liked the last one, and Eliza and Beatrix Anne preferred the one in the middle.

But Sarah selected the first one, a rose-colored silk taffeta gown, paired with white kid gloves and a white mantilla. When it turned out that the dress fit Sarah perfectly, an aging Madame Chloe secretly let out a booming belch. Altering a wedding dress could take a week, and that kind of anxiety always gave her indigestion.

The exquisite gown was carefully folded and placed into an enormous dress box. Then the spaces in between were filling with a profusion of pale pink tissue paper, and the whole thing was topped off with a pink satin bow.

The wedding was held in the east parlor at True Blue. Lowcountry weddings didn't vary all that much. The bride and groom nearly always stood beneath the chandelier facing the priest, who, in turn, had his back to the room's fireplace.

The wedding-goers sat facing the couple's backs in chairs that fanned out in a semi-circle. Funerals were often set up in the same way, although sometimes the departed was placed next to the wall opposing the fireplace instead.

Christmas, of course, was the theme of this wedding and a big fuss had been made over the flowers. Sarah hired a floral designer from Madame Chloe's studio to accompany her back to the plantation following the trip to Charleston to select the wedding dress.

Even without the flowers that were to come from Sarah's gardens, Sarah's driver had to hire two additional rigs just to transport the rented chairs, candelabras, floral stands, table cloths, and enough ribbon to encircle the whole plantation at least three times.

Even Hannah, who was down in her cuffs over Sarah's choice of bridegrooms, couldn't mask her excitement about the wedding. There was something about little gold chairs and flowers and candles and ribbons all bunched together that made a happy day.

New Year's Day was an inconvenient time of the year for a plantation wedding because it called for river travel. Charleston was more than three hours away by boat, and even though South Carolinians liked to brag that South Carolina was always warm and sunny, it wasn't.

It could get cold and windy, so fewer people attended the wedding than they would have, had it been held in Charleston. But practically everyone from the Waccamaw family showed up in high spirits.

It seemed fitting to those who knew Sarah that her entire house was filled with flowers. Even for Sarah, it had been a bumper year, especially for her hothouse plants.

Pink and white Amaryllis dwarfed their surroundings as they shot out of tall, narrow vases like trumpets.Clusters of paper-whites banded together with pink ribbons held their own against scores of pink and white potted Poinsettias, Chinese vases filled with white Camellias, and an absolute profusion of Christmas roses.

Drinking and dancing, singing and smoking cigars was the sign of a good wedding, and Sarah and Armand's wedding didn't disappoint. Except for the dropping of Sarah's ring during the hand-off between the minister and Armand, the wedding went off without a hitch.

The boisterous Heberts seemed particularly happy for Sarah. They had loved Percival, even though he was an Englishman, and they were devastated when he died so suddenly and so young.

DuBois seemed like the right sort of fellow, though, and to their delight, he was French. Perhaps they had a few reservations but nothing they couldn't scratch; they just wished Sarah's parents could have been there, too.

The Heberts were vexed over what to give the couple as a wedding gift, but Armand unknowingly tipped them off when he said that he hoped to take Sarah on a belated honeymoon to the Caribbean in the spring. What luck? The Heberts decided on the spot to offer them the use of one of their schooners and crews. Armand and Sarah seemed delighted.

Armand had agreed to live at True Blue after the wedding, although Sarah spent days talking him into it. The old Pettigrew place was coming along, he said. The guest house was almost finished; they could live there. All it needed was some wallpaper and furniture. He just felt bad about imposing on Sarah's staff, really bad, but he gave in to Sarah's wishes in the end.

CHAPTER 34

What Did You Do Then?

Everything began smoothly at first. Sarah and Armand had long walks in Sarah's gardens and wonderful conversations. But when they were alone, he was rough with her, and it reminded her of the Hanson boy.

Eliza picked up on Sarah's unhappiness from her letters, but Sarah refused when Eliza offered a shoulder to cry on. During a luncheon stopover one afternoon, Eliza spotted a bruise on Sarah's neck. When she mentioned it, Sarah withdrew. Eliza apologized, but Sarah could only cry.

Armand had chosen March 30th as the departure day for their trip to the Caribbean. They were going to visit Cuba, Haiti, and the Lesser Antilles, he announced. Sarah was horrified. She'd been to Haiti as a girl and never wanted to go again, she said. "The Dominican Republic is right next door. Perhaps we could go there instead."

She'd halfway expected a fight, but to her surprise, Armand didn't say another word. She'd grown used to him filling the spaces between them with rebukes, but she'd never seen him sulk. The sulking continued for days, and it was maddening. He pouted like a child, and her attempts to make things better only made them worse.

She didn't know that men pouted, but this one certainly did. Eventually, he agreed to speak to her, but only to whine about her not trusting him enough to tell him about her time in Haiti. When she told him that it was too painful to even think about, he pouted all the more. "How can we carry on a marriage if you don't trust me?" he said.

"I do trust you," Sarah replied. "It's just that I still have nightmares about Haiti." It would be good for them to talk about it, he insisted. A wife shouldn't have secrets from her husband; it was unseemly.

He whined, she listened, he sulked, she weakened and finally agreed to tell him about Haiti. Haiti, even hearing the name quickened her soul. What a dreadful, evil place to return to even in her dreams. She began her story by describing the giddiness that she and Eliza felt about being away from home for the first time.

"You need to skip over that part," he said, looking bored. She described their room at Carrefour—boring; the fire—also boring; and then she moved on to the beginning of the massacre.

"All right, you may start there," he said, but when she described the rebels murdering her family, he insisted on moving on.

"What happened after you escaped from the mansion, Sarah?"

"Eliza and I got lost from each other."

"Then what?"

"What do you mean?"

"I mean, what did you do after the two of you were separated? Where did you hide? Where did you go?"

"To a cave."

"And?"

"Eliza was there, and we stole a boat and sailed to Cuba."

"Oh, I think there's more to the story, my dear."

"I accidentally caught the cave on fire?"

"Yes, and what did you see when you were in the cave, Sarah?"

"Teenaged boys, and they were taunting Eliza."

"What else did you see?"

"A little island girl was wearing pearls and a Mardi Gras crown."

"Ah," he said, "and what happened to the Mardi Gras crown?"

"It fell." Sarah replied.

"Into the cave?"

"Yes, it fell into the cave."

"And then what happened?"

"The cave caught on fire, and then it collapsed."

"Did the whole thing collapse?" Armand asked.

She didn't think so.

"You're tired, my dear," Armand said in his most charming voice. "Go on up to bed. I'll be there later." Staggered by the trauma of reliving the past, Sarah called for her maid and dragged herself to bed.

"Oh, Percival," she cried into her pillow. "What have I done."

Armand didn't come to bed that night nor any other night for that matter. He prowled the Quarter, instead. Sarah was grateful for every moment she spent away from him, but she felt guilty about the women in the Quarter. Even the married ones risked beatings for refusing to accommodate him.

Sarah wanted to turn to Hannah, but how could she? If Hannah knew how unhappy Sarah was, she'd probably push Armand down the stairs. Hannah was a Christian, but she had her limits. Sarah should have listened to her.

As long as she could remember, Sarah had longed for absolution for the events in Haiti, but Armand wanted something, too. Whatever he was after had to do with Carrefour and the mushroom cave, but how did he even know about the mushroom cave?

Sarah felt as though she had been in a fog ever since the wedding, and she had convinced herself that Armand had been drugging her. She was certain of it.

He insisted upon making her drink a glass of Madeira every evening. It was good for her, he'd say. Maybe Armand was the Devil? Maybe the Devil had come to earth to punish her in person for her wicked past.

While Armand and Sarah operated like ships in the night, March 30th rolled around in the blink of an eye. Sarah had refused at least a million times to go on the cruise, but Armand said she was going whether she liked it or not, and he was used to getting his way.

So when the Hebert schooner pulled up to the landing on the morning of the 29th, Armand was there with bottles of Percival's finest Madeira. Sarah, of course, wasn't invited. Armand said if she were to appear, it would make him very unhappy. She didn't want to make him unhappy.

"No," she said, she didn't.

They were scheduled to set out on the cruise the following morning and Sarah had never felt so alone. She wasn't even allowed to take a servant.

"Whatever you need, my dear, I will do for you," Armand said, making sure that Hannah was in the room. "It will give me a chance to spoil you."

That was the last straw. As soon as Hannah could speak to Sarah without Master Armand within earshot, she spoke up. "We've got to do something. That man is evil. I'm going to kill him. I'm going to sneak up on him and kill him with a pitchfork."

"Hannah!" Sarah shouted in a whisper. "Stop!"

"Well, we've got to do something. He's going to hurt you someday, missy. I can see it in his eyes. He doesn't care about anything."

"You're wrong, Hannah. He cares deeply about something. I just can't figure out what it is."

"It's about Haiti, isn't it?"

"Yes, how did you know?"

"I hear things. When you live with a serpent, you listen real good. I'm afraid that if you go off on that boat with him, you'll never come back."

"He's not through with me yet," Sarah said. "He still needs me, at least for a while. I think he's been drugging me, but for the last week. I've dumped out my wine when he wasn't looking, and my head's getting a lot clearer. If there's an answer, I'm going to figure it out, and I'm going to save myself."

"That's pretty bold talk," Hannah said. "He's a big angry man. How are you going to fight against that?"

"I don't know, but I'm going to do it. It would be different if the boys were older or if we lived closer to my family," Sarah said. "He even reads my mail. There's no way I could get a letter to anyone."

"I could get one out," Hannah said.

"You could, couldn't you? You could send a messenger to the Heberts and Eliza. "I'll write the notes right now. You could send them tonight."

"But the morning tide," Hannah said. "It's an early tide, Miss Sarah. "We've run out of time."

Sarah and Armand and their seven-man crew set sail for Cuba the following morning. Hannah was on the landing, and she sobbed. She knew she'd never see Sarah again.

When Sarah and Armand arrived in Cuba, Sarah had a sense of being home. She'd ask Armand if they could visit Rio Seco, but he said the schedule was already set, and an out-of-the-way village like Rio Seco would hold no interest for him.

He was far more pleasant than usual, though. Perhaps it was something about being at sea. Other than his refusal to visit Rio Seco, he was actually quite gracious even to the crew.

Sarah was thankful that the crew was Heberts. She didn't know if they were freedmen like Hannah or slaves, but Armand constantly commented on their competence. He could have been doing it to ingratiate himself. Of course, he was always playing the odds, but it still made the trip more pleasant.

Two of the men were familiar to Sarah, and she sought them out. "I know you from the plantation," she said. She did, they said, and then one said he'd met her many years earlier.

"When?" she asked.

"Coming home from Cuba," he said, in a whispered voice, "you and the other Hebert children. My name's Titus Small, ma'am. I'm a freedman; your grandfather 'mancipated me for helping to bring you home safe."

"That was a long time ago, wasn't it, Mr. Small?"

"Not long enough for you, I 'spect." Titus said.

"My husband thought it might be good for me to come back to Haiti."

"What do you think, ma'am?"

"I'd rather go to hell," Sarah said, stiffening. "My husband would be very angry with me for speaking to you, but I have to ask, what if we get to Carrefour and are attacked? How would we get back to the ship?" Sarah whispered.

"You couldn't. You'd die trying if you attempt to go back the way you came. But you might stand a chance if we were to relocate the ship near the island's Western Coast. Nobody lives on that side of the island because the surf there is so treacherous."

"Then how could that save our lives?" Sarah asked.

"Because you wouldn't have to go back through Port-du-Paix to get to the ship. You could go west through the high country. You could probably do it in a half-day, but you' couldn't be seen. You'll die if you're spotted. The Haitians back in there don't like whites."

"I don't blame them, Titus, but I'm not going there to hurt them. I just want to get off the island so I can go home. Would you help me?"

"How?"

"If we don't return to Port-du-Paix on time, would you be willing to sail to that spot you told me about on the western side of the island and to wait while we try to make it back? I would pay you anything you ask. I could make you and the rest of the crew wealthy men."

"I'll do it, ma'am. I've always wanted to be rich, so I can't say I wouldn't take your money, but mostly I'll do it to help you. That husband of yours is a mean son-of-a-bitch. I know I shouldn't be saying words like that to a lady. I could be beaten for talking like that, but I don't trust him, and the other men don't, either. We don't know what we're doing here, and we're scared."

"So am I," Sarah whispered, and then she gasped.

Armand had suddenly reappeared and was walking straight toward her. Her heart leaped, and she shuddered. She had three seconds to steel herself, so she pretended to be studying the debris that was slapping against the bow of the boat. And then, through a bit of luck, her skirts got tangled up on some of the riggings. There was something so genuine about her predicament that Armand seemed to buy into it. He was even helpful as he went to his knees to free her.

"You look beautiful today," he said, flashing one of his Prince Charming smiles, "too beautiful to be so near that sickening trash. Let's go to the other side of the boat."

With that, he took her arm and gently led her away from the bow. His sweet demeanor was off-putting. She'd been the beneficiary of it before only to have him turn on her, but she found it curious. He was up to something, but again, she couldn't read it.

Hannah had been right to call him a serpent; he was the only one who knew his next move.

CHAPTER 35

Port-Du-Paix

FIVE DAYS LATER, THEY arrived at Port-du-Paix, and Sarah was shocked at the city's condition. The harbor was littered with rubbish and garbage, and many of the surrounding houses and shops had collapsed into the streets. The women of Port-du-Paix wore printed dresses with red and gold turbans, but their feet were coarse and bare, and their children were hollow-eyed.

"They're starving," Sarah said.

"They probably are, my dear, but that is none of our affair. We didn't come here to feed the hoards; we came here for something far more important."

"What would happen to us if we were to leave the ship right now?" Sarah said, feeling as though every eye on the island was glaring at her.

"We'd be killed," he snipped. That's why he'd hired bodyguards.

"We have bodyguards?"

"Bodyguards," he said with his eye.

They waited. Two hours later, ten Haitian men quick-stepped their way onto the landing, terrifying Sarah, as well as the onlookers. The men looked like gladiators as they stood next to the boat greased and sweaty and loaded to the hilt with bandoliers, machetes, and rifles.

"Our chariot awaits, dear," Armand said, intending to sound snarky. But, as he helped her onto the landing, a tired-looking landau pulled up to the landing along with two equally tired-looked open wagons. As she was helped into the landau, Sarah discovered two more gladiators sitting atop the coach, who stared at her with contempt as she pulled her skirts into her narrow seat.

Once Armand was seated, the carriage lunged forward, and Sarah begged to know why he had demanded that she return to Carrefour.

"Well, I suppose it's time you to know the whole story," Armand said, "but where shall we begin. Perhaps I should start with a tiny little fact that is so, so funny," he said with his head bobbing from side-to-side.

"You and I are cousins. Isn't that just the funniest thing?"

It was at that moment that the truth became as plain as the nose on Sarah's face. Armand was a tangle of disconnected nerves and synapses. He was insane. As she stared at him with her new understanding, he continued his disjointed soliloquy.

"I know; I'll begin with my real name, Jean-Armand Hebert. I was born at Les Cayes. My father was Georges Hebert. Isn't this just the best story ever," he said, rolling his eyes like a marionette.

"There was one little problem, though; my mother wasn't Les Cayes' mistress. She was Georges Hebert's mistress. She was quite striking, but sadly, my dear, she was a quadroon. In other words, sweetheart, I'm afraid you have married yourself a Negro."

"Georges Hebert?" Sarah said.

"Georges Hebert was Grand-Pere's youngest son. Do I have to explain everything? Now, where was I? Oh, yes, I remember. One evening my father, Georges Hebert, called me into his study and told me to deliver an urgent message to Carrefour.

"I was tall and lean and could run like a deer. When I got to Carrefour, I was escorted into Grand-Pere's study. I was shaking; Grand-Pere was my grandfather, and yet, I'd never met him. I doubt that he even knew who I was, but I stood there hoping that he would take some note of me.

"He didn't, though; he just grabbed the message out of my hand and told me to leave. However, before I had reached the door, he ordered me to find two of his grandsons—his legitimate grandsons, of course, and to bring them back to his study. He had a job for us.

"I was ecstatic. Grand-Pere had a job for us, for me. I'd never felt so important. So I rushed out of his office and ran into the courtyard. I'd passed some of the grandsons there and hurriedly told two of them to follow me.

"We were kin; we were cousins, but they told me to get lost. They shouted insults at me, but then I told them that Grand-Pere had sent me, so they dropped what they were doing and followed me.

"We knocked on Grand-Pere's door and were ordered inside.

"'Lock the door,'" Grand-Pere said.

Then Grand-Pere pointed to a wooden chest behind his desk. It was dark green and had a crest on it of some kind that looked as though it had been stenciled on.

"We were supposed to take the chest to a small cave near the border between Carrefour and Les Cayes. The white cousins knew where the cave was, but I didn't. That was only the fourth time I'd been allowed to leave Les Cayes."

Then Armand said that when he and his cousins got to Aunt Felicity's Necessary, the brothers located the hidden door. But when they struggled to get the heavy crate down the narrow stairs, one of them missed a step, and the crate slammed onto the floor. Dust flew everywhere, Armand said, and the latch that held the chest's lockset in place flew open from the concussion.

"My cousins looked at each other, and then they looked at the chest. It was a treasure chest of some sort. They were certain of that, but what could be inside? Finally, one of them dared the other to look inside, and they told me to get out of the way. I felt a wave of hatred I'd never felt before. Someday I'd get even, but not that day, so I did what I was told.

"They almost had the chest open when a skink shot out from under it, and they ran to the other side of the cave like little sissy girls.

"'You cowards,' I shouted. 'Get out of the way. I'll do it.'

"I pried open the lid and looked inside. There was a layer of purple velvet that I grabbed and threw onto the floor. And then I saw the crown."

"The Mardi Gras crown," Sarah said in a whisper.

"It wasn't a Mardi Gras crown, my dear. It was a real crown. And it was made of solid diamonds. The cousins said, 'Don't touch it.'

'Shut up!'" I said. And then I put the crown on my head and shouted,

'I'm the king of the world!'

"'You're nothing,' one of the cousins screamed.

"'I'm your cousin,' I replied.

"'You're the son of a whore!' he shouted back.

"I threw the crown back into the chest, and it got really quiet. Then I ran at the boy and kicked him. I'd kicked him so hard that it knocked me off my feet, and it gave the cousins time to get to the stairs.

"I wish I'd killed them," Armand said, looking at Sarah. "I wish I had killed them."

"Where were you that night, Armand?"

"At Les Cayes," Armand replied in a whisper.

Sarah was in tears. She felt sorry for Armand, not enough to forgive him, but enough to be able to put the pieces together.

"That was the night of the massacre, wasn't it?" Sarah asked. "The boys had golden hair?"

"Yes."

"And now I know what you wanted from me," Sarah said.

"You needed my family's connections to get you back to Haiti, and you needed me to confirm that the crown was in the cave when it collapsed."

Armand looked out the window and cried.

"The maharaja, Armand? Did you know the maharaja?"

"I knew his former valet."

"And Africa?" Sarah said.

"I worked three years before the mast on a merchant ship that sailed between Barbados and the Gold Coast. I never hunted lions, and I've never even seen an elephant. Everything I told you was a lie."

"You planned the whole thing, didn't you—the courtship, the wedding, everything. How long did it take you, Armand?"

"Four years, it took four years to make everything come together, but it was worth it because that crown belongs to me, and now you're going to help me find it."

"I can't," Sarah said. "I don't remember where the cave is."

"You were there," he said.

"But it was too dark," she said. "I could never find it again."

"Ah, but you forget that I was there, too. I'll remember some things, and you'll remember the rest."

"You grew up at Les Cayes; why didn't you know about the privy and the cave?"

"Because I was a Negro, remember? I couldn't leave the plantation without permission."

The landau suddenly came to a stop. They were at Carrefour, an open grave that contained the bones of Mimms and Beatrix and Mamma's island cousins and their priceless Russian tiaras. For a moment, Sarah remembered the glittering laughter, and then she vomited into her reticule.

"This is where we get off, dear," Armand said, opening the door to the landau. "Oh, and there's one other thing I forgot to mention; our bodyguards are all Hebert's. We're just one big, happy family." Armand's remark was intended to frighten Sarah even more, of course, but knowing that the bodyguards were at least remotely tied to the Hebert plantations made her feel safer.

"Did they recognize you? Do they know who you are?" Sarah asked.

"They haven't the slightest idea."

CHAPTER 36

Back To Carrefour

ARMAND LED SARAH TO a charred settee that had once been gold-leafed and the height of fashion. "It probably came from Paris, don't you think?," Armand said, running his hand along the back of the settee.

Sarah said she didn't know; she felt light-headed. So she sat upon the settee and was immediately covered with twenty-year-old soot. She didn't notice. All she could think about was the sound of the men rushing up the stairs to kill her family. She could hear the screams, and she could see the sprays of blood.

"Well, Sarah, like I said before; it's your turn," Armand said. "You know precisely what I want from you. What path were you following when you found the mushroom cave?"

She wasn't following a path, or not one she could see because the ground was littered with indigo stalks. She was certain that there had to be a path leading to Les Cayes, but it was getting dark, and she couldn't find it.

"So, what did you do?"

"During dinner the night before, I remembered hearing that Les Cayes was due west of Carrefour and that it was significantly lower in elevation. So I set out for the sun and made sure I was maintaining a downhill trajectory. Eliza was so frightened that she had no idea where I was going, but she stayed right behind me."

"Skip over the part about Eliza, and get on with it."

"We'd probably been running about a half-hour when we came to an outcropping of boulders, the kind that looks as though they had been thrust out of the ground sideways.

"It was really dark by then. So I went one way around the boulders, and Eliza must have gone the other way because that's when we got lost."

"The cave, Sarah, the cave," Armand said, showing his frustration.

"That's the part I can't remember because I was so scared. I remember walking around the outcropping, calling out to Eliza, but I couldn't find her, so Charlotte and I kept going downhill until the red silhouette."

"The red silhouette? And who the devil was Charlotte?"

"Charlotte was Aunt Beatrix's daughter. She was only three then. I had to take care of her. The red silhouette was Les Cayes."

Did she see the collapse of Les Cayes; he wanted to know. "Yes, part of it," Sarah said, wondering why Armand had asked. "I saw it collapse, too," he said softly. "The dependency kitchen went first, and from there, it fell in on itself like a set of dominoes. My mother died in that fire, and so did my sister."

"You never mentioned having a family, Armand."

"What difference did it make, Sarah? Now go on."

After the collapse of Les Cayes, Sarah realized how exhausted she was and started looking for shelter. That's when she spotted Aunt Felicities Necessary. It would have to do, she told herself, so she and Charlotte curled up in a dark corner and went to sleep.

"Keep going."

"I was asleep for a while, I think, but then I heard crying and was terrified that it might be Eliza. So I followed the sound and found a hidden doorway behind a fake wall.

"I opened it, and it opened onto a narrow stairway that led to a cave. It was filled with casks and wine bottles, and there were two golden-haired boys there.

"They were drunk and wearing nightclothes, and then I saw Eliza and the little girl."

"Ah, the little girl," Armand said. "Was she wearing a crown?"

"Yes, Armand, I've already told you about her." The little girl didn't interest him, he said, looking up to see if the gladiators were getting restless.

"Hurry up!" he said. "What happened to the crown?"

"It fell off the little girl's head as I jerked her up the stairs. That's when the fire started, and the cave collapsed."

"You said before that you thought only a portion of the cave collapsed, Sarah. How do you know that?"

"Because of the sounds, it made when it collapsed. It sounded like it was mostly the stairs that fell in. I can't remember," Sarah said, sobbing.

"Get up. Your job is to lead the same way you went during the massacre." Sarah stood, repositioned her bonnet, and looked around to get her bearings.

She'd escaped the house through a basement door that opened onto a small courtyard. They needed to find the courtyard, she said. The courtyard was still discernible, but nothing marked the spot where Beatrix was butchered. It was as if Beatrix had never existed. The field that Sarah and Eliza raced across to get away from the mansion had gone from being a manicured lawn to a knot of overgrown shrubs, pricker bushes, vines, and rogue indigo.

"Go!" Armand ordered as he signaled for the gladiators to follow. Sarah was thirty-six, and it had been years since she'd run, but she ran that day, just as she had so long ago. The past and the present were getting jumbled up in her head.

Eliza?

Charlotte?

No, they were fine. They were back in South Carolina, a million miles away from the terror of Carrefour.

They'd been running for about thirty minutes when Sarah spotted the outcroppings where she and Eliza became separated. It was a victory for her to have found them. At least her memory of that night was intact. The team went to the left of the rocks and continued downhill.

At this point, Armand took the lead. He knew far more about Les Cayes than Sarah; after all, it was his father's plantation. They arrived at the ruins a few minutes later, and even after all of those years, it still smelled like death.

"The privy was back up the hill to the right," Armand shouted.

"We're close."

One of the gladiators spotted the ruins less than thirty yards away, and Sarah knew there was no doubt about it being the remains of the privy because the heavy, arched door she noticed the night of the massacre was still there.

The bodyguards dropped their gear and pulled out small, collapsable shovels that Sarah hadn't noticed before. Then they moved the privy door and began to look for depressions and a soft spot in the earth with the ends of their shovels.

"Here!" one of the guards shouted suddenly.

"Dig," Armand said.

The digging only took a few minutes, just long enough to expose the original entrance into the cave. Armand was so excited that his eyes were glassed over. He was so close to the crown he could smell it.

One of the bodyguards dropped a rope ladder into the cave. By the sound of it, the end of the ladder hit the ground below in less than twenty feet; he told Armand.

"Perfect."

Then Armand ordered the smallest among the gladiators to descend the ladder holding a kerosene lantern, and Armand followed. The rest of the guards discarded their shovels and refitted themselves in their bandoliers, rifles, and machetes.

The lantern whooshed and its flickering light cast macabre shadows on the walls of the cave. The young guard was frightened, but Armand took no notice. He was obsessed with finding the crown. His cursing could be heard by Sarah and the other guards outside the hole.

They hated Armand, she could tell by the way they returned his curses, and she wondered if any of them descended from the slaves at Carrefour. Some of them must have, she knew because when they directed their gaze toward her, it was the same look that the field hands at Carrefour had given her the day she and Eliza were driven down the allee to the mansion.

She'd been shivering from the moment she'd stepped onto the landing at Port-du-Paix, but she suddenly realized that an odd sense of calm had overtaken her. She was keenly aware that she would die on the island, but she was at complete peace. Perhaps she had always been meant to die in Haiti. Perhaps she had tempted fate by surviving the massacre.

Fate was about to make up for the lost time. Armand had been sent to find her and to bring her back to Haiti so that her blood could mix with Mimms' and the rest. *It shouldn't be long,* she thought; *something terrifying was in the air.*

Armand suddenly shot out of the cave carrying a gunnysack filled with treasure. No one had to ask if he'd found what he was looking for because he had a twisted smile on his face that was frightening. The gladiators swung into action, preparing to leave the hell hole and to fight their way back to Port-du-Paix.

The first rifle shot grazed off one of the discarded shovels and pinged into the air. Sarah didn't even know what it was at first. However, the second shot got her attention because it singed her skirts and embedded itself in the heel of her shoe.

One of the guards slammed her to the ground and threw himself on top of her. The final massacre had begun. It was time to die. The rifle fire was coming from a stand of scrub bushes about a hundred yards away, the leader of the gladiators shouted.

Then he told Sarah to hand over her bonnet that he put on the end of his rifle and waved it in the air. The bonnet was destroyed in less than a second.

"There are at least five guns, sir," the youngest guard said. The leader tossed the leftovers of Sarah's bonnet back to her and ordered everyone to dig in.

"What's happening?" Sarah whispered to Armand.

"I don't know." He was clutching the gunnysack to his chest. "I found it, Sarah," Armand said. "I found the crown."

"But why were you willing to risk their lives for a make-believe crown?"

"Because it isn't a make-believe crown," he hissed. "It is the Imperial Crown of Russia. I saw the royal seal on the crate, remember?"

"I know you saw it, Armand. But you must know that it couldn't possibly be real," Sarah said as tenderly as she could. Imperial crowns don't get lost; they're always kept under lock and key. It's all in your imagination."

CHAPTER 37

All My Dreams Are Buried Here

SARAH TURNED AWAY AND took in a deep breath. So that was why Armand was willing to risk their lives. Now it all made sense. He believed the crown to be real because of the priceless Russian jewelry that he had seen the Hebert women wear when he was a boy.

Grand-Pere must have believed that a threat from the outside world would have been impossible because his treasure was protected by the Haitian jungle and a vast ocean. But he couldn't stop the threat from those nearest him. He couldn't stop the Haitian revolution. Armand's story about hiding the treasure chest the night of the massacre finally made sense.

Dust was rising from the location of the shootists, and Sarah didn't need anyone to tell her that they were on the move. It was time to get up and run; that was precisely what she did. She headed for a stand of hardwoods about two hundred yards to the west.

Because of the underbrush, she didn't know if she could run that far; because of her skirts and ruffled sleeves, she got there out of breath and trembling. She hid to one side away from the guards and as far away from Armand as she could get.

She had to pare down. She didn't stand a chance wearing petticoats and her ridiculous sleeves, so she wriggled out of her petticoats and tore away her sleeves. She couldn't do anything about her shoes, but at least they had laces and wouldn't fall off. She started to get rid of her gloves, but then she realized they would afford her some protection; she'd get rid of them when they were torn enough to get in her way.

Her hair!

Her hair was almost waist-length, and in the dash for the trees, her hairpins had fallen out. After that, her hair was free, and all she could think to do with it was to braid it hurriedly. She ripped a ribbon from her dress using her teeth and tied off her braid with it. Then she rolled the braid into a knot and cinched it into place with a section of ruffle from one of her sleeves.

There was another burst of rifle fire, and Sarah threw herself to the ground. The leaves beneath the trees were thick enough to hide in, but if she was going to save herself, she'd have to keep moving toward the boat. West, she had to keep moving west.

About thirty feet to her right was the youngest gladiator, the one Armand had ordered into the cave. He was much younger than she'd initially thought. He was perhaps no older than sixteen, almost the same age as the boy with the machete. Her skin started to crawl, and she began to tremble again.

The boy!

The boy with the machete!

Was there only blood and death in Haiti? And fires and screams and curses and eyeballs hanging from their sockets. Was there any civility left on this island, or had Satan moved his minions there?

The young bodyguard was terrified. Sarah could see it in his unpredictable mannerisms. At first, he laid on the ground, afraid to move a muscle. And then he stood up and started throwing insults at the enemy, when suddenly the back of his head exploded, and the rest of his body flew into the air.

The shootist had hit a perfect bull's eye.

The enemy, who was the enemy? Townspeople, perhaps, men who had followed them from Port-du-Paix. Or maybe they were small farmers who lived in the foothills? What difference did it make, as long as they were shooting at them?

"Sarah!" Armand shouted. "Get going!"

254

She looked around to see Armand and some of the bodyguards moving toward the west. Why were they moving west? Did they know that the boat would be there? Had Armand made a deal with the crew before they left the boat? Or was it the only direction that was open to them?

Sarah soon found herself in the island's foothills, where she discovered a forest of rogue indigo that seemed familiar. Was it because Papa had grown indigo at Rochambeau, or had she been there before? As she pushed west, Sarah kept a distance between herself and the men, especially Armand.

Two hours later, the indigo began to thin out, and the path Sarah was following led downhill into an abandoned coffee plantation. She'd never seen coffee trees before, and she struggled to keep going without stopping to study them.

Even though the plantation was overgrown, the coffee trees had glossy leaves covered with red and green coffee beans. In the distance, she saw a series of covered sheds that she guessed were used to roast and process the coffee.

She'd lost sight of the men in her group but could occasionally hear them, so she knew that they were nearby. It was midday and hot enough to bake hoecakes without a fire, as Hannah used to say. Sarah was so hot she was lightheaded, but she had to keep going.

One thing she could do, though, was to do what the women at True Blue did when they worked in the rice fields. She stopped and reached between her legs and grabbed the hem on the back of her skirt. Then she pulled the hem up between her legs and tucked it into the front of her waistband. She immediately felt cooler, and she could move so much better. No wonder men wore pants. Women should wear them, too.

As she pressed on, Sarah wondered what had happened to the enemy. Surely they hadn't given up so soon. She didn't know what they wanted, but they certainly hadn't gotten it yet. A kilometer or so beyond the coffee fields was a rise overlooking vast rice fields.

Sarah burst into tears. Would she ever see her own rice fields again? But there wasn't time for tears. It would be dark in a couple of hours, and she wouldn't have the sun to guide her. She'd be in the dark and unable to defend herself. It was the second time of the day that she lamented about not having a knife.

Sarah would have given anything for a compass, but she knew that there were other ways to tell direction during the early plantation times. The Native Americans used to notch trees to tell passersby the direction that they were going.

King's Highway on Waccamaw had dozens of notched trees because the highway had once been an important Native American trade route.

She felt like she was following some kind of path, even though it was terribly overgrown. It was still flanked by sycamore trees, mostly, and that couldn't be luck. The trees were a sign, so she started studying them, looking for notches or arrows or abbreviations cut into their soft bark. Within thirty yards, she found her first arrow.

She was thrilled but cautious. What did the arrow point to? Was it pointing the way west, or was it pointing to something else? She didn't know, but it was her best hope, so she kept looking for them.

After the third arrow, she spotted something chilling. It was an old cemetery, almost completely taken over by the undergrowth. Long fingers of Spanish moss cast shadows across the cemetery, and practically every plant to ever take root on the island, had planted itself in the cemetery, indigenous or otherwise; it didn't seem to matter.

Sarah listened for Armand and the bodyguards. She had a feeling that this was the place where the showdown would take place, and the battle would be won or lost. They weren't far. She couldn't see them yet, but she could hear them.

She decided to get off her feet for a few minutes and wait for them. The cemetery was beautiful in an eerie way because the headstones were covered with lichen and slimy black mold. The mold smelled, of course, but so did the spongy green carpet.

She sat on the nearest crypt stone and knew immediately that it was marble because of its coolness. She arched her back, and even though she'd promised herself not to look at the stone's engraving, something drew her to it. The crypt stone had a Celtic cross at its top and an engraved sentiment at the bottom:

In Memory of My Only Child,
All My Dreams Are Buried Here

Sarah jumped off the stone as if it had been set afire, never taking her eyes away from the engraved sentiment. It couldn't be, it couldn't be. It couldn't say *All My Dreams Are Buried Here.*

"Oh, Percival," she cried. "I love you so."

Suddenly she heard footsteps, and she threw herself on the ground. Then she crawled around the end of the crypt stone and was relieved to see that it was the bodyguards.

"Well, my dear, how good to see you," Armand said, walking up behind her. Sarah jumped, and Armand laughed.

"Couldn't we be civil to each other?" Sarah asked. "You came here and got what you wanted. When we get back to South Carolina, and you find a buyer for the crown, you'll be one of the wealthiest men in the country. You'll be looked up to. You'll have everything. Isn't that enough?"

"You didn't grow up like I did, Sarah. If you had, you'd understand that there will never be enough for someone like me. I'll never feel good enough, not ever, but I am willing to call a truce if you are. I know you won't believe me, but I'm sorry for the way I've treated you. You deserved better."

"Thank you, Armand."

Sarah bought time by fussing with her skirts, and then she said, "May I ask you a question?"

"Certainly," Armand replied.

"I want to know why we're going toward the west instead of south toward Port-du-Paix."

"Because the men who are after us are from Port-du-Paix, at least that's what the bodyguards told me. If we were to try to make it back to the ship, the rebel's numbers would increase, and we'd never make it. There's supposed to be an uninhabited beach on the western side of the island where we might be able to signal a fishing boat to pick us up."

CHAPTER 38

The Glint Off A Machete

SARAH WAS ABOUT TO tell him about the bargain she'd made with Mr. Small back on the Hebert ship when something caught her eye. It was on the other side of a series of headstones about fifty feet away.

She saw it again. It was the black shadow of a man with something shiny in his hand. It was the glint off of a machete!

The bodyguards surrounded Sarah and hit the ground. Then they dug their elbows into the cemetery's spongy carpet. They cocked their rifles, they pulled their daggers out of their boots, and they stared into the distance. The shadows were moving, and they were getting closer.

"If you get a shot , take it," the leader of the bodyguards shouted. Then, there was a shot, followed by a bloodcurdling scream and the sound of a body convulsing on the ground.

That's when all hell broke loose. The screams from the enemy were primordial and savage, and it was terrifying. Sarah saw one of the bodyguards thrust his dagger into a man's soft underbelly and unflinchingly force the blade up into his ribs. Blood gushed like a geyser, but the bodyguard didn't hesitate as he jerked out his knife and looked for another target.

A young guard named Samson Green didn't know much about infighting and even less about hiding from the enemy. He was on the wrong side of a crypt stone when a giant of a man slammed into him and disemboweled the seventeen-year-old with one swipe of his machete. Another of the younger men was hit next, but the wound wasn't deep.

"He'll live," Armand screamed out to the others.

"Sarah, stay down!"

The skirmish lasted less than half an hour, and what had begun as a melee ended with a whimper when the bodyguards allowed some of the injured to drag their dead away from the cemetery. The bodyguards suffered three dead with three injured, while more than twenty dead or dying attackers littered the cemetery.

There was no time to rejoice. It was obvious that a jungle was ahead, and it was getting darker by the minute. Their chances of making the beach were fleeting, but they had to try.

After a five-minute rest, the group left their dead, cared for their wounded, and set out into the jungle. In a few minutes, Armand walked over to Sarah and asked if she was all right. She was fine, she said, wondering which Armand she was talking to.

"The guards said we could make it to the western side of the island if we can make it through about five hours of the jungle.

"Do you think you're up for it, Sarah?"

"I don't have any choice. I want to get back to my children. I want to get back to my life."

"Your life before me?"

"Yes, my life before you."

Sarah half-expected him to fly into one of his rages, but he just told her to be careful. Then he said, "The guards' biggest fear is that we will get lost in this jungle. The compass we depended upon was lost in the fight, and it's too dark to follow the sun. If we had a sextant, we might be able to make it, but I'm afraid we'll wander around all night and end up back where we started."

"Let me show you something," Sarah said. "See these sycamores? The planters used these trees to mark their pathways and roads. The pathways are grown over now, but the sycamores are still here, most of them anyway. "Here's one," she said, stopping in front of the tree. Look at the bark on the tree, Armand. Tell me what you see."

"An arrow, I see an arrow pointing straight ahead."

"I've spotted dozens of arrows since we cleared the coffee plantation. You just have to know to look for them."

"Where are they pointing?" Armand said.

"I don't know, but I suspect one of two things. Either they're pointing due west, or they're pointing to a connecting plantation. Either way, we're better off than we are now, but I'm hoping they're pointing west, west to the abandoned beaches."

"May I tell the guards about the arrows, Sarah?"

"They're Taino; they should already know, but it won't hurt to tell them."

Within moments, the guards gathered around Sarah to ask her about the arrows. She pointed to the previous one and then to the next sycamore, suggesting that it would also have an arrow. When they got to the next sycamore, however, they found an arrow and three notches cut into the bark.

"Three notches," Sarah said. "Three what? Three kilometers? Three forks in a road? Three rivers? Three boulders? What could it mean?"

The company took stock. Three bodyguards were left in the cemetery dead, and three were wounded but ambulatory. Sarah and Armand were unhurt, although Armand repeatedly complained of his shoulder. Armand, of course, was burdened by the weight of the crown that he carried in a burlap shoulder pouch that was eating into his neck and shoulder. Sarah had cuts and bruises, mostly on her arms and legs.

Although most of the guards had felt animosity for Mistress DuBois initially, their admiration for her had grown. She was no sniveling female; she was a strong woman. The dead bodyguards gave the team a source of additional weapons.

Sarah turned down the offer of a rifle, admitting with ire that she didn't know how to shoot one, but she was familiar with machetes, so she selected the smallest of the extra three.

Touching the machete sent an electric shock from her hand into her heart, but she didn't flinch. She'd challenged herself to be strong since the day she'd encountered the boy with the machete, and now was her opportunity to do it. She would probably die on the island, but she was going to go down fighting.

The company set off in the direction of the arrow. The old rice plantation had given way to the jungle, and every step was treacherous. Snakes and giant spiders were everywhere. Even the biting flies were the size of moths.

Sarah found little comfort in knowing that the snakes on the island were nonpoisonous because one of the gladiators had told her that their bites alone could kill you. She was so frightened and so exhausted that giving up would have been easy, so she suggested a five-minute break to settle herself down.

"Look for another sycamore," she said. "And look for something in threes."

"Threes?" someone asked.

"Clusters of three rocks or boulders," she replied.

There wasn't a sycamore to be found, but one of the bodyguards found three distinct piles of small boulders.

"What is it trying to tell us?" Sarah said. "Are we supposed to go around them or to use them as compass points?"

"We use them as compass points," one of the younger men shouted from a cluster of trees in front of them. "I just found another pile."

Perhaps over the years, the planters had lost some of the original trees and replaced them with the boulders, Sarah suggested. "I say we keep following them." It was a rough go, though. Sarah had spider bites up and down her legs and a cut from a branch that had snapped back and hit her in the face.

Her braid was beginning to unravel, and the long, fine strands of hair were getting tangled into the maze of vines they were traversing. She had to do something, so she held the braid away from her head and lopped it off near her scalp with her machete.

"Christ's balls," one of the bodyguards whispered. "That's one bloody woman."

The floor of the jungle was getting soggier with each step, and Sarah was worried about running into a marsh or river. She remembered that there were crocodiles in Haiti, not in the inland part of the country, but the brackish regions. She reached down and scooped up a handful of water onto her lips. Salt Water.

And then she heard an inhuman screeching sound and looked to her right where she saw one of the bodyguards being tossed about by a dark shadow. "Croc!" the rest of the guards screamed in unison. "Crocodile!"

The company had kept together as a unit until then, but it became a free-for-all with the introduction of a crocodile. The bodyguards shrieked and cried out as they got up to run. Sarah guessed that they didn't even think about where they were running; they were simply running away from the crocodile.

As the bodyguard continued his death dance with the crocodile, Sarah let out a scream of her own and took off after the guards. She didn't know where Armand was; he'd been behind her when the bodyguard was attacked, but she didn't have time to look back. Her lungs were screaming at her to stop, but she was too frightened, so she just kept going.

Thistles and tree branches were tearing at her skin, and then she slammed into a tree. She fell to her knees and reached for her forehead. It was bleeding, bleeding badly, and the blood was burning her eyes, but she had to keep going. She could only see a few feet in front of her. The jungle had swallowed her whole. She wouldn't die of a Haitian rifle shot; she would disappear into the jungle.

CHAPTER 39

Salt Air

Suddenly, Sarah smelled something familiar, something wonderful. It was sea air, the sweet, wonderful smell of salt air, and although she couldn't see them, she could hear gulls and pelicans overhead.

Then the rain forest's thick canopy opened up to reveal a full moon and the shimmering edge of a sugar-white beach. They'd done the impossible.

Sarah rushed to the edge of the waterline to soothe her feet, and thought about the Hebert schooner. Would it be waiting? Did the crew keep its word, or would Sarah and Armand and the bodyguards be left to die on the beach? As she studied the surf, she realized why this side of the island was inhabitable. The surf there was unlike anything she'd ever seen.

As the waves made their way toward the shore, the ocean's bottom must have formed a narrow V, forcing the waves to grow to enormous heights. Then the bottom of the wave fell away and the top of the wave smashed upon the shore.

The biggest waves she'd ever seen were on Pawleys Island, just as the hurricane of 1804 was blowing in, but they were insignificant compared to these.

It would be impossible to swim out to a ship from this beach. There had to be another way, so Sarah scanned the shore. She spotted a sand spit about a quarter-kilometer away and hoped that it might be possible to either swim out to a boat or to be picked up by a dinghy from there.

She'd have to find the schooner first, but she'd have to wait for better light. Then she realized that she hadn't told Armand or the bodyguards about the deal she'd made with the crew of the schooner.

The schooner would have been her ace in the hole if she had needed to get away from them, but the bodyguards had saved her life, and Armand, well, perhaps he wasn't the monster she'd thought he was. She still didn't want to have anything to do with him again, but she felt sorry for him.

Armand! Where was he? She hadn't seen him since the last place they rested. She scanned the tree line leading into the jungle. No Armand, where was he? She could see the bodyguards lying on the sand at the far end of the beach, but she didn't see Armand. And then she saw a figure staggering out of the jungle.

It was Armand, but if she hadn't been looking for him, she wouldn't have recognized him. His skin was chalky white in the moonlight, and his whole body looked swollen. He had a gash on the back of his head, and he was bordering on delirium.

She rushed to him, and he fell into her arms.

"Sarah," he whispered. "Did we make it?"

"We made it out of the jungle, but I don't yet know if we will make it off the island. I made a deal with the crew of the Hebert boat to meet me here, but we have to wait for daylight to see if they kept their promise."

Then she put Armand's head onto the ground and told him she'd be right back. She owed it to the bodyguards to tell them about the boat, so she made her way across the beach to the spot where they were huddled together facing the jungle. They were surprised to see her approach, and some of them attempted to stand.

"Please, no," she said in French. "We're all too tired. She began by thanking them for saving her life and the life of her husband. Then she told them about the boat. She'd see to it that they were rewarded for their courage and that they would be returned to Port-du-Paix unless they preferred to continue on to Cuba or even to South Carolina.

It was their choice.

They opted for Cuba. Cuba it was.

The only thing to do then was to wait for the dawn. Sarah guessed it'd be a couple of hours yet, but she was so tired and turned around that she wasn't sure of anything. She went back to check on Armand, and he was so pasty she had to feel his pulse to make sure that he was breathing. *What a sad soul,* she thought.

She placed her head on Armand's chest and slept. She'd wanted to stay awake, but she was too exhausted. It was a fitful sleep, though. She kept being jolted from her sleep by nightmares, and each time she awoke, she'd jump to her feet to scan the horizon.

The last time she woke up, she almost talked herself out of looking for the boat because she'd been disappointed so many times, but she slowly rose to her knees and looked out one last time. And there it was, the Hebert schooner, bobbing up and down like a cork float, sending a signal to shore with a signal lantern.

"It's here!" she screamed. "It's here!"

The bodyguards shook each other awake and whispered the good news to their injured. Armand remained asleep, and even though Sarah shook him, he was barely conscious. "The boat, Armand. The boat is here. We're rescued. It's time to get up. There's lots to do."

"I can't," he said. "My back. It hurts."

Sarah struggled to turn him over, and then she found a neat round hole in his upper shoulder. "You've been shot; no wonder you're tired, but it doesn't look life-threatening. You'll be fine once we get you aboard."

"I can't move," he said.

"Oh, yes, you can," Sarah said between her teeth. "You started this whole mess, and now you're going to finish it. I'm not leaving you on this beach, and that's that, so get to your feet and let's get going." Armand did as he was told, but then he stumbled and fell back.

"You've got to get rid of the treasure," Sarah said. "Its weight is pulling you down."

"I can't, Sarah. If I give up the crown, I'll be nothing. I'll die without it."

Sarah was in the process of ripping the strap to the burlap bag from his shoulder when she realized that he was right. He would die without it. His entire self-worth was wrapped up in that stupid crown, so she made him a bargain. If he'd release the bag, she'd carry it to the boat for him.

"You promise, Sarah?" Armand stammered.

"I promise."

The bodyguards agreed with Sarah that their only chance was to go out onto the sand spit and swim for it. They'd form a human chain if need be. The best swimmer among the guards volunteered to go first, and his job would be to take one of the injured men with him. Sarah was in the second pairing. Her job would be to help the injured once they were aboard.

Armand was in the third pairing, and he was the one they were the most worried about. His injuries didn't appear to be as bad as the guards' injuries, but he was the weakest by far. Maybe it was because he was a gentleman, one of the guards said.

The schooner got as close to the spit's rocky outpoint as it dared and set anchor. It was dangerous business. The slightest mistake could drown them all, but there was no other way to breach the surf. When the first pairing got within twenty feet or so of the boat, two men from the boat jumped into the water and helped them get aboard.

Sarah and her bodyguard were next, and she said a prayer before they hit the water. The surf reminded her of being inside a giant washing machine, the kind the laundresses used out in the yard.

"Hold your breath!" her partner shouted.

She did as she was told, and together they were forced down by one wave and then shot to the surface by the next. She didn't think she could hold on much longer when a strong pair of hands grabbed her and pushed her toward the boat.

"Thank you," she whispered. "Thank you."

Once aboard, Sarah realized for the first time that she was wearing the burlap bag. In confusion, she'd forgotten that she had it. No wonder the surf dragged her so forcefully. She was dragging her own kind of anchor. In disgust, she ripped off the bag and threw it onto the deck.

Armand was up next, and she was frightened for him. From the deck, she watched as he and his bodyguard jumped into the surf, and she could tell from the beginning that Armand was fighting his partner.

She wondered if he even understood what was happening. His fists slapped at the water, and he was taking in great gulps of seawater. He was drowning, and he was taking his bodyguard down with him.

Through either divine intervention or voodoo magic, they got Armand aboard, but he was as white as the underbelly of a fish and barely breathing. Sarah held his hand and tried to hold his attention, but he was unconscious.

"You say he has a shoulder wound, ma'am?" the captain said.

"That's what he told me. His shoulder hurts. No, he said that his back hurt." With that, she and the captain rolled Armand onto his side and examined the lower portion of his back. Just below the waistband of his pants was a puncture wound the size of a child's fist.

"He must have fallen on something," the captain said. "I didn't know," Sarah said, crying. "I didn't know. I should have found it and tended to it."

"It was hidden beneath the waistband, ma'am. Besides, there was no repairing that wound. No one could survive a wound like that one."

Armand stopped breathing a few minutes later and slipped away before he could tell Sarah that he hadn't done anything to cause Percival's death, although he had thought about it and probably would have done it if Percival hadn't died on his own. Armand was glad he hadn't hurt Sarah in that way. She deserved better. She held his hand as he died. She would have done it for anyone, especially for a tortured soul like Armand.

After a stopover in Cuba to bury Armand and to let the bodyguards off, the magnificent schooner scarcely touched the tops of the waves as it sailed back to Mt. Pleasant.

Although Sarah and the crew arrived well after dark, they were still met by a gang of the gleeful dock and plantation workers. Sarah practically had to pinch herself to believe that she was really home. Home to her Hebert family. Home to South Carolina.

CHAPTER 40

Voodoo Got The Mistress

As Sarah was being helped ashore, one of the crew members called out to her. "Ma'am, you forget this," he said, holding out the burlap bag. Sarah reached out for the bag without a second thought. He could have been handing her anything, and she would have accepted it.

Sarah was carried up to the mansion and given over to some of the maids who were to clean her up as best they could and put her to bed. The women had been told to expect the worst, but they broke into tears when they examined her body.

Sarah's maid put the burlap bag into the bottom drawer of a large dresser, and then she carried a bowl of hot water to Sarah's bedside.

One of the men aboard the Hebert schooner had give Sarah a long coat to wear over her clothes during the journey home. Beneath the coat was the dress that she had trekked through the Haitian jungle in.

Covered with blood stains, the dress was in shreds, and it stunk. Sarah's feet were bare, with a missing toenail on her left foot and cuts on the bottom of both feet. It had been a week since her rescue, but Sarah's legs were still covered with cuts and bruises and scores of insect bites, some as big as a shot glass.

Her lips were swollen and sunburned, and the whites of her eyes were so bloodshot she was barely recognizable. The most shocking thing of all, though, was that much of her hair had been sheared off right down to her scalp. A woman from Sarah's social class would have never cut her hair, and here Miss Sarah was, as bald as a buzzard.

"It was the voodoo that got her," one of the maids said. "Voodoo done got the mistress."

Sarah slept for two days straight, and when she woke up, Edward, Sarah Elisabeth, Beatrix Anne, and five-year-old William were sitting on the edge of her bed.

"Mother!" Sarah Elisabeth exclaimed. "You're back. You're back. We were so frightened."

"You have the best black eye I've ever seen," Bea said in her matter-of-fact way.

"What happened, Mother?" Edward said, trying to sound like the head of the family.

It was a long story, she said, promising to tell them all about it when she felt better. "Right now, I'm starved."

"Say no more," Edward said, pointing to the door. That was Hannah's cue, and she didn't miss a beat.

"I heard you were hungry, so I came all the way here to Mt. Pleasant to make you some nice hot soup and one o' my special cheese biscuits. The doctor says you got to eat, so that's what we're going to do.

"And we won't be talking about your momma's hair, right Miss Sarah Elisabeth? We won't be talking about your momma's hair 'cause that would be rude. Besides, it'll grow out one of these days, so we won't be worrying about it."

Sarah had forgotten about her hair. "Oh, Hannah, I wish you hadn't reminded me. You're going to ruin my appetite."

"It'll grow back, honey. Just wait and see. Don't ask for a mirror, though. We're fresh out them, ain't we, Miss Sarah Elisabeth?"

"Yes, ma'am. We're fresh out."

Two weeks later, the Hebert family physician gave Sarah permission to return to True Blue if she promised to continue bed rest for an additional week once she got there. Sarah promised. She was feeling fine.

Sarah's maid had very little to pack, just the nightgowns that had been given to her by the family. Oh, and some medication that the doctor had prescribed. Hannah had brought some of Sarah's things from True Blue, but she didn't use much of it because the Heberts had taken such good care of her.

There was one thing, though; a burlap bag with something heavy at the end of it that Miss Sarah asked her to be sure and pack. Hannah was scared to look inside the bag, though, because the maid said it might contain a shrunken head.

CHAPTER 41

The Czar

ON HER SECOND DAY HOME, Sarah received a letter from Henri Hebert, her cousin who has saved her life so long ago. Henri said he had urgent business and begged Sarah to let him visit.

He arrived three days later.

When Henri followed Hannah into Sarah's room, Sarah gasped. He was ten times more handsome than she remembered. He was widowed, and they were only second cousins, so it wouldn't hurt to look.

He was almost as handsome as Percival, and Sarah blushed, remembering how comical she looked to him with a bald head and an enormous black eye. Then she looked over at Eliza, who was blushing, too. There was just something about men like Henri that made she and Eliza act like schoolgirls. Percival had that same effect on every woman who ever met him, including the most self-controlled woman in the world, Sarah's mother, Elisabeth Hebert.

After Sarah reintroduced Eliza to Henri and allowing Henri to adjust to the shock of seeing Sarah in her wretched state, Henri got down to business. The family had just received an official letter from Czar Alexander's Council of Ministers, he said. The letter contained allegations that Grand-Pere Hebert had purchased a shipment of jewelry that could be traced back to the Romanov family collection of imperial jewels.

The piece the Russian government was the most desperate to recover was Catherine the Great's coronation crown. At the very top of the crown, Henri said, was a red diamond weighing 398.72 carats. According to the Russians, it was priceless.

"If Grand-Pere had these things, where would he have kept them?" Sarah asked, still unwilling to believe Armand's assertion that the crown he found was real.

"We don't know," Henri replied. "Everyone who might have known was killed in the massacre."

"Not everyone," Sarah said dryly.

"What do you mean?" Henri said.

"I wasn't killed."

"I know," Henri said with renewed interest, "but I didn't expect you to know anything like that. I just hoped you and Eliza might remember something that was said during dinner the night of the massacre."

"I do remember something, Henri, but I didn't hear it at the dinner table," Sarah said.

"What are you talking about?" Henri said.

"It happened in the cave."

"The cave?" Henri said.

"The mushroom cave, not the cave on the beach," Sarah said. "Eliza and I were there the night of the massacre, but I didn't understand the importance of the jewelry I saw there until a few days ago.

"When I opened the secret door leading to the mushroom cave, I saw the little island girl at the bottom of the stairs. She was wearing pearl necklaces that came down to her knees, and what I thought to be a papier-mache Christmas crown.

"After I motioned for her to come to me, the crown fell off her head, and I could tell by the sound it made that it wasn't made of papier-mache. I've wondered about the crown for years; I even asked Mamma about it once. She suggested that it was a Mardi Gras crown."

"Sarah, you're going to have to start at the beginning," Henri said sweetly.

"It's about what happened the night before you found me in the indigo vat," Sarah said. "Remember when you told me you were searching for your cousins and your sister? I told you I hadn't seen them, but I lied. I didn't just see them, Henri. I killed them, not your sister, but the two boys, the golden-haired boys, our cousins."

"You what!"

"Let her finish," Eliza said.

"I'm sorry," Henri replied.

Sarah studied the creases on her bedsheet and wiped away a tear. She hated telling Henri about that night. He'd never forgive her, and she couldn't blame him. She had no choice; Henri had a right to know.

"Eliza and I got lost that night," she said, "lost from each other, I mean. Anyway, I looked everywhere for her, and then I realized that I couldn't go on; I was too exhausted. That's when I saw Aunt Felicia's Necessary. I don't know how long Charlotte and I slept there, but I remember waking up to hear a sound coming from the wall. Then I realized that it was coming from a small door in the wall."

"The door to the cave," Henri said.

"Yes, it was the door to the cave. I opened it and saw two boys in nightshirts, and they were taunting Eliza by twirling about with their nightgowns above their waists and pressing themselves into her face. She was covered in blood, and she was crying. I didn't know what to do. Then I saw the little girl. Remember the little island girl who was with me when you found me?"

"There were two little girls," Henri said.

"Yes, but one of them was Charlotte. I'm talking about the other little girl. When I told her to crawl to me, the crown fell off her head, and the cousins heard the sound, and they started coming after us. They were really, really drunk. They screamed at us as we frantically clawed our way up the stairs to the privy.

"Then one of them grabbed my foot, and I kicked him, and then I threw an oil lantern onto the floor of the cave. I didn't expect it to explode, but it did. The boys came after me again, but I got through the door, and then I threw the latch."

"The latch?"

"There was a latch on the door, and I locked it to keep them from reaching us, and then I blocked the door with my feet. They were screaming to get out, Henri. I could have let them out, but I was afraid they'd kill us. I didn't know the boys were my cousins."

"Would it have made a difference if you had known?" Henri said sarcastically.

She didn't know. It all happened so fast, and she was so frightened. Something was wrong with Eliza. She had a big cut on her head, and she was really confused. And there were the little girls, and everyone was screaming. Then there was a loud explosion, and the privy started to collapse, and they barely got out.

Dust was everywhere, she said, and flames and smoke, and she knew that at any moment, they'd be discovered by the rebels and killed. Then she saw the indigo vat, thinking it could be a good place to hide and perhaps not the worst place to die.

"My sister, Sarah, I need to know if my sister was in the cave?" Henri asked, reaching for Sarah's hand. I'm not angry with you for what happened. It was a long time ago, and I know it must have been terrifying, but I need to know about Ellie."

"She wasn't there, Henri. I didn't see her, and neither did Eliza or the little girl. I begged them to tell me. I promise, Henri, she wasn't there." Henri fell back against his chair, covering his eyes. His sister had been his angel.

The tall clock near Sarah's desk called out the minutes with precise indifference. All things are fleeting, its wooden works were whispering. Henri gradually regained control of his voice and his thoughts. Sarah felt a thousand years old, and Eliza was trying to anticipate Henri's next remarks.

"Let's go back to the story about the crown and the little girl's pearls," he said.

"The crown was glittery," Sarah said, "and it was too big for the little girl like I said before. It sat crooked on her head and came down over her ears. And don't forget the pearls. She was wearing a long strand of pearls like Grand-Mere used to wear. They came down to her knees, and they looked incandescent against her skin.

"The room was spinning, and everyone was crying, and the little girl's black eyes were pleading with me to help her. Something was bulging from her cheek, and she looked so very queer standing there."

"She had something in her mouth?" Henri said. "Do you know what it was?"

"I have no idea. I didn't even remember it until now."

"What happened after the privy collapsed?" Henri said cautiously.

"We climbed into the dye vat."

"No, I meant what happened to the pearls after that?" Henri said.

"One of the strands broke as the girls crawled to the bottom of the vat," Eliza interjected. "I didn't see it break, but I remember the girls grabbing at the pearls and stuffing them into their mouths."

"I was just happy for the distraction," Sarah said.

"Do you remember anything else?"

"I remember one thing more," Sarah said.

"What?"

"It didn't seem important at the time, either, but now I think it might have been. When we reached the cave on the beach, the little girl demanded that Charlotte return the pearls that she had helped her save. Then she found a rag of some sort and tied them together."

"Was that all?"

"No, there was one more thing," she said.

"Even though Charlotte and the little girl didn't stay together once we got to Cuba, they played with each other during the day. And I know that the little girl gave Charlotte a present just before we reached Mt. Pleasant."

"What was it?" Henri asked.

"I don't know," Sarah replied, "but we could ask Charlotte."

"Charlotte!" Henri shouted, louder than he had intended to. "She's here?"

"No, but she wrote that she's coming tomorrow."

The following afternoon, Sarah heard rambunctious footsteps on the stairway when Henri and Charlotte suddenly burst into the room. Charlotte looked like she was being kidnapped.

"I'm sorry, Sarah," Henri said. "It was rude of me to come unannounced, but I've been waiting all morning for Charlotte to arrive, and she's finally here." Charlotte rushed to Sarah's bedside, as Sarah scolded Henri for upsetting Charlotte.

"You frightened her half to death."

"I'm sorry, Charlotte," Henri said remorsefully. "I didn't intend to frighten you, but we have something very important to ask you. It's about something that happened in Haiti while you and Sarah were hiding in the indigo vat."

Did she remember hiding there? She did, she said. "I remember asking Sarah if the bad men were coming."

"That's right," Sarah said, "but something else happened while we were there. Do you remember the pearls the little island girl was wearing?"

"You mean Kai?"

"Yes, Kai," Charlotte said. "She told me she'd found the pearls in a pirates' chest."

"A pirates' chest?" Henri said, jumping to his feet.

"A pirates' chest. I was too young to know what was going on at the time, but I do remember that Kai and Sookie didn't continue on to Mt. Pleasant; they exited the boat in Cuba," Charlotte said.

"As they were leaving the boat, Kai gave me a present. I thought she was going to give me a pearl, of course, but she gave me something else instead.

"It was a smooth red stone about the size of a partridge's egg. It wasn't faceted or anything, and it was irregular in shape, but it was beautiful. Kia said it broke off of her fairy crown back in the mushroom cave, but I just laughed because she didn't have a crown by the time I saw her. She said when the cave caught on fire; she hid the stone in her mouth. I've always thought it was beach glass."

Henri stared at Sarah and Eliza with his mouth ajar. His brain was spinning fast enough to produce steam, but his words were stuck in his throat. And Eliza had rolled off Sarah's bed and onto the floor with the giggles, so it was up to Sarah to do the shouting.

"A bright red stone!" Sarah shouted, tossing a bed pillow at Eliza. "Really and truly?"

"Really and truly," Charlotte replied, stunned by Sarah's response. "It was just a piece of beach glass. I don't understand why everyone's so excited."

"Well, you will, my darling girl," Henri said, kissing her on the cheek.

"But we've forgotten something," Eliza pointed out. "Does Charlotte still have the stone?" Three sets of eyes suddenly locked onto Charlotte's face with the intensity of sunlight pouring through a peephole.

Where was the stone? Where was the insignificant piece of beach glass that just happened to be one of the most important precious stones in the history of the world? "Where is the stone, now?" Henri said, moving within inches of Charlotte's delicate face.

"Why is it so important?" Charlotte said on the verge of tears.

"Just tell us, sweetheart," Sarah said.

"Tell us where the stone is. Please, please, please tell us that you still have it."

"I saved it for my girls," she said, referring to her twin daughters.

"But where is the stone right now, Charlotte?" Sarah asked. "If Jesus walked through that door and asked you to show it to him, could you do it?"

"I could," she said. "It's on the windowsill in my daughters' room."

"She said yes! She said yes!" Eliza shouted, jumping up and down on the end of Sarah's bed.

"Oh, my sweet, sweet cousin," Henri said, "you have saved the day. Sweet, sweet Jesus!"

"That's it," Charlotte said in a voice shrill enough to break glass. "If you don't tell me what's going on this minute, I'm going home. The three of you have gone completely daft."

"I'll be right back, and then we'll tell you everything," Henri said after asking Sarah if the Madeira was still stored in the garret. Then Henri rushed out of the room, and the door to the attic suddenly flew open. He could be heard taking the stairs two at a time. Seconds later, and out of breath, he stood at the door with a magnum of Percival's best Madeira.

"We need a toast," he said, "a toast to Charlotte, a toast to beach glass, and a toast to the czar."

"You're all demented!" Charlotte said, preparing to leave. "That's it!"

Eliza took Charlotte by the arm and said, "We're sorry, Charlotte, we won't tease you anymore. Sit with Sarah, and we'll tell you the whole story. "Be prepared to make a toast, though. After you hear the story, you'll want to make lots of them."

Charlotte got just as silly as the rest of them after Sarah told her the story of the red stone. How many times had she lost that stone only to find it again? "I can't tell you how many times the girls have played with it in the surf. It disappeared at least a hundred times last summer, but it always reappeared.

"Perhaps the stone is enchanted," Charlotte suggested. "Maybe the reason it was cherished by the Russian imperial family had nothing to do with its beauty," she mused. "Perhaps they knew it had magical powers, and with the turmoil going on there now, the czar could use some magic."

"So, where do we go from here?" Sarah asked, smiling.

"We put together a team to go to Haiti and recover the crown," Henri said. "By the way, why did you and your new husband risk going there?"

"He made me go," Sarah said. "I didn't want to, but I have to admit he had a pretty good reason."

"And what could possibly be important enough to die for?" Henri said.

"I'll show you," Sarah said, digging beneath the pillows on her bed. "We went for this," she said, handing Henri a grubby-looking burlap bag.

"Look inside; I promise it won't bite." Henri took the bag from Sarah and set it next to her on her bed. And then he reached inside and touched the crown.

"I think we all need to pack our trunks because we'll be going on a very long trip," he said, laughing.

"And where shall we be going?" Sarah said, going along with the joke.

"To Mother Russia."

"To Russia?" Charlotte and Eliza said in unison.

"Yes," Henri said, pulling the crown from the bag and placing it on Sarah's head. "We have important business with the czar."

Epilogue 2025

In 1999, my husband and I built a house on the former grounds of True Blue Plantation in present-day Pawleys Island, SC. Near an allee of live oaks was a small cemetery covered with pricker bushes except for the ground surrounding a single crypt stone that reads, Sacred to the Memory of Sarah Richards Vaux, 1783-1823.

A picket fence surrounded the cemetery, and I was in the process of scaling it one day when I spotted a huge skink and about a billion termites boiling up out of one of the other graves. I changed my mind.

The connection I felt with Sarah that day was palpable. Who was she, and who were the people buried there with her? One of my new neighbors told me that house servants were buried there. Another said that Sarah Vaux had been a witch and that she was buried sitting upright in a rocking chair.

The only thing they agreed on was that I needed to speak to Donna Phillips, whose grandparents had been the plantation's caretakers during the 1950s.

Donna and I became fast friends. I'd visit, she'd ply me with cookies, and then she'd tell me stories about the plantation. To this day, Donna cries when she talks about True Blue. She's the only person I know who loves the plantation more than I do. I had intended to sell Donna's story to a magazine, but it dawned on me one day that I was in the midst of writing a book about Sarah, eventually titled SARAH'S SECRET.

Percival Pawley I, the first member of the Pawley family to own True Blue, received a colonial land grant for the plantation in 1711. In return for the land that he paid a pittance for, he was sworn to build a dwelling house and to produce a cash crop approved by the English crown. During colonial times, that crop was indigo.

Following the Revolutionary War, Lowcountry planters turned to rice. Most people are surprised to learn that rice generated more wealth than any of the other plantation crops, including cotton. No wonder the planters of rice were often called rice princes.

True Blue Plantation was prized because of its location on the Waccamaw River, one of South Carolina's five great rivers that are subject to the tide. On-demand flooding is an absolute requirement when growing rice, so dikes and floodgates were constructed along the river's edge, enabling workers to flood the fields during high tide and to drain them when the tide receded. During the mid-1800s, South Carolina produced two-thirds of the world's rice.

After the War of the Confederacy, the plantations lay fallow. Rice was a demanding crop that had to be grown on a large scale to be profitable. Most of the plantation owners lost everything during the war, and even if they did have the funds necessary to pay their former slaves, the former slaves refused to return to the plantation.

So nature reclaimed the dikes and floodgates, and the rice fields disappeared. True Blue was eventually divided into subsistence farms and parceled out to former slaves.

Although only seven headstones remain at the True Blue Cemetery, notations made years ago in the margins of a parish registry kept at All Saints Church state that True Blue's cemetery has many more souls, including four generations of masters and their wives; two spinsters; two veterans of the Revolutionary War (one American and one English); an English woman; and four unnamed infants.

In 2004, I founded a nonprofit to restore the cemetery at True Blue. The first fundraiser was held at the cemetery at dusk, and costumed reenactors told the story of True Blue based on my research. We exceeded our expectations that night. One couple gave us a check for five thousand dollars, and a woman who worked at a local bar gave us the contents of her tip jar. I cried when I went to pick it up.

Today I live in Charlotte, NC, where I give plantation and cemetery tours and prepare my other manuscripts for publication.

In SARAH'S SECRET, Sarah and her husband, Percival, were a love match. I believe that was true in real life, too. The real Sarah was seventeen when she married and went on to have ten children with Percival. She died in childbirth at forty-one, after giving birth to her second healthy child in one calendar year. Imagine a sixty-year-old doing that today,

Percival outlived her by seventeen years but never remarried. He was an extremely wealthy man and relatively young. One would think he would have remarried.

Even though my characters are fictionalized, they are based on actual people when possible. The names of the enslaved people, for example, were taken from the actual plantation documents. There are a number of real people and real events in the story.

The History Behind Sarah's Secret

The real SARAH and PERCIVAL VAUX had ten children, five of whom lived into adulthood.

JAMES LAYTON RICHARDS or RICHARDSON (1748-1804) was Sarah Vaux's father.

Elisabeth NICHOLS RICHARDS (1751-1797) was Sarah Vaux's mother.

The HAITIAN REVOLUTION (1791–1804) was a slave rebellion in the French colony of Saint-Domingue (Haiti's colonial name) that resulted in the founding of the independent Republic of Haiti.

The ghost story about ALICE FLAGG is a legend in South Carolina. The real Alice is buried at All Saint's Church in Pawleys Island, and I've visited her grave many times. I've never seen anyone else there, but seashells, coins, and dimestore engagement rings can always be found there. Last year, my friend's daughter spotted a real engagement ring on Alice's grave. I'd like to think its still there.

ELIZA LUCAS PAGET is the fictionalized granddaughter of ELIZA LUCAS PINCKNEY (1722-1793). While still in her teens, Eliza Lucas Pinckney transformed South Carolina's pre-Revolutionary economy through her successful cultivation of indigo and her willingness to share her seed and her findings with her fellow planters.

Pinckney continued her research of all things agricultural, including silkworms, until her death at seventy-one. At his own request, George Washington served as one of her pallbearers.

The IMPERIAL CROWN OF RUSSIA was made for Catherine

the Great (Catherine II), who wore the crown for her official portrait following her coronation in 1762. The nine-pound crown contains five thousand diamonds and a 398.72-carat gemstone called a spinel.

My fictionalized story is simply that. The notion of a 398-carat red diamond is ridiculous. Currently, the largest red diamond in the world is the Moussaieff Red, a diamond measuring 5.11 carats.

As it turns out, however, my fictionalized story pales by comparison to the crown's true history. The Imperial Crown of Russia was used by the Emperors of Russia until Nicholas II's abduction and the abolishment of the monarchy in 1917. It is currently displayed at the Kremlin. There are many rumors about the crown.

My favorite is that in the late 1700s—a hundred years before Nicholas II's coronation—the crown was sent to London to be held as collateral on a loan from the Irish government, whereupon it disappeared on the train ride there and was lost for a hundred years before its return to the Kremlin.

When I read that account, I decided to create a story of what might have happened to the stone during that time. That is the reason I began Sarah's story in Haiti. I wanted to start off big, which that storyline enabled me to do. It also helped me to eventually get Sarah back to Haiti so the story could come full circle.

I love Sarah. My children have reluctantly promised to rake my ashes into the little Vaux cemetery someday. I just hope they don't have to do it anytime soon.

The headstone for Ann Morrall Vaux, one of Sarah's baby daughters:
Credit: Nancy Rogers

The Pawley-Vaux family cemetery at True
Blue Plantation. Credit: Nancy Rogers

About the Author

NANCY ROGERS'S passion for history is the result of having spent many years living on the remains of an eighteenth-century rice plantation in Pawleys Island, South Carolina. She is a former biographer of the South Carolina Hall of Fame and is a former docent at Historic Columbia, in Columbia, South Carolina, and Latta House, in Charlotte, North Carolina.

Nancy's freelance work has appeared in numerous magazines and newspapers, including *The New York Times. The Women of Abbey Plantation* is a sequel to Nancy's first novel, *Sarah's Secret,* a story inspired by a real-life plantation mistress who died in 1723.

Nancy currently lives in Charlotte, where she takes part in various civic projects, gives historic lectures, and occasionally gives cemetery tours specializing in iconography. For more information about Nancy and/or her novels, go to www.nancysnovels.com.